FLESH PEDDLERS

A SOPHIE STAR SERIES BOOK THREE

L.J.WEBB

FLESH PEDDLERS
BY L. J. WEBB

Cover by Adebayo S. Oluwatosin

eBook ISBN 978-1-7330939-5-8
Paperback ISBN 978-1-7330939-4-1

Library of Congress Control Number: 2020916238

This is a work of fiction. The characters, dialogues, and incidents are a creation of the author's imagination and are not intended to be taken as real. Any similarity to any persons, living or dead, is entirely coincidental. Any discrepancies to actual police policies or processes were made to move the storyline along and were not intended to reflect exact police procedure.

Although the names of some gangs are real. The use of them and how they operate is strictly a fictional account and intended to move the story plot along. It is not intended to reflect the reality of organized crime or how they think or operate.

TABLE OF CONTENTS

...for the LORD seeth not as man seeth; for man looketh on the outward appearance, but the LORD looketh on the heart.

I Samuel 16:7 (KJV)

CHAPTER ONE

Four months ago Izumi Nori was commissioned by his Kumicho to purchase 20 million counterfeit $100 bills. The transaction was simple. Izumi was to send 10 million dollars to the Yon syndicate, and in exchange, they would send the counterfeit bills. Yon Se-bin and his two brothers ran and operated their lucrative business, selling their goods all over the world from North Korea. The North Korean leader allowed it because a considerable portion of the profits went to him, which he in turn, used to support his pet project, the nuclear missile program.

It was the first time the Akuza, an ancient Japanese mafia organization founded hundreds of years ago, had ventured into counterfeit money. Izumi waited at the specified location to pick up the trunk; however, when he opened it, there was only paper in it.

Izumi immediately contacted Yon Min-ji, Yon Se-bin's son, who was his contact and demanded an explanation. When Yon Min-ji responded that the money was in the trunk and inspected by his man as requested, Izumi was furious. He told him he had sent no one to inspect the merchandise and requested no such thing. He felt that Yon had pulled a 'con' on him. Izumi gave him a two-hour window to return the ten million or face the consequences. No response came. Izumi called on Akuza assassins in Japan to behead the family in retaliation. They were all dead but Yon Min-ji, who had disappeared.

Izumi Nori walked into the assembly room of the Kumicho. It was the fifth time in less than four months he was to witness punishment.

Izumi was 5'11", built like a man who spent time training for military action. He stood two inches taller than the Kumicho, who was his stepfather. A man with a small frame but a commanding presence.

As the Saiko Komon, (senior advisor), Izumi had to be a witness to any discipline, such as yubitsume. (The offender must shorten his own finger). Punishment ran from yubitsume for small offenses to beheadings for more serious ones. He knew one day it would be his turn. One day he would walk into his stepfather's court, and the red carpet would be down for him.

Izumi expected the debacle with the North Koreans would cost him his life. But the Kumicho decided that his quick and decisive response was worthy of a reprieve. However it did nothing to quench his anger about the betrayal from the Yon organization. The Kumicho was angry, he wanted his money back. He had been sending men out to locate Yon Min-ji and his money for the last four months, with no results.

Izumi was weary of this life, at 14 he was old enough to be a 'kobun' he was immensely proud. He even bragged about his exploits and his connection to the Kumicho. His mother had made sure Izumi could speak several languages. She knew it would make him valuable to whoever he worked for in the Akuza or hopefully outside it. Now he wished he could turn back the clock and start again. Run from his family and have a different life. He tired of the cruelty and the evil perpetrated by the businesses the Akuza maintained. *There has to be more to life than this,* he thought late at night as he paced his four-room suite in the west wing on the second floor. His room was directly across from the Kumicho's suite, so he could be at his beck and call all hour's day or night.

4

He didn't think he would ever marry. The life of a *saiko komon* belonged only to his Kumicho. He didn't want a marriage in name only.

His only friend was the *so*-honbucho (headquarters chief), Kato Yori. They grew up together, Kato lived with Izumi because he was abandoned by his parents when he was six. He was the only person who knew how he felt.

Izumi walked into the Kumicho's presence and bowed. He waited for the Kumicho to offer him a seat and the ceremonial tea. They spoke in English most of the time, depending on the Kumicho's mood.

"Izumi. It has been almost four months, and everyone I have sent to locate our stolen ten million dollars has failed. What are you doing about it?"

"Sir, our men have searched the earth for your money, without success. But there are rumors of a woman with an extraordinary ability to locate anyone or anything."

"Do you believe it?"

"If she can do only half of what I heard, it is worth a try. No one else has accomplished what we need."

The Kumicho finished his sake and ordered Kato to bring in his 'underboss.' He stood in the middle of the platform that was on the east end of an expansive empty meeting room. The only furniture was on the raised platform that had a separate entrance. There were four stairs that allowed access from the space below. No one sat when they met with the Kumicho, except the Kumicho if he decided to use his Victoria Armchair. There was a four-panel bamboo black room divider hand painted with traditional Japanese scenery on the left side that hid the separate entrance. It also hid the matching Victoria love seat. A small black lacquer table with four modern floor pillows, two with backs, one with a free-standing armrest, sat just behind the divider.

The 'underboss' Fujio came in and saw the red carpet, he knew what it meant. He bowed and waited for the Kumicho to address him.

"Fujio, have you located my money?"

"Honorable Kumicho, I have gone to the ends of the earth seeking answers for you. It is an impossible task."

"You mean to insult me by saying I ask too much of you!"

Izumi knew it was the wrong thing for Fujio to try to give an excuse. But it wouldn't have mattered. The Kumicho planned on killing him as an example. The last four men who disappointed him were ordered to sever the upper part of their own pinkies in his presence. The Kumicho was done being patient. He waved his hand to the *So*-honbucho, and without another word, the man knelt bowed his head and Kato severed it.

"Make sure you send a message to every Akuza in the country that this is what happens to anyone who disappoints their Kumicho."

Kato nodded, and several men came in to help him take the body out and roll up the carpet. The carpet would be disposed of and another take its place when needed.

"Do you know her name." He picked up the conversation as if nothing had happened and moved back to his tea at the table.

"I do, her name is Sophie Star."

"Can you bring her to me?"

"Yes, sir. As soon as I locate her."

CHAPTER TWO

S ophie was on the computer finishing up her purchase of nine tickets on the 50-yard line for the Thanksgiving Day's football game at MetLife Stadium. It was going to be so much fun. Sophie was excited to be spending her first holidays with Houston as husband and wife. She smiled as she grabbed a covered elastic to pull back her thick auburn hair. She would have to control the amount of holiday treats she consumed; she'd already gained five pounds since her wedding day. She managed to reconcile that by telling herself happiness weighed five pounds. She could live with that.

Houston's mother, Lily, and his sister, Spring, had agreed they could move the Thanksgiving meal to Friday. They all knew it would be an experience no one would ever forget. The sale went through as the phone rang.

"Hello."

"Sophie?" Captain Cartwright was calling.

Sophie met Don when he was a detective investigating the beating she took at the hands of her then boyfriend, who ran a notorious drug empire, Nikko Morano. She knew she had to run or he would end up killing her. During her escape attempt from the hospital she nearly collapsed on the street going to meet the man helping her disappear. Detective Cartwright caught her and helped her get to her destination. She never would have made it on her own. In essence he helped save her life and she's never forgotten it.

"Yes, hi, Don. How are you?"

"I'm well, but I'm still working the desk until one of the precinct captains retires. I'm alright with that, but I do like having the rank. I'm actually calling to ask a favor." At forty Cartwright was one of the youngest Captains to be offered a precinct in New York.

It was in large part due to the collars Sophie insisted he take credit for. Sophie came out of hiding to take down Nikko's empire. She approached the DEA and they formed a task force to initiate her plan. She insisted Don be included. Since then whenever her Task Force missions included New York she made sure his department was a part of it and got the collar.

"You know I'd do anything for you."

He laughed, "I know Sophie. I got a called from the emergency room doctor about a woman at the hospital. She won't say how she got roughed up. I was hoping she might open up to you," he said. He wouldn't be handling things like this once he got his own Precinct to run, but they called him because she was a high-profile victim.

"Don, I can do that, but what makes you think she'll open up to me?"

"She knows who you are. It's Gail Turner"

"The field reporter?" Sophie interrupted, "I'll come, but I can't promise anything. Which hospital?"

"Bellevue Hospital Center. She's still in emergency."

"I'll be there as soon as I can."

"Thanks, Sophie."

She called Houston to tell him where she was going, in case he tried to get ahold of her, he was still in Trenton working on the apartment six plex they purchased. He told her to call the town car, and when he got home, she could tell him all about it.

Sophie was in the emergency room in thirty minutes. Cartwright met her at the door and brought her back to Ms. Turner's room.

She didn't turn her head to them when they came in.

"Captain, I told you I don't want to talk to you."

"I heard you, but I have someone here you may want to talk to."

She turned to look; she didn't recognize Sophie. "Who is she?"

Sophie saw one of her light blue eyes was swollen and bruised, she had a cut on her lips, and several bruises on her face. Her blond hair matted in places with blood most likely from her bloody nose.

"This is Sophie Star, as you know she was in an abusive relationship. I thought you may want to talk to someone." The Captain's introduction roused her memory.

"Alright, I'll talk to her."

The Captain said he would wait outside and left them alone.

"Well, Ms. Star, I have a lot of questions about your arrest and subsequently dropped charges."

"I'm not here to talk about me, Ms. Turner."

"It never smelled right. When I tried to dig deeper, I ran into a brick wall." She ignored Sophie's response.

"Ms. Turner, if someone is abusing you, you need to report it and get away from the abuser. Everyone thinks they can change an abusive man, but it seldom happens."

"Ms. Star, I wasn't abused, I was assaulted." She went on to tell the chain of events that landed her in the hospital.

A young woman, Halina Taru, here from the Philippines on a scholarship, came to her office. She'd been trying to get a green card for her sister, Dajao, so she could come to the US but was unsuccessful. They were living with their uncle, who's a real piece of work. Halina only got away from him because of a contest she entered and won. The prize was a full ride scholarship to Manhattan College in the Bronx. Her sister got tired of waiting and signed up to be a domestic worker, they promised to bring her to the US. She hasn't been heard from since. That was 2 weeks ago; she's only fourteen.

"I was able to get a line on the boat she got on in the Philippines and tracked them here to New York. It appears I was getting too close because the next tip that came in took me to the place I got assaulted." Gail finished her story with difficulty.

"Ms. Turner, you can't be investigating on your own, these men are extremely dangerous. Why not talk to Captain Cartwright, he will follow whatever leads you give him. You can trust him."

"Why is it a criminal, like you, wants me to trust a policeman."

Sophie didn't answer. While working with the Task Force to take down Nikko Morano's drug empire, she had to work undercover as a criminal. In order to protect her, the decision was made not to expose the fact she was working with the police. A fact that has helped her now that she is part of the FBI DC Task Force, when working undercover.

"With your underworld connections, you may be able to help me, Ms. Star."

"I would only help if Captain Cartwright were part of it," Sophie replied. "And you would have to sign a non-disclosure statement. I can't have you writing about me or people I may bring into this."

"That's very extreme, Ms. Star."

"I'm sorry it's the only way I'll help."

The nurse came in with discharge papers. The doctor wanted her to stay for observation but she refused. Gail had to be in pain even with the pain killers the nurses gave her, but she was determined to leave. They insisted she not drive so Sophie told Ms. Turner she would drive her to Cartwright's office. Sophie gave her some privacy to get dressed and went to talk to the Captain.

"What did she say?" Cartwright asked as he closed the gap between them. He was waiting at the nurse's station across the hall.

Sophie explained everything Gail had told her. "I'm going to give her a ride to your office. The Doctor doesn't want her driving on the pain killers she's on," Sophie said.

Captain Cartwright led them into one of the interrogation rooms.

"Are the cameras and mics off, I would like this to be confidential?" Ms. Turner asked.

"Yes, they're off," the Captain answered.

She told him what she had relayed to Sophie earlier and added a description of the assailant.

"He knew enough about my job that beating my face would keep me off-camera for a while. He said next time he would use a knife." Saying it out loud shook her up.

"Ms. Turner, you had no business trying to do this alone, it's a miracle he didn't kill you. Can you give me your notes and I'll start an investigation?" The Captain responded.

"You're going to think I'm shallow for worrying about this instead of that girl. But this is my scoop and I want in on it." She was fingering her notepad she'd taken out of her purse.

"Ms. Turner," Sophie interrupted. "I understand this is your job, just like it's the Captain's job to protect you and find this young woman. We will give you the information as it comes in. If you give us your word, not to report anything until the Captain says it's alright," Sophie explained.

"We? What exactly will *you* be doing and why would Captain Cartwright let you help and not me?" She asked.

"Ms. Turner, Sophie, has connections that she can use that aren't available to me. And her husband can make sure she's safe." The Captain said.

He asked her to give them all she had on the men that took the girl and where she tracked them to.

Sophie turned to her outside the police station, "Ms. Turner, I know you don't plan on leaving this alone. Will you at least call me before you go out on your own again?"

Gail thought about it. She didn't know if she could trust Sophie, although the Captain seem to trust her. Finally she decided she wasn't getting anywhere on her own.

"Yes. I've gone as far as I can alone. If you do find anything out from your connections will you promise to tell me what you tell the Captain? I could use your help," Gail confessed.

Sophie agreed to call Ms. Turner as soon as she had any information. Sophie insisted on driving her home.

Houston hadn't gotten home yet, so Sophie decided to contact Director Cosby in DC at FBI headquarters. He had gotten another promotion. The Task Force he assembled, just brought down ten terrorist cells in the US. Along with confiscating the plates from the most prolific counterfeiting operation in the world. Both contributing factors for his promotion.

"Hi, Cassi, is he in?"

"Oh, Sophie, I thought you'd avoid all contact while the Task Force was on hiatus?" She laughed.

"That was my plan, but I need a favor."

"I'm afraid he's in a meeting with the 'muckety-mucks'," she said.

"Gotcha. Ok, can you have him call me when he's free?"

"If it's important, I can interrupt him. He always takes your call."

"No, it's a personal favor, I can wait. But thank you."

"Alright, I'll give him the message as soon as he gets back."

"Thank you. Goodbye."

Sophie was answering the return call from Cosby when Houston walked in. She motioned for him to come sit with her, while she put the phone on speaker. He kissed the crown of her head before he sat down.

"Ms. Star, I'm surprised to hear from you. Cassi said you need a favor."

"Yes sir, Captain Cartwright of the NYPD contacted me today." She went on to tell him the whole story. "What I was hoping to do was use some of the task force's resources to find the traffickers who took this young girl. If I think there's a way to take the network down, then I'll approach you about making it a task force operation."

"You do have one thing going for you. The First Lady has targeted human trafficking as one of her personal projects. I don't have a problem with you doing some initial research on your own and letting me know. If you don't find anything, we'll give what you have to ICE."

"Thank you, sir, I need Matt or Sissy. I'll call them tomorrow."

Matt Mathews and Sissy Corban were the computer experts, in Sissy's case more like expert hacker, on the Task Force.

Sophie explained the events of the day, after giving Houston a proper hello kiss.

"How deep do you plan on getting into this, do you need me to take some time off to help?" Houston questioned.

"I don't think so sweetheart but thank you for asking. I don't know what I even have yet." She scooted closer to him.

"Promise me there will be no fieldwork unless I know about it and you have backup."

"I don't plan on doing anything dangerous, but I will keep you updated."

Houston got up and told her he was going to take a shower and wanted to take her out to dinner. Sophie went to change; she was always up for a dinner date.

Sophie was able to get ahold of Matt in the morning. She asked if he wanted to help her out. He was all in. Sophie told him the whole story.

"All Gail was able to find out was that either the Tongs or some other Chinese gangsters transported her to New York's Chinatown. They told her she would have a job as a domestic worker waiting for her." She took a breath.

"It's the worst kind of evil to enslave someone for any reason. I really want to find this girl, Matt."

"If it's possible, we'll do it. I'll get Sissy to help. Give me everything you know about her. Do we have a picture?" Matt asked.

"Yes, I'll send it to you. Thanks, Matt."

After saying goodbye, she decided to do some research on her own. She found the names of the Chinese gangs that trafficked girls and boys to New York. She went back to the date she would have entered the US and started checking the docks to see what kind of ships came in. It was a long shot, but every lead had to be followed. Sophie was in her mini-command center when her phone rang.

"Hello."

"Ms. Star, this is Gail Turner. I have a lead I'm going to

check it out. Do you want to come?"

"Ms. Turner, you can't go chasing leads without backup, that's how you ended up in the hospital, last time."

"I tried to call the Captain, but they said he was at the scene of a murder and would be gone all day. I'm going, I don't know how long this tip will be good. All I plan on doing is staking out the place and taking pictures. How dangerous can it be?"

"Very. You can't go alone. Where are you?"

"I'm in my office, but the lead is in North Bergen, New Jersey by North Hudson County Park."

"Wait for me at your office, I'm going to call Houston and see if he can give us back up."

"Alright, but hurry." She wanted to get there before dark.

Sophie tried to get Houston or Fons, but they were out on protective detail. She left a message and headed to meet Gail. She couldn't let her go by herself.

They made it to the address on 79th a couple of hours before dark. There were lots of cars on the street, so they blended in and scooted down in their seats. Sophie had the binoculars and Gail had a camera, with a zoom lens and the flash off. There was a light mist falling, but it didn't hinder their view.

Gail explained she had an informant that was an outlier of the Chinatown street gangs. He said he heard some men talking about a brothel, he thought it might be the one she was looking for. Gail planned to get pictures of everyone who came in and out. She wasn't sure what she could do with the photos yet, but it was a start. All her other leads had fizzled out.

Sophie was surveilling the area; they were positioned in front of the house about six cars down. The house was two stories about 3000 sq. feet. It was not well tended; the paint was peeling, and the roof needed work. The yard was unkept, mostly dirt with splotches of grass or weeds. She could only see one lookout, but there could be more around the perimeter.

Sophie didn't see cameras, but there had to be some. She kept looking and spotted one above the front door and one on the side of the house.

The fact that the clients weren't in and out in less than a minute gave credence to the fact that the merchandise they were selling wasn't drugs. The light mist ended but the night was setting in. Gail wanted to peek in the windows to see if she could see any of the women. Sophie showed her there were cameras on the perimeter and probably more lookouts.

Gail kept taking photos until there was no light left at all, then she noticed the lookout went inside.

"This is our chance, Ms. Star." She started to get out of the car.

"It's too risky." Sophie grabbed her arm and held her.

"Then stay here, I'm going."

Sophie knew she couldn't stop her. "It looks like there could be a blind spot. Follow me." Sophie learned a great deal about surveillance since she's been part of the Task Force.

"First, let me try the Captain again, someone needs to know where we are." She called, but it went to voice mail. She left a detailed message.

They got out of the car, both had on flats and dark clothes; that was helpful. Gail had the camera on a strap around her neck. Sophie judged the blind spot and they ran to the left side of the house and flattened themselves against it. The windows were low to the ground and lights were on, allowing them to see in easily. Sophie poked her head around the window to see what was going on inside. There were mini blinds, but they weren't turned down. There were five men in what looked like a living room. She could see them eating and talking.

Gail moved to the other side to see for herself. The men were heavily tattooed, most likely Tong. There was little doubt this was a brothel. Gail wanted to take photos, but Sophie shook her head. They moved to the next window, there was no

16

covering on that one, the kitchen, it was empty. The next window had curtains, but they weren't closed all the way. It was a small bedroom, divided by a sheet hanging from the ceiling. They could only see the bed on this side of the sheet. A woman was laying on it, she looked like she was pretty drugged up. Gail took her picture.

They heard the door in the front open again. "We have to get out of here," Sophie whispered. She peeked around the corner to the back door, no one was there. As they stepped around the house, the door opened. One of the men spotted them. He hollered and another man came out. Sophie grabbed Gail's arm and ran. The two men started chasing them. The car was too close, the men would grab them as they tried to get in; so they ran. They had to stay in the housing development, there were more places to hide. If they got pushed to the park, they would be wide open. Sophie weaved them back and forth between houses trying to get far enough ahead to find a place to hide. The men were gaining on them. They took a couple of turns, there was a house with no lights on up ahead. They ran into the back yard and saw an RV.

"Lord, please let it be unlocked." Sophie tried the handle. It opened.

They hurried in and closed and locked the door behind them, sitting on the floor against the door. Sophie could hear voices from the street. She peeked out the window, two of the gang members were in the road looking around. Sophie took out her phone and dialed the Captain.

"Captain, we need your help," she whispered.

"Sophie, I got your last message, tell me you didn't go in the field alone." His voice was gruff.

"I couldn't let her go by herself. Anyway, were being chased, I need you to come get us. We're hiding in an RV behind a house. I'm not sure where we are, we started out on 79th, but we've been weaving in and out."

17

"I'll have one of my techs ping your phone. I'm on my way, but it will take about 30 minutes from where I am. Do you want me to send a patrol car?"

"No, we'll be alright." She didn't want them to move that brothel until NYPD and ICE could come and raid it. Seeing uniformed police would make them relocate it for sure.

After she hung up, she peeked out again, the men were searching the back yard. They came to the RV and tried the handle when it didn't open they moved on.

"Thank you, Lord." She breathed to herself. They were both sitting on the floor in front of the door. Knees bent close to their bodies, trying to be as invisible as they could. Sophie's heart rate was still up as she imagined Gail's was too.

While they were waiting, they discussed their next step.

"We'll give this information and those photos to the Captain; he can shut it down and get the women out of there." Sophie was glad something good might come of this fiasco.

"I'm alright with that, but I want to be there, so I get the story. That's only fair," Gail added.

About twenty minutes later, they heard a car door slam. The Captain must have been driving way over the speed limit to get there that fast. Sophie peeked out and saw the Captain heading for the RV. They got up and headed out to meet him.

On the way back to the station, Gail rambled on about all that happened. She insisted she wanted to be there when they raided the place tonight. But Sophie could see the Captain was upset. She kept quiet.

When they got into the station, he took them to an interview room, and they sat down.

"Ms. Turner, do you realize what would have happened if those men found you?"

Surprised at the anger in his voice, Gail said, "I knew it was a risk. But I was willing to take it."

"I'm sure all you were thinking about was a Pulitzer. Did you stop to think you weren't just putting yourself in danger but Ms. Star too? And anyone else who would have had to come to rescue you." The Captain's voice raised.

"She didn't have to come. I was perfectly willing to go alone." Gail defended herself.

"Sophie would never let you go alone. And for your information, if she hadn't been with you, you'd probably be dead right now or one of their newest *girls*." He slammed his hand down on the table.

"What's with you, I'm handing you a very nice collar."

As they were speaking Houston and Fons walked into the room. Gail didn't know who the two very handsome men were that just came in, but it was apparent they had some authority. By the look on their faces, they were not happy.

"Captain, can I speak to you please." Houston gestured to the hallway.

They could hear Houston reading the Captain the riot act. The Captain took it, he knew it was Houston's anxiety over what could have happened. When he calmed down the Captain explained what he knew.

The Captain came back into the room after speaking with the SWAT team. "Ms. Turner, the SWAT team and ICE are almost ready to raid the brothel. I got permission for you to come, but you have to stay in the mobile staging unit." Houston and Fons waited outside the interview room.

"Ms. Star, are you coming?" Gail asked.

Sophie looked at Houston, who hadn't said a word to her. "No, I'm going home."

She went to the Captain and gave him a quick hug, "Thank you for coming for us."

"Sophie, I'll always be there for you, but you can't go off on your own again. Promise?"

Sophie nodded. She could tell Gail didn't understand the deference the Captain showed her.

They were in Fons's SUV, he took them to the News Station to pick up Sophie's vehicle. No one was talking.

She had seen Houston angry before, but never at her and never like this. She tried to take his hand when they were driving home, but he pulled it away. When they got to the condo, he sat at the kitchen table, she went to him.

"Houston, I understand why you're upset, but I couldn't let her go alone. I tried to get you and Fons before I left. Even the Captain was unreachable." She was sitting next to him.

"Did you even *think* about me before you went on this suicide mission?" His voice was calm but cold as ice.

"I told you, I tried to call."

"You promised me you would not do any fieldwork on this without discussing it with me." Houston stood up. "When we took our vows, we became one, that means whatever happens to you affects me. Did you even *consider* me, Sophie!" He asked her again. She stood up and faced him. He cupped her shoulders, "do you have any idea what they would have done to you if they had caught you?"

"Houston, I'm sorry."

"That's not good enough." He went to the bedroom, changed, and headed to the spare bedroom.

"Houston, please don't walk away."

"I can't talk to you right now, I'm afraid I'll say things I can't take back." With that, he shut the door.

She sat back down at the table, shocked, "Lord, what have I done."

Sophie finally headed to bed. She prayed, asking God to help her make this right with her husband. She couldn't sleep. She got up and went into the spare bedroom and sat at the edge of his bed. He didn't even move; she knew he wasn't asleep.

Sophie started crying, "Houston, please, what can I do. I can't stand the thought of you not loving me anymore." She held her head in her hands and wept bitterly.

Houston sat up, *Lord, I know I'm handling this all wrong. Please help me,* he prayed. He turned to her, his voice softened, "Sophie, you misinterpret my anger. There is nothing you could ever do to make me stop loving you. It's the opposite, every day, every minute I love you more. That's why I'm so angry. If you felt the same way about me, you wouldn't have put yourself in danger like that. I'm hurt Sophie, my anger reflects my hurt."

He finally broke down and held her. She was still sobbing.

"I can't lose you, Houston, you're everything to me," Sophie spoke through her sobs.

He started stroking her hair, "I'm sorry, sweetheart, I was too angry to explain myself better. The thought of what those men would have done to you, kept running through my mind on the way to the police station. It was torture, Sophie." He moved a little, so he could see her face. "I know my job is dangerous. When I wasn't married, Fons and I would do careless things, impulsive things on our job. Things that could have gotten us killed or injured. I don't do that now, I follow protocol. I may still get hurt, but not because I'm reckless. I wouldn't do that to you." He held her close again, "I always expected you to do the same for me, that's all."

"Houston, I'm so sorry, I didn't mean to make you feel I don't consider you. I do, I love you. I faced a dilemma today, whether to let her go alone or go with her. I did what I felt was right. It may have been bad judgment, but it felt like the right thing to do," Sophie explained.

"But, you know better, you should have stopped her."

"Houston, you can't expect me to stand by and let someone get hurt and not try to help. I'm not built that way."

"I know you care too much. But that's not what I'm talking about. This was reckless, unnecessary. That's what makes it different. There was no hurry at the time. You could have waited for backup."

"Your right, it was unnecessary. We could have waited for the Captain and given him the information. I won't let that happen again. But please know, this was not intended as a disregard for your feeling. It was bad judgment. I love you more than my life."

Sophie held him close and promise him she would be more considerate of him when she made her decisions. He wasn't over it, but he knew how much she loved him. He needed to put his hurt aside and think of her. They headed back to their bedroom when the phone rang.

"Hello."

"Houston, tell Sophie we raided the place. There were 25 girls in that house, Dajao wasn't one of them. We arrested five gang members and ten johns. The girls are at the hospital, I don't think a couple of them are going to make it. They were in bad shape Houston...they're young. It's bad." His voice trailed.

"I'll let her know Captain, thank you. And I'm sorry for reading you the riot act, I know it wasn't your fault."

"Houston, I understand. Sophie has the heart of a lion, she's always willing to put herself at risk for others; we all know that. We're going to have to do our best to be there when she needs us."

He was right, God gave her a heart of a lion, she has no hesitation when it comes to protecting someone. Why would he want to make her less than what God intended? Living with it

22

was going to be a challenge.

Houston woke up in the middle of the night, he never wanted to make Sophie cry like that again. He should have controlled himself better, explained how he was feeling. God made her, now he needed God to teach him how to get through to her without hurting her.

When Sophie woke up, she could hear Houston in the kitchen, making breakfast. She took her shower and dressed. He was in front of the stove when Sophie came out. She wrapped her arms around him from behind and laid her head on his back.

"I love you so much, Houston. I'm sorry I disappointed you," she whispered.

He turned to her, "Sophie, you didn't disappoint me, marriage is new to both of us. We have to navigate around things that are important to each of us and figure them out in a way we both can live with. I know you didn't mean to make me feel you didn't consider me by your actions, but now you know how important the issue is to me. I expect you to keep it in mind. Next time it will be me doing something that upsets you, and I will have to learn to adjust my actions." He kissed her.

Sophie put her hands on his face, "You will never disappoint me, that's the problem, you're perfect."

Houston laughed, "Oh, how I wish that were true. Disappointing you will be the worst day of my life."

They ate breakfast and Houston left for work.

In the next couple of weeks, Matt and Sissy helped Sophie isolate ten other brothels. They were in and around Chinatown in the lower east side of Manhattan. The problem wasn't a lack of information but an abundance of it. There were so many gangs, cartels, syndicates, whatever they called themselves, that peddled in flesh. And most of them also operated opium dens, gambling dens, and some of the more sophisticated ones cloned credit cards. Others trafficking in guns, drugs and human beings. Sophie turned the information over to the Captain. She insisted he include Gail in the raids since she was the one who brought them the initial data. The Captain's SWAT team and ICE raided the brothels, but Dajao was not in any of them.

ICE interviewed all the women; none came from the same province Dajao came from. It was still gratifying to get these women their freedom. Sophie knew the gangs would just replace the women. They hadn't done anything to take down the trafficking network itself. Right now that wasn't the goal, she wanted to find Dajao Taru.

CHAPTER THREE

I t was Thanksgiving week, Sophie finally told Houston her surprise. After kissing her, he immediately got on the phone to Fons, his dad and his brothers. They decided they wanted to tailgate before the game. Houston and Fons asked for Thursday and Friday off. His boss approved it, but they would have to work Saturday, and Sunday after church in exchange. It was a fair compromise.

On Thanksgiving Day Sam and Teddy headed to the MetLife Stadium early. They had to get spots reserved for their trucks to tailgate. By the time Houston, Sophie and Fons got there they were setting things up. The men got right in to help, and Sophie worked on the food with Lily and Spring. She had never tailgated; now she understood why it was so popular. People from other vehicles came over to visit and share food. It felt like a small-town community.

By 1:30 pm they had everything cleaned up and they headed to their seats on the 50-yard line. Sophie was the designated videographer. She intended to record the game, but she spent most of her time documenting the men's reaction. It was more fun to watch.

They all made it back to Trenton at about 7 pm. By the time they unloaded everything, they were exhausted and stayed the night in Trenton.

Sophie got up and dressed the next morning and went downstairs to help. Lily and Spring were already working on the big meal. Houston, Jack, and Fons were still asleep. The plan was to eat at noon when the rest of the family got there. That way the men could watch another game on TV. It wouldn't be the same as being there, but they would enjoy it.

They headed home around 8 pm, Fons and Houston had to work the next day and Sunday. They decided to attend the Church Fons's family went to in Armonk, about 34 miles north of Manhattan, instead of driving back to Trenton. They recapped the weekend as they road home. Fons was in the front seat. Sophie had the back seat to herself. They had left Bully with Cody and Anne Maxwell, the owners of Bully's parents. Fons turned in his seat to face Sophie and spoke in his most persuasive voice. "Sophie, when are you going to set me up with Carol?"

Sophie could see Houston's pleading eyes through the rearview mirror. "Alright already, I'll do it. We'll have a BBQ at our condo and invite some friends, she will be one of them. If you're really nice to me, maybe you can come too," she laughed.

Fons fist bumped Houston, who had a big smile on his face. They went back to discussing the big game again.

"Thank you for such a great gift, Sophie. My family will never forget it," Houston said.

"I had ulterior motives. I have in my possession digital proof of the other side of Houston Townsend to show our children. A glimpse of their always calm, cool, and collected US Marshal father being a crazy football fan." Sophie raised the camera as proof.

"That is blackmail, princess," Houston chuckled. "I have every intention of showing our children that side of me."

Sophie let the men banter back and forth the rest of the way home, sitting back and enjoying it.

Matt had managed to locate the headquarters of one of the Tong gangs called the White Tigers. Sophie asked Captain Cartwright to get warrants for surveillance and computer forensics. Fortunately, human trafficking was a hot button for Jurists. After getting the orders, Sissy managed to hack into the White Tigers computer. She could see they weren't as organized as the Triad's who ran like a fortune five hundred company. The Tong ran more like a small business. In her snooping, she found they had forged visas for the forced labor domestic workers they trafficked. It allowed them to sell to more affluent customers.

They had names and locations of six brothels, but still, no indication of where Dajao may be. Her name didn't show up on any lists. Sophie handed the information over to the Captain.

The NYPD SWAT took down the six brothels. They interviewed the women, but still, no one from the province of the Philippines Dajao was from.

Cosby was in the loop and he let the First Lady know the number of women freed by the raids. Whenever he talked to Sophie his tone made it crystal clear he was not happy that she was giving the collar to the NYPD and ICE, instead of operating through the Task Force. But he knew how she worked. Her contract allowed her that freedom.

When Houston got home, she let him know where they were on the case. The good news was that many prostitution houses were being closed. But he knew Sophie would never stop until she found the girl she was looking for.

"We need to agree in prayer about this Sophie, the enemy is smart, but God knows all things, and he knows where she is." He took her hand, and they began to pray.

After getting changed, Houston asked if she would like to go out for an early dinner. They decided on Italian again.

It took over a week for Izumi to finally locate Sophie Star. He got word from his men on the street that she and her husband were eating at a casual Italian restaurant in Manhattan. He pulled up in front of the popular restaurant in a small limo with two SUV's one in lead one behind.

Izumi stepped out of the limo and buttoned his custom-made suit, made from silk imported from Japan, tailored to fit him perfectly, as were all his suits. He could see her sitting alone. He was a little surprised by her youth and beauty, although he wasn't sure what he was expecting. Izumi new she wouldn't be alone so he looked around to find her husband. He was paying the check at the front counter. Izumi could see that Mr. Townsend would not be one easily intimidated. He would have to use diplomacy, but if that didn't work he had five of his best enforcers with him to take her by force if need be.

Izumi initially planned on entering alone but thought better of it and motioned for his men to come with him. He walked into the restaurant; his men spread out around the perimeter of the seating area as a show of strength. It was brazened, but Izumi needed to make a statement to Sophie's husband that it would be futile to refuse his request. It was also a powerful reminder to the public that the Akuza were still around and a force to be regarded.

Houston had just paid the bill when he noticed the six men entering. He knew exactly who they were. During his years as a DEA agent. He studied every gang, syndicate, cartel and mafia in New York. He knew their tats, their choice of apparel, their mannerisms and how they acted in public. He knew these men were Akuza. One of the most secretive underground organized crime syndicates in the country. More akin to the mafia than a street gang. They normally stayed out of the limelight, letting the street gangs get all the attention, and thus the wrath from law enforcement. The Akuza members were extremely loyal and as far as Houston knew not one of them had ever been turned to become an informant. That's why prosecuting members above the lowest level grunts hadn't happened. Their history went back centuries and they still had strong ties to their affiliates in Japan who they still answered to.

The men were dressed in suits, all but one was ill fitting. The men, except for the obvious leader, didn't try to hide the fact they were carrying weapons under their suit jackets. He moved to take Sophie out of harm's way when the man in the fitted suit stepped up to them. He came across as a wealthy businessman.

"Ms. Star, Mr. Townsend, my name is Izumi Nori," Houston hid the fact he recognized the name, "I'm sorry to interrupt your evening but I must insist Ms. Star comes with me, she has been summoned to meet with my Kumicho." He stepped a little closer.

Houston stepped in front of his wife. "That's not happening."

Izumi tried to move around him, "Mr. Townsend, I know you are a trained bodyguard you must have noticed I did not come alone."

"Do you plan on shooting up this place in broad daylight? I'm sure the management has already called the police."

Sophie moved around Houston and placed her hand around his forearm. "Mr. Izumi, please explain yourself."

"You will not be harmed Ms. Star; I have only come to escort you to this meeting." He made a gesture with his hand indicating he wanted to escort her.

When Izumi moved his arm Houston notice his buttoned sleeve move above a Patek Philippe time piece, an extremely expensive watch. He recognized it because Sophie had wanted to buy him one as a birthday gift but he chose a more practical watch.

"What don't you understand! She goes nowhere on demand and certainly not without me!" Houston spoke up and put his hand in a stop position.

"I'm afraid he's right Mr. Izumi, if indeed your Kumicho wants to speak with me then he must honor my request to bring my husband along or I won't go willingly. That doesn't promote trust, if in fact, you intend me no harm." Sophie's voice did not betray the fear she was feeling.

Houston was ready to break this guy's neck which would end up getting him shot by the others and unable to protect his wife, so he thought better of it.

"All right, Ms. Star, I will allow it." He gestured toward the door, "please come with me."

They were led to a waiting limousine, Mr. Izumi and two enforcers got in with Houston and Sophie. The others went into the lead and tail black SUV's waiting with their engines running. The privacy window was up between the driver and the passengers and the other windows were tinted, totally isolating those inside. Or maybe it was to keep them from seeing where they were being taken. Izumi said the trip would be just over an hour and he offered them something to drink. They refused. He poured himself a drink, a burnt amber color that was most likely bourbon.

Sophie noticed he was young maybe mid thirty, he was handsome, taller than most Asian men she had met and in excellent physical shape. She saw Houston was watching the men. She knew his mind was racing, working on ways to incapacitate them if necessary and protect her. They were totally off the radar, no one knew where they were or that they were in trouble. It was all on him.

About forty-five minutes into the ride the limonene stopped and Mr. Izumi spoke again.

"Ms. Star, I'm afraid your husband will have to wait in one of the SUV's here until you come back."

The men tried to force Houston out of the car. He was fighting them and managed to get one of them off him.

"STOP!" Sophie screamed. Her voice thundered through the enclosed setting and startled the men, halting their assault for a moment.

"Mr. Izumi, I need a minute with my husband."

He motioned to the men to get out and he exited behind them. Sophie wiped some blood from Houston's lip with a napkin she took off the bar.

"Houston, you can't overpower these men. Please let them take me. I really believe they don't intend to hurt me." Sophie cupped his battered face.

"NO, don't you dare ask me to leave you. I won't do it." Houston was shaken and out of breath. Then his voice softened, "please, I couldn't live with myself if something happened to you and I stayed behind safe." She knew it would crush him. She decided it was better to face what might come together.

"Alright, sweetheart, I'll do my best." The door was still ajar and they stepped out of the limo.

"Mr. Izumi, as you can see, my husband will fight to his death to protect me…"

Izumi interrupted her, "I am happy to accommodate him, Ms. Star." She knew Houston would love to slap that smirk off Izumi's face.

"*But then*, you see, you would have to kill me too, and how would your Kumicho take that news?" It was obvious her statement startled Houston; he would never want her putting herself on the line for him.

Izumi stared at her for a moment, he believed her. "What do you propose Ms. Star."

"Let him come with us, he can wait in an outer room of wherever your taking me. I can see no harm in that."

He thought for a moment, then agreed. They got back into the limo and headed to their destination.

The estate was isolated, there was maybe fifteen acres of plush landscaping. A twelve-foot rock wall with concertina wire attached to the top surrounded the compound. There were woods all around the outside of the wall. The men on the rod iron gate recognized the limo and the gate opened. As they passed through the headquarters became visible. It had to be ten thousand square feet on each level. There was an ornately fenced area to the left that appeared to be some sort of garden or courtyard. There was a garage that held at least ten vehicles and a large rectangular structure that was probably a barracks for his soldiers and servants.

When the limo stopped, the men manhandled Houston out of the limo, but he gave no resistance. He was with his wife, that's all he cared about.

They were escorted to a beautifully decorated sitting area in the main building. Several stunning glossy black lacquer dividers were placed around the room as part of the furnishings, they had scenes on them that looked like they were carved from ivory. Izumi seated them and went into a room that appeared to be a large meeting hall. The door was guarded by two men.

"Sir, I have brought Ms. Star here as you requested." He spoke as he bowed. He told him everything that happened and why he brought her husband with them.

"Bring her in." The Kumicho said. Izumi bowed again and left the room.

Izumi stood in front of Sophie offering his hand to indicate she was to go with him. He directed her on how to address the man who summoned her. She was told to call him sir or Kumicho and she was instructed to bow. She touched Houston's hand, knowing he wanted to come in with her but he stayed seated.

They entered and walked within a few feet of the raised platform. Izumi made the expected 30-degree bow of submission as Sophie made a slight bow as a respectful greeting. It was a huge assembly room over two thousand square feet, no furniture other than a very ornate chair on the platform. There was a four-panel divider on one side of the raised platform, but she couldn't see what was behind it.

The man standing at military rest, feet apart hands clasped behind his back, was several inches shorter than Izumi and although he was slim he appeared strong. He was dressed in a black British power suit with a light gray silk shirt and a darker gray tie.

The man did not move or say anything for what seemed like a long time.

"Thank you for coming, Ms. Star, your reputation precedes you." He changed his stance and moved closer to the edge of the platform that stood maybe four feet off the main floor.

"I didn't think I had a choice, Kumicho. Not a good start if you want me to do something for you." Sophie didn't look away from his face.

"I do apologize but it was necessary. I needed to ensure you would come." He responded then added, "can I offer you some tea?" He gestured to the stairs that led to the platform. Sophie noticed his gold cufflinks but no bulge from a watch when he gestured with his arm.

Izumi led her up the stairs and behind the divider where there was a traditional low table and floor chairs. The Kumicho offered her one of the pillows with no back so she could kneel on the pillow with her legs to the side; the traditional feminine posture for sitting.

Sophie smoothed her skirt over her knees and knelt on the pillow.

The Kumicho then seated himself in the traditional male cross-legged position and offered her tea, which she graciously accepted. Izumi moved to the side, out of the way, where Kato, the headquarters chief, was standing.

"You are a beautiful woman, as was my wife, Ms. Star." He finally spoke.

"By that statement I take it she has passed away, I am sorry for your loss," she responded.

"Yes, Izumi's mother," he gestured to him, "Suki…she died several years ago." Sophie was shocked that the Kumicho was related to Izumi. There was no warmth between them at all.

He sipped his tea, "do you like your tea, Ms. Star?"

She sipped some more, "yes, your tea is excellent, Kumicho."

Sophie was familiar with the Japanese customs. As a child she spent years living overseas with her father, a Jag officer in the Army, when he was stationed abroad. The American run school taught protocols and customs to their students for every country in the United Nations. The Japanese felt it was rude to get immediately into the business at hand. She waited for him to bring up the reason she was whisked up and brought here.

"I understand your husband refused to let you come by yourself?" He remarked, lifting his cup again to take a sip, "I'm surprised in this day and age that an American woman would allow her husband to tell her what to do."

"My husband and I have made agreements and vows to each other and we do our best to keep them."

"Ms. Star, I asked you here because I have a problem that my men tell me I am being unreasonable in asking them to solve. My senior advisor," he pointed to Izumi, "told me he heard rumors of a woman who can locate anyone or anything. You can understand my hesitation to believe such rumors, but I was intrigued enough to want to meet you." The Kumicho was obviously weighing her up.

Sophie smiled, "I'm afraid my abilities have been greatly exaggerated through time and the grape vine, sir."

"Please call me Katsumi." He requested.

"I would have agreed with your statement before I met you, but now I'm not so sure." He continued.

"What is it you think I can do for you Mr. Katsumi?"

"About four months ago, I made a purchase, but somewhere during the transfer of the product it was stolen. The seller then disappeared with the money I paid for it. We have not been able to retrieve the money or the product. As you can see," he gestured around suggesting his home and property. "Money is no object for me, but I can't let it get around someone can steal from me and get away with it or it could happen again."

"I see, and you want me to find the money or the product?"

"Yes, I will pay you whatever you ask, if you will do it."

"Mr. Katsumi, money is no longer an issue for me either, and although you are a charming host, there is no incentive for me to get involved." Sophie pauses for a moment, "what happens if I can't do as you wish? You may retaliate and harm me or my husband. I won't put us in that position."

"Ms. Star, I am not used to negotiating with anyone, usually my requests are considered mandates. I realize you do not know me, but you must realize saying no to me would not be wise."

"I am aware, but if I do this under duress how would you know if I did my best. And if you retaliated against me, then the next time you need help, who would you go to?"

"Yes, but if you refuse me what need do I have for you anyway."

Sophie sipped on her tea as she considered her options. She could continue to refuse but she was convinced that she was put in this position for a reason. Deciding that having a favor owed to her by a man such as the Kumicho could be of great value in her line of work. Thinking she might find herself in need of it someday, she changed her mind.

"Mr. Katsumi, if I felt we could come to a fair and equitable agreement I wouldn't refuse your request."

"So, your refusal has to do with equitability?"

"Yes, and the fact I don't know I can trust you not to retaliate if you don't like what I find out."

"Ms. Star, state your terms." Sophie could see Katsumi was getting impatient.

"Mr. Katsumi let me explain. I do not recover items or persons, I find them. What I would do for you is find out where your money is and where your product is. In return I would like a favor from you when I need it and your word that if you are not happy with my results you will not retaliate."

"Ms. Star, you are a formidable woman, I can see why these stories grow." He tapped his fingers on the table for a while and drank some of his tea.

"I will accept your terms. Whatever favor you ask of me I will do, in return."

"I have your word on the terms, with Mr. Izumi as our witness."

"Yes." Katsumi stood up and went to her chair and put his hand out to her to help her up. She took his hand and gracefully stood. He walked her to the door and opened it for her. She turned to him, made a slight bow, thanked him, and walked out.

Izumi followed her, he was in disbelief at the extent of the Kumicho's attention and deference to her. He had never seen him treat anyone, except his mother with that much respect.

They were escorted back to the limo. The enforcers roughly shoved Houston into the car still angry at his earlier resistance. Izumi spoke harshly to the men in Japanese. Their demeanor changed instantly and their faces reflected surprise. Izumi dismissed the men with him and slid into the limo alone.

After they had left the compound Izumi spoke. "Ms. Star, you have made quite an impression on the Kumicho, I have not seen him give in to demands from anyone. You don't need to worry about being harmed, you are now under his protection." He offered them a drink again. They refused asking instead for water. He handed them water, then poured a drink for himself.

"I've been instructed to tell you the whole story, so you know where to begin your search."

Izumi went on to tell them the story from his perspective. Sophie asked why he didn't believe Yon Min-ji when he gave Izumi his theory that someone had hacked his account and confiscated the counterfeit money in transit. If his reputation prior to that was impeccable. Izumi said they would have been satisfied with the return of their money. In fact, he was sure Yon Min-ji would just explain to his father what had happened and return it. When Yon didn't respond to their two-hour deadline, he sent in the assassins in retaliation.

"Yon Min-ji was not there and has not been heard from since. That is the reason we feel he was the one who stole it. The Kumicho is a proud man, his reputation for being ruthless is an issue of importance to him, he doesn't tolerate failure. Yon Min-ji failed him. It isn't the money it's his reputation at stake. Since then he has had five of his highest ranking and best men working on this, all to no avail. He beheaded the last man who failed."

Sophie knew they were a brutal organization, but hearing it put that way was disturbing. She said she would find out what happened and when she had some news she would contact him.

He handed her his card. "I wouldn't take too long Ms. Star," Izumi responded. Once they were back at the restaurant he let them out at their vehicle and said goodbye.

Now that it was all over Sophie's knees became weak. Houston wrapped his coat around her and helped her to the car.

"It's just the aftereffects of the adrenalin, Sophie. I am so sorry I couldn't stop them from taking you." He held her for a moment until she stopped shaking.

"Houston, you did the right thing. I can't explain it but although I was frightened I had peace about it." She turned to look at him in the car. "Why would the Lord put us in the path of such evil men?"

"The story of Jonah in the Bible comes to mind. God wanted Nineveh to hear God's word and repent or he was going to destroy them. Jonah didn't want to go preach to them; it was an evil city. You know the story; it took some doing but he ended up going to Nineveh. When Jonah finally preached to

Nineveh they repented. Jonah, like so many of us would, had judged Nineveh unworthy and got angry with God. He still wanted them destroyed fearing the city would think his preaching of destruction was a lie. He was worried for his reputation and not for the lives of thousands of people. But God had a different plan. He wanted to show his greatness by revealing his ability to change hearts." Houston thought for a moment and continued. "In Ezekiel 36:26 the word says, 'I will give you a new heart and put a new spirit within you; I will take the heart of stone out of your flesh and give you a heart of flesh.'"

"I don't want to get in God's way, Houston. What do you think we should do?" Houston started the car. He didn't have an answer. He certainly didn't want his wife involved with the Akuza, one of the most brutal underground crime syndicates in the world.

"I don't know, sweetheart. We'll have to pray about it. Do you think we need to get the Task Force involved with this?"

"I'm not sure yet."

CHAPTER FOUR

Katsumi couldn't get Sophie off his mind, there was something about her that reminded him of his late wife. Suki was kind, gentle and very feminine. *If Suki had only lived she would have given me a daughter as formidable as Ms. Star*, he thought.

Katsumi looked up Sophie on the computer and read all the news articles, he became angry when he read of the terrible beating she endured from Nikko Morano. If he weren't already dead he would have had him killed.

Izumi came in and asked permission to speak. Katsumi granted it.

"Sir, I gave Ms. Star all the necessary information to do what you ask."

"That's good Nori."

Izumi hadn't heard his stepfather use his given name in years.

"Are you alright, sir?" Then feared he shouldn't have asked.

"Yes, I was just looking up information on Ms. Star, are you aware of her history?"

"Yes, sir, it was the lead story in the news for a long time. But they dropped the charges. What will you do to her if she does not find the answers you seek?"

Katsumi looked up at him perturbed, "have you ever known me to go back on my word?"

"No sir, I was just surprised you accepted her entreaties."

"That's not your concern." Katsumi dismissed him with the wave of his hand.

Izumi was puzzled at the interest Katsumi had in Ms. Star.

After Houston and Sophie prayed about it and discussed it at length, they decided to include Fons and Director Cosby. Houston called Fons asking him to come over. They changed their clothes and Houston made some coffee while waiting for Fons to show up. Then they all went into the mini-command center and video called Cosby who was at home.

"Hello?"

"Sir, Sophie and Agent Rodriguez are here with me. Sorry to bother you at such a late hour, but Sophie and I just got abducted by Izumi Nori. He took us to the Akuza headquarters and Sophie had an audience with the Kumicho." Houston relayed what happened except for his scuffles with the enforcers.

You could see by Cosby's expression he was concerned; he noticed a cut lip and a swollen cheek on Houston. "Does he know you were the ones that orchestrated the loss of his money?" Cosby took out a pad and started writing some notes.

"No, just the opposite, he wants Sophie to find it."

"How did he even get her name?" Cosby was concerned about leaks in his department.

"It appears, my name is floating out there among the criminal elite. They think I have special abilities to find anything," Sophie broke in.

"What can you tell us about where you were taken?"

"I'm sure Houston will be able to figure it out," Sophie

related.

She told him the entire conversation with the Kumicho and described him. She knew his surname was Katsumi. Which was more than any agency had on the man since he was inducted as Kumicho in the US, many years ago.

"Do we need to get you protection?" Cosby asked. Her valued to the government made her an asset he couldn't afford to lose.

"No, apparently I'm under his protection. At least until I get him what he wants," she explained.

They discussed what this could mean. Was there any way they could use this to tear down that organization for good? Sophie didn't think that was likely, the Akuza wasn't like other crime syndicates. The government had declared war on them once and thought they had crippled them, but they run like a family, they just rebuilt and kept going. No one would ever testify against the others. Even to the cruelest leader, they were fiercely loyal.

"What is it you want to do, Ms. Star."

"If I don't redirect him he's going to find Yon Min-ji eventually; he's a sitting duck in prison. I need to come up with a scenario of where his money is that will satisfy him."

"How?" Cosby wanted to know.

"By telling him the truth, that he lost his money to the government because he branched out into a field the government keeps a close eye on. I'll get a cohesive plan and let you know."

"Alright, Ms. Star. Can I have a minute with Agent Townsend and Agent Rodriguez?"

"Of course, I'll call you when I have something. Goodnight, Mr. Cosby."

"Goodnight, Ms. Star."

After she left the room, Cosby grilled Houston about the real danger they were in. He told him it was a serious situation but for now he felt the Kumicho would keep his word, he wanted to know where his money went. It was a matter of honor. Cosby wanted to know if there was any way this could lead to taking the Akuza down. Houston couldn't answer that at this time.

"I need to think about the danger for you and your wife, we may need to relocate you for a while."

Houston wasn't keen on the idea but he also wouldn't rule it out. He remembered the bloodbath in North Korea brought on by Izumi. Cosby ended the conversation and signed off.

After Houston left for work in the morning, Sophie got ahold of Gail, she hadn't talked to her since the incident on 79th street. Sophie had been working with the Captain. He was keeping Gail informed. Now she felt she needed to press Gail for more information, she felt Gail wasn't telling her everything. She called and asked her to come over.

Gail knocked on her door and hour later. "Come in Ms. Turner, it's good to see you again."

"This is a nice place you have Ms. Star. I wonder how you made the money to afford it." Gail's insinuation was evident in her condescending and self-righteous tone. "I got the impression you were avoiding me." Gail hadn't mastered the art of disguising her feelings. It was obvious she didn't like being summoned by Sophie.

They sat at the dining room table. Sophie ignored her insult and brought out the non-disclosure agreement she had prepared. Sophie placed it in front of Gail.

"Ms. Turner, I would like to have you sign this before we begin."

Gail was a little reluctant, but she had already agreed to it before, so she signed.

"Is that why you brought me here?" Gail said, put out.

"No. Ms. Turner, the information I have been feeding you about locations of brothels has garnered you a lot of attention from your News station. But, we haven't gotten any closer to our target, Ms. Taru. Are you sure your informant can't tell us more?"

Gail sat there for a while weighing things up. "You're right, the information you've provided Sophie... may I call you Sophie?" She nodded. "Has shut down, seventeen brothels. I'm sure it's put a dent in the Tong's business. I really had no need for my informant anymore; I cut him loose. My bosses are happy with my reporting and my numbers." She bragged.

"I thought you were in this to save a fourteen-year-old girl from a fate worse than death. That's the reason I signed on. I'm not interested in boosting your career, Gail." Sophie was liking this woman less and less.

"Do you really care what my motives are if we're able to shut those places down?"

"Yes, I'm done with supplying you information, I'll find Dajao Taru myself. You can go it alone from here." Sophie stood up; this conversation was over.

Gail changed her attitude; she knew her ratings would drop as soon as she lost her front-page stores. "Wait, I really am interested in finding Dajao. It's just this has boosted my career exponentially. I don't have the contacts you do."

"If I agree to keep you in the loop, you can't report any of it from here on until we find Dajao, understood?"

"I have to fill airtime to keep my contract at the station."

"Then you'll have to get other stories, or follow your own leads for those, but you cannot use anything I bring to the table." She was adamant. "And I want to talk to your CI. He knows more than he's telling."

"Alright, but you can't cut me out of this, it's my story!" Gail demanded. She wanted to be sure she wasn't getting the boot.

"Let me know when you arrange a face to face with your CI, Ms. Turner." She walked to the door. Sophie was done with her.

Gail followed, "alright, I'll do what I can." She said goodbye and left.

Sophie was angry, feeling used. She had to get over it, she stilled needed to find Dajao Taru. Sophie called Houston to vent.

Sophie called back Director Cosby. She wanted to let him know she had a plan. Her objective was to stop the Kumicho from retaliating on the Yon family. She needed to settle this situation permanently. She told him she wanted to give the Kumicho a way to save face by letting it be believed he was able to hack into the governments banking system and retrieve his money. Of course, they would never even get close but the rumor would be sufficient to appease him. Cosby didn't like the idea of the US government looking like it got hacked, of course they would deny it. Sissy would just go as far as she could. Sophie suggested Director Cosby sell it to the Treasures Department by saying it was a test of their cyber security. It really didn't matter if she only got to the first level the rumors would take care of the rest.

"Ms. Star, you have a lot of clout right now because of all the brothels you've identified and shut down and the women who have been rescued. The First Lady is extremely happy, so I'm not going to say no to you, but you are really pushing the limits here... Do what you have to, I'll back it up."

That ended the conversation and he was gone.

A few days later, Houston was again waiting in the sitting room at the Akuza headquarters. Izumi escorted Sophie into the big assembly room. The Kumicho got up from his chair and went to greet her, leading her to the ceremonial table and pouring her tea.

"I am delighted to see you again Ms. Star." He finally spoke.

"That's kind of you to say."

"I must tell you, I looked you up on the net after you left our last meeting. You do have quite a history." He sipped his tea and offered her a plate filled with traditional Japanese green tea cookies.

"Your interest in my past is understandable, it's important to know who you're dealing with." Sophie said as she took a cookie and placed them on the plate provided.

"Indeed, it is, but you do not know anything about me, Ms. Star."

"I wouldn't presume to be so fortunate." The more she knew about him and the organization the better, she may need the information. The law enforcement knowledge of him and how he runs the Akuza is slim at best.

Katsumi told Ms. Star his life's story. She was not surprised to hear of his harsh and loveless upbringing by his father who was an Oyabun under a Kumicho in Japan. When the Akuza council decided to expand to America Katsumi was promoted to Saiko Komon to the newly inducted Kumicho that would run the territory.

"My rise to Kumicho was my destiny, would you agree, Ms. Star."

"Who am I to agree or disagree. The fact you are the Kumicho says it all."

"After our business is complete, I would like it very much if you would come back on Saturday and have dinner with me."

"After our business is concluded you may wish to take back that offer." Sophie smiled.

"I doubt it Ms. Star." He returned her smile.

"It is an honor to be invited but I would not have dinner alone with a man without my husband, Mr., Katsumi." He frowned; he wasn't used to rejection.

"Not even your father?"

"Of course, with my father, but my father would love me and my husband and would want to dine with both of us." Sophie was confused by his persistence.

"Then, of course, bring your husband, and Izumi will join us too." Katsumi said, pleased with himself.

"It will be our pleasure."

"Now, Ms. Star, what news do you have for me?"

"May we speak in private?" She requested.

The Kumicho waved Izumi and Kato off. They stepped through the platform door to the other side.

"As you are aware a few years ago the government declared war on the Akuza and a few other organized crime syndicates. According to their inner memos they felt they had done a great deal of damage to the Akuza organization nationwide, although they did not wipe you out. After that deluge they backed off thinking you would eventually fade away. They lost interest in you."

"All that is true, but what does that have to do with my stolen money?" She could tell bringing their misfortune up annoyed him. Although it happened before he became Kumicho.

"When you decided to delve into counterfeit American currency it got their attention. The government responds quickly to crimes that do harm to the economy. You were already on the watch list when you decided to expand, it brought you back onto their radar. The FBI or the Secret Service must have found out about your deal and hijacked it, and the counterfeit bills.

I tracked the money from account to account all over the world, it finally landed in DC, in a special government appropriation account." Sophie waited for a response. When there wasn't one she went on. "I'm sorry but I wouldn't recommend trying to retrieve it." She waited now until he spoke.

"And what of Yon Min-ji?" She knew if he couldn't get his money he would want Yon's head.

Sophie hesitated, "I was able to track Yon Min-ji from North Korea to Hong Kong, then he came to the United States. After he left here he went back to Hong Kong and it appeared he was going to start up a new business until he got spooked. Something happened there that caused him to run. His plane landed in Japan and then it was seen again in Mexico City and disappeared from there. It's possible he may have sought asylum with the Mexican cartels. That's all I can give you on him sir, but it is evident he does not have your money. He was telling the truth.

"Ms. Star, you have accomplished more than all my men were able to do. But I cannot just let it go, my power is in large part imbedded in the respect I have from my men. They have to see me as insuperable." His voice was somber.

"Would you think me too disrespectful if I offered a solution?" She asked.

"I will listen first and then decide."

"I would be willing, at great risk to myself, to hack into the governments banking system. It could then be rumored that you, the great Kumicho, outwitted the government and stole your money back."

"Is that possible, Ms. Star?" His voice perked up with his interest.

"No, I may be able to get into the very outer regions of it, but that won't matter, the rumor would be out, of course they would deny it. They would never admit to being hacked even just at the edges. That's the beauty of it, the people who matter to you will believe it and yet you will have no risk of waking the lion against you again. I would be the only one in jeopardy. If I get caught they would put me in jail. But I have no connection to you, so you would not be in their crosshairs. It would end there" Sophie took a breath. "This of course is predicated on a few things."

"Why would you do this for me, Ms. Star, and what conditions would need to be met?"

Sophie took a bite of her cookie and sipped some tea while looking him in the eye. "I don't feel I was able to accomplish my goal for you. So this would allow me to try to make you whole by giving you what you really want. An untarnished reputation as a leader to be feared and respected. One not afraid to go up against the mighty government of the United States. Consider it the successful completion of my assignment and a gift for your gracious invitation to dine with you."

"And your conditions?" He kept eye contact with her.

"If I do this you must give up the idea of retaliating against the government or Yon Min-ji and his family. If you don't then everyone will know you did not make yourself whole and my risk would have been for nothing." Sophie put her tea down and finished her cookie while she waited for his answer.

Katsumi did not speak for a long time; she knew he was weighing up his options. She waited patiently for his response.

"Ms. Star, giving advice to a Kumicho without being asked is a dangerous thing to do. However, you are not a member of Akuza so you do not know our ways. Now you do, so I suggest you don't repeat that mistake. Is that understood?" Katsumi had to maintain his position of power over her. The Kumicho is a god to his men. A god does not need or ask for advice. It couldn't get out that he took direction from her. She understood that.

"Yes of course." She got up to leave.

"Sit, please." He gestured to her pillow. "I do feel this plan may do what I need. I can't be responsible for rumors whether true or false that may come up about the Akuza. I could resist retaliation against Yon Min-ji in order to keep you from being found out, as a courtesy. I would not, of course, expect anyone to misrepresent facts to my subordinates." Sophie understood the insinuation.

"Of course not. But you can't be held responsible for rumors that get out about you. Good or bad." She said with a slight grin.

"No, that is true."

At that, he got up and asked Izumi to return. Then he went to where she was seated and offered his hand to her and walked her out of the assembly room. Izumi followed. She felt he had given his word not to track down Yon Min-ji or as close to it as she was going to get.

They were escorted back to town and dropped off at their condo.

Sophie called Sissy when she got home and asked her to come over, so they could commence with the plan. Sophie was watching Sissy work; she really was a genius. Sissy managed to get into three levels of the government treasury, before being detected. Normally at that point the FBI would be knocking down their door, but since this was sanctioned the right people knew about it. Needless to say, the Treasury Department was not happy she was able to get so far and hired her to fix the flaws in the system.

Sissy laughed, "as long as I'm around you, I'll have consulting jobs for life." They both laughed.

It was now Sophie's job to get the rumor to the right

people. She called Gail and let her know she found out that the Treasury Department was hacked. She told Gail she had no way of verifying it, knowing Gail couldn't use it if she didn't get another source to confirm it. Sophie told Gail she was giving her this tidbit because she felt bad she was so abrupt with her the other day. By Gail trying to get a second source it would spread the rumor all around the city. She also let it slip it might have been the Akuza trying to retrieve some confiscated funds.

Sophie would normally feel bad about using someone like this, but this time it didn't bother her at all.

Houston was not sure accepting the invitation to dinner with the head of the Akuza was a good idea. But Sophie was convinced there could be some benefits down the line.

Sophie had chosen a silk cream top and a navy silk skirt for the dinner at the compound. Houston was in a dark suit and light green tie. Izumi picked them up in the limo at 6 pm.

Mr. Katsumi greeted Houston first, then came to Sophie and crooked his elbow for her so he could lead them into the formal dining room. There were two large crystal chandeliers hanging from the twelve-foot ceiling. The table was at least twenty feet long, with matching chairs that had carvings on the sides, the legs and the backs. It was breathtaking. He took her to the seat next to his and pulled the chair for her. Houston and Izumi seated themselves. Houston sat next to Sophie and Izumi on the opposite side next to his father who was at the head.

The servants brought out the first course. As it was laid in front of her she said, "Itadaki-masu." (I humbly receive.) Mr. Katsumi was impressed. The first course was an appetizer, (Sakizuke), the second course (Hassun), was sushi. Each course was exquisite. They were offered sake; she knew it was not impolite to refuse it and asked for tea. The meal continued for twelve courses.

Mr. Katsumi spoke first, "Ms. Star, you might be interested in a rumor that has come to my attention through several of my Oyabuns. They say it has been reported that the United States Government Treasury account has been hacked. Do you think that is interesting?"

"I do indeed sir, are there any reports of who may have dared such a risky endeavor?" Sophie smiled at him.

"Yes, it appears that the Akuza are being blamed. Of course, we would deny any such criminal activity," Katsumi said. "Many of my men, however, believe it and have congratulated me on my success in retrieving what was ours."

"Of course the Akuza cannot be responsible for unsubstantiated rumors," she responded.

As the meal continued she asked Mr. Katsumi to honor them with some tales of his childhood. He seemed pleased to do so and told some very amusing stories of the antics he and his friends were involved with as children in Japan. They laughed and enjoyed it, even Mr. Katsumi chuckled a few times. Izumi and Houston also told of some of their misdeeds as youth.

At the end of the meal Mr. Katsumi asked if she would tell a story. Apparently, Katsumi's love for hearing elaborate stories followed him from his youth. Izumi confirmed that when his mother was alive she would always tell them stories after dinner.

Mr. Katsumi ordered the table cleared and fresh cups of tea brought. Then he settled in to hear a story.

"I am honored that you should ask me, I hope I don't disappoint you. I would like to tell you a true story. The story I learned as a child about the God my father served."

Sophie started at the beginning, using flourishes and elaborate descriptions of how God created the earth.

"But before God created the earth he created the Angels.

One Angel, Lucifer, was more beautiful and powerful than all the other angels. But Lucifer let pride take him over and he decided he would set his own throne above God's. For this act of treachery he was expelled from Heaven for eternity. How can the one created tell the Creator, 'I am greater than you'?

But the angels were made for service, not companionship. God wanted someone made in His own image to commune with. So he created Adam and Eve and placed them in the beautiful garden he had prepared for them on earth. God loved Adam and Eve so much that He would come down from Heaven every evening to talk with them. But he wanted them to love Him by choice, so he placed one tree in the garden and told them that all He had was theirs but the fruit on that one tree. If they ate of that fruit they would die. He spoke of a spiritual death, a separation from Him, not a physical death. He knew if they loved him they would not disobey Him and would not want to be separated from Him."

Katsumi and Izumi were listening intently to the story and made animated faces when they were surprised by something said. Sophie continued after taking a sip of tea.

"Satan hated Adam and Eve because God loved them so much. Lucifer wanted to hurt God because he was expelled from Heaven. He thought the way to hurt God was to take away the one thing God loved more than anything else. His companions.

One day Eve was walking in the garden and stopped at the forbidden tree. Satan came as a beautiful tempter in the form of a snake. He told her that her Father, God, had lied to her and that this fruit would not kill her but indeed would make her equal to Him. The snake said that was the reason He didn't want them to eat of it. Eve hesitated but the snake kept pushing his words on her, enticing her to disobey the One who loved her, who gave her everything. She took the fruit and ate it, then she went to Adam and convinced him to eat it too.

That night when God came to visit them, they hid. They knew they had sinned and were afraid. When God asked them why they ate of the fruit of the forbidden tree, Adam said the woman enticed him, and the woman said the snake enticed her. But, in truth, they made a choice to disobey the One who gave them life. God could no longer visit with them since He is so Holy He could not look upon their sin. The Angels removed them from the perfect garden and to this day the entry to the garden is hidden and no one can enter.

Adam and Eve were now on their own. God no longer would be their companion, but He would always be their Father. He had lost his children to sin in the perfect world he had made for them." (Genesis chapters 1-3)

Mr. Katsumi clapped. "A true Japanese tragedy, Ms. Star, very good. Next time you come for dinner I would like you to tell another story."

"This true story has many volumes and has a happy ending, Mr. Katsumi."

"Then you will have to come many times to share it all," he smiled.

Houston had been watching Izumi during Sophie's story, he was intently listening and it seemed like he had been moved by it. *This is extraordinary* he thought, to be at the home of the most brutal crime lords in the United States. Telling them stories from the Bible. He was convinced, God is no respecter of persons. He was brought back to the moment when Sophie said.

"Is that another invitation, Mr. Katsumi?"

"Yes, musume it is another invitation for next Saturday." She smiled at him quizzically at the name he called her.

Izumi could tell she was uncertain of the meaning so he

told her in Japanese it meant 'daughter'.

It was 11:30 pm by the time they got home. Houston had spent the ride home talking to Izumi. He asked him what he thought of the story Sophie told. Izumi said he had never heard of a God like that. Houston didn't push the subject any further, that was enough for now.

When they finally made it into bed Houston asked, "Sophie, what do you think is going on, why are we involved with these people?"

"I have no idea, but God is doing a work of some kind. I know one thing for sure. Everyone gets the opportunity to accept or deny Jesus as their Savior. This may be the only chance either, Katsumi or his son will have to hear the Gospel."

"If he gets angry at you, the fallout will be at a level we haven't dealt with yet," Houston said.

She turned to him and touched his face, "that's not our problem, Houston. If God has orchestrated this then it's His responsibility to keep us safe. As Paul said, 'For to me, to live is Christ to die is gain'." (Phil 1:21)

Houston knew that was true, but it was hard for him to let go of his concern.

CHAPTER FIVE

Houston and Sophie hurried home from Trenton after Church to get ready for the BBQ they promised Fons. Matt and Sissy were also coming. Fons came over to help set up, he was excited to finally get a formal introduction to Carol.

Sophie was on the balcony of the condo putting the finishing touches on the table they set up outside. She moved into the dining room to call Captain Cartwright and get away from Houston and Fons who were discussing the right way to grill the steaks; loudly.

"Don, do you want to come over and have dinner with us? Houston and Fons are BBQing." She glanced through the French doors, as she sat down on one of the dining room chairs and saw Houston and Fons laughing. She loved the layout of their Manhattan penthouse.

"Thanks for the invite but I have work to do. Besides, I hate feeling like a third wheel."

"Don't give me that. You, Fons and Houston have no trouble mixing it up." She heard him laugh but didn't give him a chance to answer. "When are you going to start looking for a good Christian woman? You are too good a catch to stay a bachelor." She knew plenty of young women who would love to date this handsome African American man with dark eyes, who kept himself in excellent physical condition.

"I've been thinking about it a lot. I used to date. Then I got wrapped up in the job. Now I have my dream job but I'm alone.

I guess you have to find a balance in every part of your life. There are lots of single women in my Church. I just need to take the time to get to know some of them," his voice had gotten melancholy talking about it. He told Houston once that he hadn't always been so picky about who he dated. But when he saw how good Houston's relationship with Sophie was, he decided he wouldn't settle for anything less.

Sophie didn't want to end the conversation with him sounding so melancholy. "Please come over, Don."

"I would Sophie but I really do have reports that need finished today. I promise I'll come next time, and I'll bring a date." He tried to lift his voice with the last sentence.

"I will hold you to that Don."

"I know you will, Sophie. You're a good friend."

They said their goodbyes but the conversation weighed on her for a long time. Sophie would start praying that God would bring the right woman his way. She would have to tell Houston about it. He would find time to meet with Don and encourage him.

Lilly had sent a nice pasta salad home with them; Sophie made a green salad and got some rolls out to heat up. Fons was preparing the steaks and Brocks for the grill while Houston got the spices and utensils ready. They had a patio heater, so it would be warm enough.

Matt and Sissy showed up together, Carol made it a few minutes later and brought a beautiful cake. They were all seated when Sophie spoke up.

"Carol, let me introduce you to our friends." She gestured to Matt and Sissy, "this is Matt Mathews and Sissy Corban." She motioned to Fons, "and this is Alfonso Rodriguez." She ended with a big smile.

"It's so nice to actually meet you all, Sophie says such nice things about you." Carol turned to Fons, "I've seen you several times but we never got past hello." Fons was a good-looking Latino man, about 6 feet tall, black hair, brown eyes in his early thirties.

The dinner talk was light and fun. Carol showed herself to be witty and engaging. The men's banter was always an amusing addition. During dinner Matt wanted to spill his secret; at least he thought it was. Everyone else had already figured it out.

Matt stood, "I just want to let everyone know, Sissy and I have been dating the last few months." He sat down with a smile. The others clapped and acted surprised.

Bully was going from guest to guest getting scraps until Houston caught him and exiled him inside the house. Sophie watched as Bully laid down in front of the French doors, his head on his front legs, banished from all the food...and fun.

"Houston, he's so sad...*look*," Sophie said as he walked back to his chair to finish his meal.

"He'll get over it," he replied.

Houston saw Matt and Fons snickering. They were enjoying the exchange, waiting to see who would win this little battle. It didn't take long for Bully to worm his way back outside.

After everyone helped to clean up, Fons came over to Sophie, "do you think she'd be up to going to the movies, if we all went?"

"Would it be a date?" Sophie teased.

"More like an 'almost' date, like you and Houston had. Just until she feels comfortable with me to go on a real date."

"Alright," she said.

Sophie got everyone's attention. "It's still early to end the evening, would everyone be agreeable to going to a movie?" She waited for the response. It looked like a unanimous vote.

Sissy and Carol looked up what was playing. They decided on a kidnapping drama and they headed out in two cars. Carol and Fons rode with them.

Sophie spent her time watching the couples, she felt like a den mother. Matt and Sissy were sharing popcorn and whispering back and forth. Fons and Carol were more animated. He was trying to deflect her attention from the movie to him with his comments about it. He would get her to laugh and she would tell him to be quiet and watch the movie. The people in front of them kept shushing them. Houston had ahold of Sophie's hand and was just enjoying being with her. They chatted quietly through some of the movie, it wasn't particularly good.

On the way home Fons asked Carol if she wanted to go ice skating with him next Saturday. She said yes and then addressed Sophie, "Fons wants to go ice skating Saturday, want to come?"

Sophie turned her head to the back seat to respond. But Houston looked in the rearview mirror at Fons who was looking at him shaking his head.

"That would be...." Sophie started to respond when Huston interrupted.

"That would be wonderful Carol, but we already have plans." Then he squeezed Sophie's hand, so she would understand.

"Maybe next time." Sophie responded.

When they got to the condo parking garage, Fons walked Sissy to her car and made sure she got off safe before leaving. Houston was helping his wife out of the car when he caught something in his peripheral vision. He quickly turned but there was no one there. It spooked him. He didn't want to scare

Sophie, so he just ushered her into the building and got her safely inside.

They were getting ready for bed when her phone rang. "Sophie, I had such a great time tonight. Thanks for introducing Fons to me, he is so handsome and funny."

"He is a wonderful man Carol; I hope things work out between you."

"Thanks, I just met him, so I know it's a long shot, but of the men I've known he meets my 'must haves' better than anyone else."

"What are your 'must haves'?"

"He must be a Christian, have a job, a kind heart, be funny and handsome, and love me the way Houston loves you."

"That's not asking so much, you deserve that."

"I'm going to hold out until I find someone that meets them all. He's already at the top of the list."

"Call me after your date on Saturday. I know you have to go back to DC this week. Will you have time to make our meals? If not, it's alright." As Sophie's private chef Carol made three meals a week for them, so all Sophie had to do was pop them in the oven.

"I've already put time in my schedule for them. I'll bring them on Tuesday before I leave." They said goodbye and hung up.

While she was on the phone with Carol, Fons had called Houston and told him how much he liked Carol. Houston teased him about how she had him acting like a lovesick schoolboy.

"You're going to chide me about being a lovesick schoolboy. Did you forget who your talking to? Remember, I was your chaperone with Sophie?"

"Yeah, Yeah, I remember." They both laughed.

"Fons, after you left I thought I saw someone in the parking lot watching us, did you see anything?"

"No. Do you want me to come over, we can check it out?" Fons said. his voice changing from lighthearted to concerned.

"It's fine, I have the alarm on and Bully would bark if he heard something. I'll see you tomorrow."

Houston had gone to work and Sophie was in her mini-command office when Gail called.

"Sophie, I finally got a text from my CI. He said we could meet at an abandoned auto shop about ten miles from here. What do you want me to tell him?"

"Let me ask Houston what time he and Fons can come with us, I'll call you right back."

Sophie called and told Houston about the CI. He said to set the meet for 6 pm. Sophie called Gail back and set it up. They would pick her up at the News Station. Then Sophie called the Captain to let him know.

"Are you sure you have enough backup Sophie; I could send some plain clothes men with you."

"No, I think we'll be alright, Houston and Fons will escort us and Gail says she's worked with this man for years."

"I'd insist on coming but I have my third dead Tong member today. It looks like their trying to find the mole giving us the locations of the brothels. The raids are really starting to hurt the Chinese gangs, they're losing girls, money and enforcers."

"Alright Captain, I'll fill you in tomorrow." She said goodbye.

Sophie had been working with Sissy all morning, trying to locate more gang headquarters they could hack into to find lists of the girls they trafficked. They were running out of leads.

Houston just picked Gail up at the News Station and was driving to the address the CI gave her. When they got close, the demographics changed in just a few blocks. It went from nice working-class well-kept homes to homes spaced further apart, unkept, some even dilapidated. It was a disturbing transition.

Fons was up front with Houston, he pointed out the auto shop. Houston pulled over on the opposite side of the street to stake it out. They deliberately got there early to see it in the light.

"I don't know, Fons, something doesn't feel right." Houston was still edgy from last night.

"Don't worry Mr. Townsend, I've known this CI for years, he's never lied to me."

They sat in the car and waited until 6 pm. It was strange they never saw the CI's car pull up.

"Maybe he's inside?" Gail offered.

"What's his name?"

"He goes by Santos." They were losing the light.

"Sophie, you and Gail stay here, Fons and I will check it out first." He grabbed his flashlight and they got out of the car. Sophie and Gail were in the back seat, watching the men go around the building.

"This is ridiculous, they're going to spook him. We need to go in there," Gail said.

"Don't you dare leave this car." Sophie grabbed her arm.

"Alright, let go of me." Gail pulled her arm away.

The Captain was at another crime scene. This body was in a dumpster behind a fabric manufacturer's warehouse. Three Tong members dead in the last few days. Add in one Triad, that's a lot when there isn't a gang war going on. His first thought would usually be a turf war, but there were no rumblings on the street about that. The only other thing happening was the pressure from the raids. The bosses had to believe there was a mole. They had no idea Sophie and her team existed. The bodies had been tortured which gave credence to his mole theory.

"Detective, do you have any ID on the man?" The Captain asked as he strolled over to the dumpster to see the body.

"We ran his tattoos, he's a Tong member named Santos."

Sophie was getting worried; the men hadn't come back yet. It was too dark at the auto shop to see anything now. A few minutes later she saw motion. The figures moved closer then stopped. Sophie gasped, five Tong members surrounded Houston and Fons. They had them on their knees, with guns to their head. It looked like there had been a fight. Houston and Fons were disheveled, she couldn't see their faces clearly, but it looked like their mouths were taped.

"Ms. Turner, I hear your looking for information. I'm afraid your informant is no longer with us." The man yelled and then laughed. "I have your bodyguards, if you want them back in one piece, I need you to come and talk to me."

"We need to get out of here!" Gail was frantic.

"I'm not leaving my husband and Fons. They'll be killed," Sophie said.

"And if I go out there, they'll kill me."

"It's dark, we're the same height, give me your hat. They won't know the difference until I get close."

"If you go out there, they'll just kill all of you," she said as she gave her the ballcap.

"Our times are in God's hands, Ms. Turner." Sophie opened the door.

She told Gail to call the Captain and tell him what's going on.

"Ms. Turner, I'm not a patient man," the Tong hollered again.

Sophie got out of the car. She told Gail to stay down, so they didn't see her.

"What's your name. I like to know to whom I'm speaking."

"Chan. Now move closer," he insisted.

"Not going to happen. I'm not stupid. You send my men back and we can talk."

Houston knew Sophie's voice. He was afraid of this; he knew she would take Gail's place. She was going to get killed if they didn't do something. He had to come up with a plan, fast.

"I don't think so, you come closer."

"No, what do you want to talk about?"

"Why are you targeting our business. We've done nothing to you. I don't want to kill you, but I will, if you persist."

"What exactly do you think I am doing to your business?"

"We know you are the one giving information to the police on the location of our brothels."

"Who told you that?"

"Santos." There was no point in denying it any longer.

"You, have a girl I'm looking for and until I find her, I will take down your business piece by piece."

"What's her name?"

"I'll send you a picture and her name. As soon as you let us go. You give me the girl, then you're off my radar. You can go back to business as usual."

"You're doing all this for one girl?"

"Yes."

"I'm afraid I don't believe you Ms. Turner. No one would do this for one girl. What's the real reason."

"I'm telling you the truth; I can't help it if you don't believe me. If you kill me you will get more attention on your business and you'll lose much more than a few brothels. Let my men go!" Sophie said.

"How about we do a trade? You for them."

"What do you want from me…" She didn't get a chance to finish her sentence. Houston took that moment to rear up and forcefully threw his head back, giving the guy behind him a headbutt. Fons did the same and followed his lead. They started to run toward Sophie. She was headed toward her husband when shots rang out, but not at them. Houston turned and saw one of their captors go down. The others took cover. Sophie knew Houston couldn't defend himself taped up. She ran to him and ripped off the tape on his hands and mouth as they ran for cover. Then she did the same for Fons. Their guns had been taken; they had no way to fire back. More shots rang out. This time toward them.

"Fons did they get both your guns?" Houston made sure his body was protecting Sophie's from the bullets.

"Yeah, I've got nothing."

"I'm going to create a diversion; you get Sophie to the car and get her out of here," he ordered.

"No, I'm not going without you." She reached for him.

He ignored her, "on three." He started counting but heard his name called behind him. He turned, ready to fight. He was startled to see Kato. Kato handed him a gun and pointed in the direction the men had gone.

"Take her Fons, as soon as we start shooting."

Kato and Houston started shooting while running toward the building. Fons grabbed Sophie's hand but she fought him, "No, Fons I won't leave him."

He took her shoulders, "Sophie, listen to me, I can either

stay here and backup Houston and Kato or I can babysit you. What do you want me to do?"

She instantly stopped struggling, "go back him up. I'll take Gail out of here and make sure the Captain is on his way."

"Good, don't come back Sophie. Houston won't forgive me for letting you go on your own as it is. If you get hurt, I'll lose my best friend."

"I promise."

"Ok, run now." He protected her with his body until she was at the car. Then he ran to catch up with his partner.

Sophie got in the driver's seat; the keys were still in the ignition. She started the car and gunned it down the street. She didn't stop until she saw an open gas station with lots of lights. Gail crawled up into the front seat and kept looking behind them to see if anyone was following. Sophie called the Captain to see how close he was. She could hear sirens as she was connecting to him.

"Where are you?" Her voice was shaking.

"I'm almost there, Sophie, tell me what's happening."

She told him the whole story and where she and Gail were.

"Stay there, I'll send uniformed police to protect you."

"Please hurry, Captain, they need help."

Houston and Kato were scoping out the body shop, checking the perimeter. The men that grabbed them were inside. They were coming back around the front when Fons caught up to them.

"Can we hold them until the police get here?" Houston asked.

"Do you want to hold them or just leave? Your wife is out of harm's way," Kato asked.

"I'm afraid Ms. Turner and my wife won't be safe if the

information Gail's CI gave these men gets out to any of the other gangs. If they're in jail they can't hurt her."

"No, but they can still talk." Kato knew what he had to do.

"That's true but we'll deal with one thing at a time," Houston replied.

One of the men who were in the auto shop opened the door to see if it was clear. Kato and Houston started shooting to keep them inside. Kato's shot killed the man, that left three alive. The first man shot in the initial shootout, was dead out front. Kato suggested they needed to cover both exits, "you two stay here I'll cover the back. "

Kato quietly slipped in the back door. One of the men was looking out the window trying to spot the shooter. Another was pulling the dead man inside so they could shut the door. The third was punching numbers on his phone, walking away from the others. The room was dark, Kato had to get to him before it connected. He came up behind him and covered his mouth with his hand and put his knife to his throat. He dragged him backwards a few feet and slit his throat. He quietly lowered him to the ground.

Kato heard the sirens getting closer. He had to hurry, if these men passed on what they knew Ms. Star would be in jeopardy. His orders were to keep her safe.

"Chan, did you call for help?" The one closest to the door asked. When he didn't get a response, he came looking for him. That gave Kato an opportunity to grab him. He cut his throat and lowered him to the ground. He snuck up behind the third man who was being a vigilant lookout and killed him in the same manner. Kato slipped out the back door and disappeared.

Six police cars pulled up at once out front. Houston sent Fons to let them know the situation. Fons saw the Captain get out of one of the vehicles and went directly to him.

Moving to the front of the building behind cover, the Captain called out to the men inside to come out. After the third call to come out, he ordered the men to breach the shop and take the suspects into custody.

When the police breached the doors of the abandoned auto shop they found the men inside were dead.

"Houston, what happened here?" The Captain asked as they walked through the dead bodies.

"There was another man here, I recognized him as a member of another gang. He must have done this." The Captain didn't inquire further.

"Captain, these men took our weapons. After CSI is done can we get them back from you?" He then questioned the Captain about his wife's whereabouts. He knew the Captain would have made sure she was protected.

One of the officers drove them to the gas station where Houston saw Sophie pacing. Gail was interviewing one of the officers, who looked annoyed. When she saw the police car pull up she waited to see who stepped out. When she saw Houston, she ran and threw her arms around him.

"I was so afraid for you." She kissed him. He held her tight. This was a close call for all of them.

"The Captain wants us at the precinct for statements tonight," Fons said.

"I'm good with that, let's get out of here," Houston responded.

Fons went to tell Gail so she could ride to the precinct with them. They got in their vehicle and headed downtown.

In the morning Sophie got up before Houston and took Bully for a run. She thought she noticed someone following her, so she cut it short and headed home. She was making breakfast when Houston came out ready for work. She turned to put his plate on the table and noticed the bruises that formed overnight on his face. She was sure there were more all over his body. He and Fons would not have been taken quietly last night. She touched his face delicately and kissed his bruises.

Houston smiled, "You can be my nurse anytime." He wrapped his arms around her snugly and pulled her down to his lap.

"Houston, I think someone might have been following me when I took Bully for a run this morning." She got up and sat in her chair.

"Sophie, maybe it's time I get protection for you again. This case involves dangerous people. They're not afraid to eliminate a problem. I'll contact the News Station about getting protection for Gail too." He put his hand on hers.

"Houston, I don't think they know who I am and I hate having my movements restricted again." She had her fill of it when she was dealing with Nikko.

"Unless you're finished with this case and turn it over to me, the Captain, and Fons, you're going to need protection, Sophie."

"No, I can't let go of the case. I want to find this girl; to know what's happened to her. If she's still alive she needs to be rescued. I just hate losing my freedom again."

He got up and went to her chair, lifted her up and wrapped his arms around her again.

"We have to be getting close, it won't be forever. If you want to ask Cosby to make it a Task Force operation we would be able to protect you ourselves. Do you want to do that?"

"I don't think so, the NYPD has done a great job with this. I don't want to step on their toes and you know if we make it a Task Force operation, Cosby will insist on the team getting the collars."

"Alright, I'll talk to Cosby about getting you protection when I'm not home."

He cleaned off the table and kissed her goodbye.

Sophie and Sissy were working together remotely. They had tons of material they had collected from the warrants but going through it was time consuming. They were looking for anything that pointed to addresses of the individual clan's headquarters. They needed to locate more trafficked girls. It was taking precious time with just the two of them.

Sophie heard a knock on the door. "Sissy, someone's here, I'll get back to you."

Usually the doorman called before someone was allowed up. She looked through the peep hole and saw Izumi and opened the door.

"Mr. Izumi, welcome, please come in. I'll fix us some tea." She led him into the kitchen area.

"You are very gracious, Ms. Star, but I'm here at the request of the Kumicho, he wishes to see you." He remained standing.

"Of course, when did he want us to come."

"Now," he replied.

"Mr. Izumi, my husband isn't here right now. I don't want to offend the Kumicho, but I'd rather wait for my husband to come with me."

"Please, Ms. Star, the Kumicho, heard of the incident last night and wants to see that you're alright. He is concerned."

"Let me call Houston and see what he thinks." She moved to the patio and called her husband.

"Houston, Izumi's here, he says the Kumicho has asked to see me, right now. I don't think he plans me any harm, but I will do whatever makes you feel comfortable."

"Kato is the one that saved our lives last night. It will seem very ungrateful if you turn around and reject his invitation. But you can't forget these are dangerous men. If I left now, I could be there about the same time you get there. Let me talk to Izumi."

She handed Izumi the phone explaining Houston wanted to talk to him.

Houston asked if there was any reason for him to be concerned. Izumi assured him that Ms. Star was under the protection of the Kumicho, no Akuza would dare touch her. He asked if he could meet them there to drive her home. Izumi felt that would be acceptable and gave him GPS coordinates. Izumi had no idea Houston had already located the headquarters on his own.

Sophie did a quick change of clothes and grabbed her purse and jacket before she left with Izumi.

The Kumicho was pacing when Izumi came in to let him know Sophie was in the sitting area.

"Bring her in." When she came in the door he stopped pacing. Kato stood a few feet away, off to the side of him. Katsumi stopped on the edge of the platform in the traditional command stance. Feet apart, hands clasped behind his back. She stopped in front of him on the lower level and bowed slightly in a respectful greeting.

"Ms. Star, I need you to explain yourself," he ordered.

"I apologize, Mr. Katsumi, but I don't know what you mean."

"Explain to me why you have gotten tangled up with Tong and Triad gangsters."

"Of course, Mr. Katsumi. Before I do, I must thank you on behalf of my husband and myself for your protection. My husband said it was your So-honbucho, Kato," she turned her head and nodded to acknowledge him. He reciprocated. "Who saved our lives. It was a trap and the men overtook Houston and Mr. Rodriguez."

"Yes, I know, Kato explained to me that they had Houston at gunpoint and you were going to offer up yourself in exchange. You are reckless with your life, Ms. Star. Women have no place in this type of business. Explain yourself."

Sophie was a little annoyed at his sexist declaration, but this wasn't the time to debate it.

"Mr. Katsumi, I have a new client, much like yourself, this client Ms. Turner needs me to locate someone. Ms. Turner is a field reporter for the local News Station. A young woman came to her telling the story of her sister who she believes has been trafficked from the Philippines to New York and sold to a Chinese gang. I have been hacking the gang's computers trying to find a record of this girl. I can't seem to find her so I'm applying pressure. I'm sending the police the information I come across of the location of their brothels. I'll take them down one by one if I have to, until I get the location of that girl."

"Ms. Star, you will wish they killed you if they ever get their hands on you. Do you not understand that? I cannot go to war with the Tong, Triad or any other Chinese street gang, to protect a woman. If they kill one of my soldiers I have cause but for a woman who is not Akuza; it would not be tolerated by the other 'crime lords'." His voice was raised.

"Mr. Katsumi, although I can never thank you enough for last night, I do not expect you to protect me. I am not your responsibility," Sophie calmed herself. "I'm sorry if I have done something to offend you."

"If you were my daughter I would control you, you have no business getting involved with this."

"I will not leave a fourteen-year-old girl in the hands of men like that. Every day I fail her, she faces abuses no one should have to endure. I won't stop until I find her. My father would not want a coward for a daughter!" She matched his volume.

Katsumi finally sat down, *she has the heart of a warrior*, he thought. He was proud and angry at her at the same time.

"Unfortunately, I have no say in your life, I had wished you would respect me enough to listen to me. But I see I hoped for too much." She could see he was disheartened.

Sophie moved up the stairs next to his chair and squatted down next to it. A gesture no one else would have been allowed. She put her hand on his arm, "Mr. Katsumi, I can't tell you how much your concern means to me. But, I am not a porcelain doll, I plan on making my life count."

"It will not count for much if your dead, Ms. Star, but there is no sense in trying to convince you." He stood up, and she followed suit. He had forgotten how much it hurt to care about someone and risk losing them. Katsumi thought he had built up walls around his heart but apparently, they weren't strong enough. It brought back his pain. He said goodbye to her and left the room.

Izumi walked her out. Houston was in the sitting room waiting for her.

"Izumi, why is he so upset with me?" Sophie needed to know.

"He hasn't cared for anyone since my mother died, he thinks of you as a daughter, he's worried you'll get yourself killed."

"I'm sorry to disappoint him, but I won't stop looking for

this girl, Izumi."

"I know, and there's a part of him, I'm sure, that is very proud of you."

They said goodbye and Houston drove her home. Sophie told him all that happened.

"Houston, I'm afraid our chance to tell him more about Jesus has probably come to an end. He was pretty upset with me. Maybe I should have handled it differently."

"Princess, you've done what you can. Now if God wants us to do more, He will have to work on Mr. Katsumi from the inside."

Houston told her he talked to Cosby and told him what happened. He said he would get you a bodyguard from the Secret Service teams we work with. He'll be out of uniform, so our cover isn't compromised. She was comfortable with that; she knew most of the men on that team. Houston said Cosby was pushing to get us to turn this over to the Task Force, it was getting a lot of good press.

Izumi was summoned to Katsumi's private residence again for breakfast. This was the fifth day in a row. When his mother was alive they ate breakfast together every morning. He entered the room and bowed. Katsumi gestured him to sit down.

"Your sister is going to get herself killed, Nori. She is too stubborn to stop this crusade." His countenance was still disheartened from the conversation with her.

Izumi thought for a moment wondering if it was wise to be so forward with his response, "watashi no Chichi, (my father), why is it you and my mother never had children?"

Katsumi's surprise showed on his face at the personal question. "We wanted children, very much, but it never happened for us. You were her only child." Izumi could see it was a painful memory for him.

"Watashi no Chichi, if you had a blood daughter, she would have your warrior heart and spirit. She would be brave and wise like her father and beautiful and strong willed like her mother. Just like Ms. Star. Would she not?" He didn't wait for an answer, "that would make you proud, not angry?"

A smile came on his face, "yes, of course, she would be the reflection of me and Suki. That's true." He started to eat his breakfast. "But my blood I could control, this woman does not listen to me."

"She listens to you and cares for you, she's just determined to do what she thinks is right, whether it puts her in danger or not." Izumi sipped his tea.

"Indeed. Increase her protection, but make sure she doesn't see them. She can't think I approve of her reckless behavior. Help her find this girl so she will be done with this."

"Yes sir. But I'm sure her husband will also have men protecting her. We don't want an incident between the men."

"You are right. Just send Kato. She knows him, that should prevent problems."

"Yes, sir." Izumi ate a few bites before going on. "She thinks you don't want to see her anymore, that you no longer care for her."

"She has a tender heart, like your mother. Contact her and remind her of our dinner on Saturday. She will understand."

"I must say Chichi, I am proud of her fearlessness. Kato said she faced those gangsters down."

"Her fearlessness today could mean her death tomorrow, watashi no musuko (my son)."

"Of course, your right, Chichi." He hesitated to ask this

next question. "Chichi have you ever wanted a different life than the Akuza?"

Katsumi's first expression was one of anger that Izumi would ask such a question of the Kumicho. Then his face softened.

"One night when your mother and I were alone, I told her I would give her anything she asked of me. Her response was to ask if we could leave the Akuza and live a life away from all this cruelty and danger. She wanted a different life for you. I agreed. She knew I had to wait for my Kumicho to pass on, my contract with him was for his lifetime, as yours is to me. She was willing to wait, my Kumicho was an old man his days were numbered. But your mother died before I could be released.

By the time my Kumicho died, I had no reason to leave and I was inducted as the new Kumicho." He took a breath; saw the surprise on Izumi's face. "I was so angry with Suki for dying, for leaving me here without her. I wanted to kill myself, so I could be with her. But as you know, a Saiko-Komon cannot do that without permission from his Kumicho, and he would never have allowed it." He paused and looked directly at Izumi, "I could have let you go when she died…Not force you to stay with me and eventually make you my Saiko-Komon. Insisting you stay, was my punishment to her."

Izumi was pleased at this new revelation. His mother had wanted a different life for him. That's where this desire came from, to live away from all this brutality. "Thank you for telling me that. Of course, I was honored, as I should have been, when you named me your Saiko-Komon at your induction, Chichi." He didn't dare say his true feelings, even in this unusually tender exchange about his mother.

CHAPTER SIX

S ophie woke up with a new thought. Maybe they're looking in the wrong direction. She contacted Sissy to see what she thought about it.

"Sissy, what if we're looking at this all wrong. Maybe Dajao was sold into forced labor, domestic slavery. We haven't gone down that road yet." Sophie had new hope.

"If that's where we're going, I'll need to go back to the beginning and go through the gang's computer files again. I didn't see a forced labor or domestic file listed with the names of women in the brothels."

"You work on that; I'll try to get some other leads."

Sophie called Houston to tell him the direction she was going with this.

"As long as you don't go in the field alone, Sophie. I do think it makes sense to look at all avenues." His boss called his name; he said goodbye and went back to work.

Her phone pinged; she saw Izumi's text.

> **The Kumicho wants to remind you of your dinner invitation on Saturday.**

She responded,

> **I'm surprised; I didn't think he wanted to see me again.**

His response,

> **He cares about your safety, as do I.**

She responded,

> **That is kind of you, Izumi. Do you have time to talk?**

He responded,

I'll be there in an hour.

Sophie texted Houston to let him know her plan and that she invited Izumi over. Houston didn't feel she was in danger. He texts back that security would be there today.

Sophie prepared a nice salad and tea for Izumi. She wanted him to be in a favorable mood.

Izumi arrived on time; she seated him at the more formal dining room table. Bully came up to him to see if he was friend or foe. He must be friend because Bully walked away and decided he wanted to go out on the balcony. Sophie indulged him.

"I'm afraid, my sister, you are trying to butter me up." He said, laughing after she fed him.

"Am I that transparent? I'm sorry, I know your culture prefers subtlety." She smiled, filling his tea again.

He sat looking at her to give it up, but she was trying to be a good host. "Alright, what is it you want of me?" He feigned annoyance.

"I've decided I need to change my strategy. I think I've been looking in the wrong place for this girl. Maybe she was brought from that Province to be a domestic slave. There isn't as much money in it, but it's still a good revenue stream. Can you think of any gang that specializes in that? In the research I've done, it looks like the Triads…"

Izumi interrupted her, "You cannot tangle with the Triad, they are strong and organized, much more so than the Tong. You cannot trifle with them." Izumi straightened up in his chair and spoke bluntly.

"I have no intention of trifling with them. I plan on getting back this girl, and I will do it with or without your help." Sophie pushed back.

"I believe you, Ms. Star, for that reason, the Kumicho has ordered me to help you. He wants this crusade of yours over."

She was surprised that the Kumicho would consider helping her in any way. "Does that mean you'll answer some questions for me?"

"Yes," he relented.

"How are the trafficked girls distributed throughout the country? And how would I find the ones slotted for domestic slavery instead of prostitution?"

He hesitated, "there are many organized street gangs and mafias that traffic in flesh. The most notorious are the Tongs and the Triads. The Triads alone have four clans that traffic in flesh. They do not broadcast the fact they have migrated to the five boroughs."

"Which one would be your educated guess?"

"There is no way to know. But if you understand how they operate, it may help. Long gone are the days a gang does all its own transporting and holding. They lost too much merchandise and members that way. And understand this, those women are considered merchandise to these men.

Now different clans in the groups specialize in certain areas. That way if they are caught, they cannot take down the whole organization. Other clans hire them as transporters; thus, they only pay for product that arrives alive. Getting caught is their problem. They contract with holding facilities not associated with their Chinatown gangs. They pick up the women when they have room for them in a brothel or a request for purchase of forced labor. The women sold as domestic slaves must be in good health so the rich buyers will pay a premium for them. The contracted facilities take better care of them."

It made Sophie sick to hear of human beings spoken of like chattel. It must have shown on her face.

"Ms. Star, you must understand there are many cultures where women have little or no value. I know that is distasteful to your western sensibilities." She knew what he said was true, but it was still repugnant.

"Why would they pay someone else to hold their women?"

"The chances of a raid is highest when the women first come in. Their own headquarters are under surveillance from the police constantly."

"Do you have any idea where any of these holding facilities are?"

Izumi let out a deep breath; he did not want to tell her. "I only know of one. The facility is in an innocuous office building on the edge of town."

"I'd like to go check it out, will you take me?"

"Absolutely not! Let your husband check it out. I don't want you to go anywhere near it. If you do, I will not help you again, Ms. Star." Izumi immediately stood to leave. She was getting accustomed to his mannerisms. There was no doubt he was angry with her.

"I'm sorry, Izumi, I shouldn't have asked. I'll talk to Houston about it." He wrote down the address and handed it to her.

Sophie didn't want to have him leave upset, so she asked about dinner Saturday night as she walked him to the door.

"Will Katsumi still be cross with me when I come?"

"No, his mind is settled. He knows he has no control over your actions. He will want to hear another story, however. As will I." Izumi softened his voice.

"I would love to tell another story. I'll tell of a great warrior named David." She relaxed and smiled at him. "These stories come from the Bible. Have you ever read it?"

"No, but I know of it, it tells of the Christian God, but we are not encouraged to believe in any god but our Kumicho. We must give 100% allegiance to our Kumicho. We offer our lives totally to him and our brother Akuza. If we believed in a god other than him, we would have split allegiance. Most of our men are Shintoists.

"I have never heard of Shinto, who are the gods?"

"It is not the belief in god as you would understand it. They believe all things have a spirit or kami. So there are many shrines and idols. They believe the kami of their ancestors can protect them, for instance. There is a kami of wind, rain and so on. But their belief does not interfere with their absolute loyalty to their Kumicho. There is even a shrine at the headquarters."

"In that private courtyard, you can see when you drive up to the headquarters?'

"Yes, the Kumicho allows it for the men," Izumi said.

"Then why does your Kumicho allow me to tell these stories?" She knew it was only God, but she wanted to know what Izumi thought.

"I do not know. It is a mystery. It is possible my Kumicho likes to hear you speak. A woman's voice is very pleasant." He laughed.

"I will do my best to make it pleasant." She opened the door for him.

"I look forward to it, Ms. Star."

"Thank you, Izumi. For your help. I know I seem ungrateful at times...I just want to find this girl." She said as an apology.

"I understand you, Ms. Star, you can only offend me if you get yourself killed."

Sophie laughed, "I will try very hard not to offend you then." She noticed Special Agent Ted Poleck walking the hallway. She waited for Izumi to get in the elevator before she acknowledged him.

"Special Agent Poleck, I'm sorry you got stuck with this detail. I'm sure you would prefer something more noteworthy."

"Ms. Star, you undervalue yourself. It's an honor to be trusted." He was checking out the hallway security cameras to make sure they were working.

"You're too generous but thank you. Can you come in."

"No, they don't want us too close, they want to protect your cover. I was just doing my rounds when you saw me."

"Alright. Houston will probably be home at six. He can take over from there."

"That is the plan, for now, Ms. Star."

She wondered what he meant by 'for now', but she went into the condo and closed the door. Sophie needed to talk to Houston about checking out the address.

Houston and Fons weren't on protection detail today. They could come and go as they pleased, as long as their reports were done. They arrived at the condo at 4 pm and headed to the address Izumi gave Sophie a few minutes later. With the traffic, the drive took an hour. Houston was using binoculars, and Fons was taking pictures. The name on the sign out front was Global Enterprises Ltd. There were a few cars parked in the parking lot, but little foot traffic. About the time they arrived, a few people came out of the building and left in the parked cars. Fons emailed the pictures he took to Sissy and Matt, who were researching as information came in. Matt worked on the faces while Sissy researched the company name and address to see who owned it. The brick structure was in pristine condition, the grounds meticulous. The properties slope made the basement visible only from the back of the property. It had another parking lot, at the basement level.

"Let's go around back, maybe that's where the action is," Fons suggested.

Houston found a spot with some bushes that would partially hide the SUV. The tinted windows were enough that a casual look in their direction would not reveal them. By 6:30 pm, it was beginning to get dark. Houston's switched on the binocular's night vision.

"I want some toys like that." Sophie was in the back seat. She scooted herself up and leaned in between the bucket seats to get a better view.

"I'll share with you, sweetheart." Houston handed her his binoculars.

They were beginning to think this was not going to be a successful stakeout when they saw a utility van pull up. There were no windows except for the two front ones and windshield. The van pulled up to the door, backed in, and stopped. She handed the binoculars back to Houston. Fons had the camera on video to capture whatever happened next. Two men got out and opened the van door; ten girls were ushered out, cuffed together in twos.

"I recognize the tats on those men; their Triad." Houston was still looking through the binoculars.

Fons enlarged the pictures of the girls on his camera. Most of them had looked around when they got out of the van, allowing Fons to get a full-face picture on most of them. He sent the video to Matt. Dajao wasn't one of the girls. Houston had told Sophie it was a long shot, but ever the optimist, she had her hopes up.

"If we have NYPD raid the facility now, we'll lose our chance to keep it under surveillance. They'll end up moving the operation to another privately contracted facility, and we will lose the chance to see if Dajao comes through here."

"But if we don't take it down, who knows what will happen to them in there," Sophie lamented. Houston knew this was a tough call.

Fons was still watching the video he captured. "The tattoos are definitely Triad," he said.

"We can follow the vans that take these women to the brothels. Take them down there." Houston watched the door, waiting to see if anyone was going to come out.

"Houston, how do I justify giving up these girls for Dajao. But how do I save Dajao if I don't." The catch twenty-two was painful for Sophie.

Houston didn't answer her; he knew she would carry the guilt for the rest of her life if she made this decision. No matter what they did, some of the girls would be left behind. There was no right answer. He knew what he had to do.

"Sophie, you are going to be upset with me for this, but I have to take the decision out of your hands. As a US Marshal, I can't sit by and let a crime be committed right in front of me. Fons and I are taking over; you can't have any say in our decision."

At first, Fons was confused by Houston's statement, Sophie always had a say; she was part of the team. Then he realized what he was doing. He was taking this burden off her shoulders.

"Houston? You can't cut me out of this."

"I'm sorry, Sophie, but I agree with Houston. We can't consider your opinion on this." Fons backed his partner up.

"What are you going to do?" The relief of not having to make this decision was immediately evident in her demeanor.

As Houston and Fons discussed it, the back door opened, and the two Triad members got in the van and left.

"Ok, then we agree. If a van comes to take girls tonight, we will call the Captain. He can get a SWAT team together in an hour. I'll ask him to send someone to take over the surveillance here too. That way, we can have backup if we need it." Houston said.

"I think we should call him now and give him a heads up on what we're doing."

"Your right Fons." Houston dialed the Captain's number. "Captain?"

"Yes, Houston, what can I do for you?"

"We have a situation." He went on to tell him all that happened so far. "If we take down this facility, they will move it. But if we wait to see where they move the women, we can rescue the women there, and take down the brothel. They'll think it's part of the new NYPD's initiative, just like the others that you raided." NYPD told the press it was a 'clean up the streets' initiative. They used that cover to keep the public from digging up the real purpose behind the raids and protect Sophie's identity.

"Can you have a SWAT team on standby in case they move some of these women tonight? And we need someone to relieve us. This place needs 24-hour surveillance."

"Houston, I can do this tonight, but the brass upstairs is wanting me to hand this over to the Gang and Vice Units." The Captain was still in his office. He got up from his desk to wave at one of his men to come in.

"I understand," Houston replied.

"What started as a rescue mission has turned into an all-out war against sex traffickers. It's out of our department's purview." The Captain scribbled a note to the officer to get SWAT on the line. "I'll be standing by for your call, and I'll send someone to take over surveillance and free you up."

"Thanks, Captain. How soon should we expect someone to relieve us?"

"I'll see someone is there in a half-hour."

Houston gave the Captain his location and ended the call.

The Captain picked up the call to SWAT, now on another line.

"Houston, what happens if they take some of these women to a private purchaser. Just because they're domestics, doesn't mean they aren't abused physically or sexually?" Sophie asked.

"We'll have units follow them and take down the addresses. If we raid them one at a time like the brothels, the others are likely to get rid of the women. We need to take them down all at once. I'm sorry, Sophie, but it's the best we can do."

"Look." Fons poked Houston and pointed at the van pulling up. He took pictures of the men as they backed the van in and left the vehicle. Houston had the binoculars. "These guys are Tong."

"Sophie, can you pass up the go-bag? There should be some trackers in there. I think we should put one on the vehicle in case it gets away from us." She passed it up; Fons dug into it.

Houston checked the perimeter for cameras with his binoculars. There were several. They decided if Fons went straight in from the east side, it was dark enough the camera might not pick him up. He was wearing black, so that would help. It was their only choice. Fons headed out as Houston watched the door.

Sophie's phone pinged a text; it was from Matt,

> **Received your intel-- am running the men and the girls through facial recognition. I will let you know what I find.**

She responded,

> **Thank you.**

Fons was at the front of the vehicle placing the tracker. He made it back without incident.

"How long did the Captain say it would take SWAT to be ready?" Sophie asked.

"Probably an hour," Fons replied.

Houston was the first to see the door open. The same men were leading six women into the van. Fons took their pictures.

"We need to follow that van, but one of us is going to have to stay here. They may bring another vehicle to take other girls out." Relief would be there in twenty minutes.

"I'll stay here, leave me the go-bag. And I'll call the Captain and let him know what's happening." He quietly got out of the SUV and took the bag with him; he stayed hidden in the bushes. Sophie crawled up in the front seat, and they waited for the van to pull out.

She had the tracking receiver in her hand. They waited for the van to get almost out of sight before they pulled out with their lights off. When they mingled with other cars, they turned their lights on. They stayed four cars behind; that would give them time to react if they turned. The street they were on would pass Fordham University about a mile down the road. They kept driving passing by strip malls and restaurants, it was an upscale part of town. Fifteen minutes later, the van pulled into a parking lot of a private business. It was an old building but painted and clean. The front was a barbershop, but the building was much too big for that one business. It was a perfect front. No one would think anything unusual about men coming in and out of a barbershop.

The van pulled in the back alley where merchandise generally gets delivered. Houston went up the street and turned around. He parked where they had a view of the back of the building. He got on his cell with the Captain. Sophie had been texting him their locations as they were following the van. The Captain said SWAT needed another 30 minutes.

They watched as the men led the girls through the back door. It was dark so they couldn't see much when the door opened.

Houston called to tell Fons what was happening on his end. He said SWAT was 30 minutes out. Fons said his relief came, and he was in the car with an NYPD detective named Becker. They were watching the building.

"Houston, I don't want those girls harmed," Sophie said.

"SWAT will be here as soon as they can." He was just as anxious; the girls were young.

Houston saw the SWAT team vans. They drove past their SUV and parked up the street. He watched as a team of ten men in their black tactical gear filed out of the vans. They lined up across the street out of sight of the back of the building, waiting for orders. Houston got out and met up with the Captain. Sophie stayed in the car. The SWAT team's Lieutenant Jenkins got his men ready to breach the back door.

Once the Lieutenant gave the order, they breached the building. Sophie rolled down her window so she could hear the shouts and commands coming from the open door. "Get down on the ground... hands up," repeated over and over. It was a tactic law enforcement used to create panic and confusion.

Twenty minutes later, several ambulances pulled up. Sophie got out of the SUV; she wanted to make sure Houston hadn't gotten injured. She ran to the building as he was coming out. Captain Cartwright caught her before she made it to the door.

"Sophie, you can't go in there," he said, holding her back by her arm. "It's bad. The conditions the girls were in were deplorable. They're taking some by ambulance the rest we'll transport by bus to the hospital. All of them need attention."

"Bus? How many girls are there?"

"At least forty."

"Forty!" She couldn't believe she heard right.

Houston saw her and went over.

"Captain, I'm going to go pick up Fons. Is that alright with you? Fons and I will write up our statements at your office tomorrow."

"Yes, of course, Houston. Thanks for the heads up on this."

Houston started walking with Sophie to their SUV.

"What about the girls we followed? Where are they? Were they hurt?" Sophie asked as Houston opened the door for her.

"No, Sophie, the new girls are alright. They weren't drugged or hurt." He got in and started the car. He didn't tell her the worst of it. What he saw and smelled would stay with him for a long time. He never wanted those images in her mind.

"What happens to the girls from here?" She never asked about that before.

"It depends on the age and where they're from. First, the women will be checked out at the hospital. Then they will go to one of many facilities the State and some non-profits have set up for these victims." She could see he was very disturbed by tonight's events. "Social workers, public defenders, translators, and ICE will get involved. They will determine who will go back to their country of origin or who can get U-Visa's to stay in the US."

Sophie didn't ask him any more questions. He needed some space.

"We need to go pick up Fons." He didn't talk much on the way there.

Fons was in a car with Detective Becker. They were still waiting to see if anyone came for the other women tonight. He grabbed the go-bag and got in the back seat of the SUV.

"We were listening to the raid on Becker's radio. I heard a few of the men gagging when they saw the conditions those women were living in. It must have been bad," Fons stated.

"It was, Fons. I've never worked Vice; I don't know how they do it."

"Is the Captain taking over from here?" Fons asked.

"Yes, he'll handle all the surveillance from here and keep us informed."

They dropped Fons off at the US Marshal's office, where he left his car and headed home.

All Houston wanted was to go to bed and hold his wife. He needed to get those images out of his head.

It was the middle of the night when Sophie woke up. She reached for Houston, but he wasn't in bed. She heard him in the other room. Quietly, she went into the living room and saw him on his knees by the couch, weeping and praying. She could see that the Lord had laid a heavy burden on him. Sophie went back to her room and prayed for all the souls caught in this. All these women wanted was a way to a better life. Instead, they were stolen away by these despicable men and forced into a life of anguish. She also prayed for peace of mind for her husband.

Katsumi summoned his Saiko Komon (senior advisor) into the assembly room. He heard about the raid on the brothel in the Bronx, that belonged to the Tongs.

Izumi came in, bowed and waited. Katsumi was pacing.

"Do you know if your sister is the one who took down the brothel of the Tongs."

"Yes, I believe she is."

"I hear rumblings of retaliation. They do not know who is responsible, but they are diligently searching. They are torturing anyone who acts suspiciously in their ranks. They have already killed several of their own men seeking out the mole. How close is she to locating the girl she searches for?"

"She feels she is making progress."

"Help her, Izumi, before they find out there is no mole, and it is her doing this."

"Yes, sir." He left the room and went to talk to Kato.

Kato was in the kitchen eating lunch with one of the housemaids. She got up and left when Izumi came in.

"She is very pretty," Kato was still watching her walk away, a smile on his face.

"Yes, she is." Izumi sat down next to him and took half of his sandwich. "Kato, what do you know about the gangs that traffic young girls?"

"Probably the same things you do. The gangs with the most houses of prostitution are the Tongs and Triads. They pay specific clans to take girls from all over the world for their brothels."

"What about women sold into domestic slavery?"

"Fewer do that since it is less lucrative. It's more of an on-demand side business."

"Who would know how they run their operation?"

"The Kumicho's gardener was Triad before he became a member of the Akuza. The question of how that happened has always been fodder for rumors. But for some reason, the Kumicho allowed it. No one knows the real story."

"I often wondered myself. The Kumicho must have owed him. It's the only logical explanation," Izumi added.

"Is the Kumicho considering expanding into domestic slavery or prostitution?" He looked bothered by the idea.

"No, I just need information."

Izumi would talk to the gardener next.

"Kato, have you ever thought what you would do if you weren't Akuza?"

"No, I'm satisfied with my life. Our Kumicho is fair and has made the Akuza very profitable and he shares the wealth with us. Few of us go to jail anymore. We can thank your father for that." He stopped and looked Izumi in the eyes. "It is not all that great out there on your own."

"You never think of having a family and living free, without violence? Away from all this?"

"You are kidding yourself, my friend, if you think the grass is greener on the other side. It's brutal and cruel everywhere, not just here." Kato took another bite of his sandwich.

Izumi didn't push it any further, Kato was right in some respects. The world, in general, is a cruel place. But Izumi has seen a softer side, the side Sophie lives in. He was going to find that someday. But not today, today he had to help Sophie find the missing girl. And that meant delving into the abyss of evil — the human trafficking trade.

Houston decided not to wake his wife when he left for work. He still felt the effects of the night before. He should have never brought her on the stakeout. What he saw was seared into his mind. His phone rang.

"Hello, sweetheart." Houston answered.

"How are you this morning? You left without waking me."

"I'm fine; there was no need to wake you. I'll be home early. Would you like to go out to dinner?"

"Is this a date?" She teased.

"Only if the answer is yes." He closed the file he was working on and smiled.

"Then, yes. Which means it's customary to bring your date flowers and a gift." She cradled the phone against her cheek so she could use both hands to gather her hair into a ponytail.

"Now, you ruined my surprise."

"Call me before you leave so I have time to get ready, you know how long it takes a princess to get ready."

"Alright, princess. I love you." She heard the sadness still present in his voice.

"I love you too. You are the man of my dreams."

He smiled and immediately called the florist to order some flowers to pick up on the way home. He'd have to stop by a Quick Stop to grab her some Twizzlers.

Sophie put down the phone, hoping she lifted his spirit for a moment. She headed to the mini command center in her office to get ahold of Lieutenant Jenkins.

She made the call, "Good morning, Lieutenant. How are the women this morning?"

"Good morning Ms. Star. I'm sorry to say one of the women died in the hospital last night; two others are still there. The rest of the women were treated for various injuries and diseases. We transported them to designated housing. Their identities will be confirmed, and their futures determined." She could hear him shuffling papers in the background.

"I understand there are special 'U Visas' available for victims."

"Yes ma'am, the victim's advocates will sort out all the details."

"What's happening at Global Enterprises?" Getting information from him was like pulling teeth. She already knew from Sissy that it was a shell corporation inside a shell corporation. She was able to track the registered agent back to a suburb of New York. However, she had not found the girls' identities or the identities of the men handling them from last night.

"We still have it under surveillance. No other women left the building since last night. I made a request to the FBI for an infrared reading. They hesitated to help at first but when I mentioned Houston's name they approved it. The reading showed ten people in the basement."

Lieutenant Jenkins said the main level is a legitimate importing business, specializing in importing toys from India and China. The basement has six cages. They saw eight figures are in cages; two others they assume are guards outside the cells.

"Did the raid spook them?"

"No ma'am. Everything is business as usual. They have no idea their facility is under surveillance."

Sophie relayed all the new information to Sissy via a video call. "Do you think the address of the registered agent you found might be Triad?"

"I don't think so. The owner has no connection to the gangs that I can find. I'll try to hack into Global's computers. They have a good firewall."

"Thanks, Sissy, let me know. I've got to get ready for a date with my husband." Sissy laughed.

"How are you and Matt doing. Is there a future in it?"

Sophie could tell Sissy was smiling by her voice. "He is such a great guy. He treats me special; I like that. It helps we have the same interests. Computer geeks like us like to talk about it, *a lot*, which gets in the way if you're not into it. I found that out the hard way. We have a date Saturday. I have to say I look forward to it every time." Sophie heard Sissy start typing again.

"That's great news; you make a beautiful couple. We'll all have to go out together again." Sophie went on to tell the gossip about Fons, "Fons has another date with Carol. Their going ice-skating Saturday."

"I'm glad; they looked like they were having fun Sunday. Does he know she was a champion ice skater on her way to the Winter Olympics?"

Sophie couldn't help but laugh. "I'm not telling him. I am going to let him find out the hard way."

"You are a wicked one," Sissy said playfully.

With that, they said their goodbyes and Sissy got back to work.

By the time Houston made his two stops and fought the traffic, it was 6 pm when he got home. He walked in, and Sophie came to greet him. He handed her the flowers and candy. She held them in one hand and wrapped her other arm around his neck to pull his lips down to hers and kissed him.

He wrapped his arms around her and held her close. She leaned back and smiled at him.

"Well, Mr. Townsend, are you trying to win points with me?"

"Mrs. Townsend, to get points with you, I would do anything. You still make my heart race." He whispered in her ear.

"In that case, I'll take advantage and ask you to take me to the ballet when the 'Nutcracker' comes to town." She patted his chest with the flat of her hand.

"You have me under your spell, princess."

"You're so easy, Houston. You never say no to me. I feel guilty," she smiled.

"No, you don't. Anyway, you can make it up to me." He responded with a big smile, then went to change for dinner.

Houston and Sophie walked to their favorite Italian restaurant and enjoyed the evening. They both needed a break.

After they settled in bed for the night, Houston said. "Sweetheart. There is a non-profit that I'd like to support. It's one of the organizations that are taking in the women we are freeing from these brothels. The group has a trade school and provides emotional and medical services. I'd like to give a substantial donation to support them." Sophie sat up and turned to him.

"Honey, that's a splendid idea. During my research, I found a Christian non-profit that works out of India and the Philippines. They pay to buy women out of brothels. They teach the women how to support themselves, so they don't end up back where they started. I'd like to support them too."

"Yes, of course. I would love to be a part of that."

They both had substantial wealth. Houston's came from investing in his father's wildcatting business. A majority of Sophies came from reward money generated by Nikko's funds and properties after his takedown. She received a percentage of everything that was confiscated by the Task Force. It was one of the largest payouts ever given as a reward.

"There's one other thing we need to talk about. I'm not ready to turn this over to the Task Force yet, but I can't hold out much longer. I had no idea it was going to take this long or involve so much when I started this. Cosby's been pushing for it."

"I hadn't had a chance to tell you yet. The Captain told me tonight that the brass wants him to turn all new leads over to the NYPD Gang and Vice Units. So this might be good timing," Houston said.

"I want to hold out as long as I can. I'd really like to work it from here, rather than DC."

"Did Sissy find out who owns Global yet?"

"No. She tracked down the registered agent. The name may be legit but we found out the address is bogus."

"Even after we find Dajao, I would like to track down the traffickers and find a way to disrupt their businesses in a more significant way."

"Why them and not the gangs, Houston?"

"I was talking to Lieutenant Jenkins about it. It's the sheer depravity of it. They steal these tender age girls and lie to the older ones who are desperate and told they are going to get honest work. Then they force them into prostitution. It's despicable. Disrupting the traffickers will also affect the brothels."

"Of course, I'm behind your decision completely. But how much good will it do, Houston? Realistically, I doubt we can make much of a dent in human trafficking no matter how hard we try."

"Don't ask me that! I don't care if it only stops it for six months, it's that many girls who have a chance at a decent life." He got out of bed and went to the kitchen for some water. He knew it would not end the problem, but he couldn't think about that.

When he came back to bed, Sophie snuggled up to him and laid her head on his chest. He put his arm around her, and they fell asleep.

CHAPTER SEVEN

On Friday, an NYPD officer surveilling Global Enterprises followed a van with two women taken to private homes. They logged the addresses into the system.

Sissy worked from the secure mini command at Sophie's. Matt logged in remotely. They had spent the previous day hacking into the computers at Global. They found files of women they held for the Triad with the names, addresses, and purchase prices of women sold into forced labor, and ones taken to brothels. Names of traffickers who dropped off the girls, including their country of origin. They hadn't opened the Tong files yet but expected the same. Sophie was printing out the information and organizing it on the whiteboard hanging on the wall. She was formulating a plan.

They worked until Houston got home at 6 pm.

After kissing Houston hello, Sophie said, "Matt just disconnected. He has dinner with his parents tonight." She smiled at him then added, "I think he's going to tell them about his relationship with Sissy. Their relationship could be getting serious."

"He hasn't said anything to me," Houston told her as he walked into the bedroom to change.

It was 9 pm when Sissy finally left. They were organizing the material they had acquired earlier. Sophie offered her dinner, but Sissy said she had plans. Houston and Sophie warmed leftovers for dinner and spent some time with Bully on the balcony.

It was Saturday morning. Bully hadn't had a walk in days, so after breakfast, Houston and Sophie took him on a long walk. They spent a little time analyzing information, before they left for dinner with Mr. Katsumi.

Sophie wore a very stylish royal blue dress. Houston was in a suit and tie. Izumi came to pick them up in the limo at 5:30 pm.

It was another fabulous twelve-course meal, with the men keeping a lively conversation going. Even Katsumi was enjoying himself. After the meal, Mr. Katsumi ordered the table cleared and fresh tea.

"Do you have a story for me, musume?" He asked, sitting back into his chair, waiting.

"Tonight, I would like to tell you a true story from the Bible of a great warrior named David.

Many years after Adam and Eve disobeyed their Father and left the Garden of Eden. God still wanted a people who could be called by His name. He would be their God, and they would be His people. A people who chose to love and obey Him.

There was a man named Abraham, who loved God and lived according to the laws of God. God said to Abraham. 'And I will make thy seed as the dust of the earth, so that if a man could number the dust of the earth, then shall thy seed also be numbered.' (Gen 13:16 KJV) His people increased in number, so God set Judges over them. In time, the people wanted to be like other nations and have a king, so God gave them a King. He was a very handsome, strong man, a mighty warrior who stood head and shoulders over other men. The people were pleased to have Saul as their King. God blessed His people when they walked in His statutes. And in war, God gave them victory over their enemies.

But the King moved away from the ordinances of God and did not always seek His counsel." Sophie stopped for a moment to take a sip of tea.

"There was a young man in Israel, the descendant of Abraham, who loved God with all his heart. He would worship and praise Him with song and with his harp. His brothers were in Saul's army, he was too young to join them, so his Father kept him home to tend the sheep. But God knew David's heart, that he was a great warrior.

Now the armies of the mighty Israelites went out to fight the powerful armies of the Philistines. But they had forgotten in whom they believed and all the mighty battles where God had given them victory.

Every day the Philistine army stood in battle-ready lines on one hill. The Israelite army stood in battle-ready formation on the other hill, with a valley between them. The Philistine army had a warrior, a giant who was over nine feet tall, strong, and powerful.

The giant would taunt the armies of Israel and say, why should we war. Send one of your best warriors to fight me. If I win, then the Israelites will become our slaves. If your warrior wins, the Philistines will become your slaves. The giant scared Saul's army, and they hid from him.

David's father sent David to bring food to his brothers in the army. When he got there, he heard the giant taunt the army of God and asked his brothers why no one had gone out to kill him. They told him everyone was afraid. So David said he would go and defeat him."

The Kumicho ordered Kato to stand at the door; no one was to disturb dinner with his guests. Kato knew firsthand there had been no joy in the Kumicho's life since his wife died; and years since he heard him laugh. He hoped Ms. Star might be the vehicle of change for that.

At 9 pm, Mr. Zhao, second in command of the Tong's White Tigers in Chinatown, came uninvited and was stopped at the front gate. The guards called Kato, and he allowed him to enter the compound, escorted by Kato's men.

"I demand to see the Kumicho immediately."

"No one demands an audience with the Kumicho; one may only seek one." Kato responded.

The Chinese Street gangs' lack of discipline and respect for the old ways and customs, caused the Akuza to treat them with contempt. He escorted Zhao to the sitting area, away from the dining room, so that he couldn't overhear the Kumicho and his guests. He explained the Kumicho was in a meeting and would let him know he was waiting as soon as the meeting was over.

Sophie continued her story. "Saul heard of the young man's boasting, saying he would fight Goliath. So Saul summoned him.

'How will you fight this giant; you are just a boy?' The King said.

'Your servant has been keeping his Father's sheep. When a lion or a bear came and carried off a sheep from the flock, I went after it, struck it and rescued the sheep from its mouth; and when it arose against me I grabbed it by its beard and struck and killed it. Your servant has killed both lion and bear; this uncircumcised Philistine will be like one of them, seeing he has defied the armies of the living God. The Lord who rescued me from the paw of the lion and the paw of the bear will rescue me from the hand of this Philistine.'" (1 Samuel 17:34-37 NKJV)

She went on to tell him how Saul tried to give David his armor; it was too big for him, so David chose not to use it. He took five smooth stones and his sling and went to meet the giant. Sophie continued.

"The giant saw David and was offended that they sent out a boy to fight him. 'So the Philistine said to David, am I a dog that you come to me with sticks?' (1 Sam. 17:43 NKJV) David replied, 'You come against me with a sword, with a spear and with a javelin. But I come against you in the name of the Lord of host, the God of the armies of Israel, whom you have defiled. This day the Lord will deliver you into my hands, and I will strike you down and take your head from you. And this day I will give the carcasses of the camp of the Philistines to the birds of the air and the wild beast of the earth, that all the earth may know that there is a God in Israel. Then all this assembly shall know that the Lord does not save with sword or spear; for the battle is the Lord's, and he will give you into our hands.' (1 Sam. 17: 45-47 NKJV)

As the Philistine moved closer to attack, David ran quickly toward the battle line to meet the giant. He reached into his bag and taking out a stone, slung it, and struck the Philistine, and he fell face down on the ground. David triumphed over the Philistine with a sling and a stone.

David ran and stood over the giant. He took hold of the Philistine's sword and drew it from the sheath. After he killed him, he cut off his head with the sword.

When the Philistines saw that their hero was dead, they turned and ran. Then the men of Israel and Judah surged forward with a shout and pursued the Philistines and killed them."

She paused for a moment. "And that is just one of the true stories of the mighty warrior David." Katsumi and Izumi clapped; she could see they enjoyed it.

"I like this David; he would have been a mighty samurai in Japan," Katsumi said.

"Indeed, Mr. Katsumi, I'm so glad the story pleased you."

"Will you honor us with your presence again next Saturday, musume?"

"How could we refuse such a gracious and charming host as you, Mr. Katsumi. But won't you grow weary of me?"

"Can the moon grow weary of the stars?" He laughed.

While they were finishing their evening, Kato came in and whispered to Izumi. Izumi excused himself for a moment and went to talk to the Tong leader waiting in the sitting room.

"What do you mean by showing up here without an invitation?" He demanded.

"Mr. Izumi, my name is Mr. Zhao..." He bowed low.

"I know who you are, Mr. Zhao."

"I must speak to the Kumicho. Someone is betraying us; we need his help." His voice was respectful.

"I will ask him if he will give you an audience. Wait here." Izumi had to make sure Ms. Star left unseen by Mr. Zhao or the men that accompanied him waiting at the gate.

He went to Kato and told him to bring the limo to the back of the building and send his best soldiers.

Izumi went back into the dining room, where they were still visiting.

"Izumi, it is rude to leave our guest, come back and sit down," Katsumi said in a jovial voice. Izumi whispered in his ear; he nodded his head and stood.

Katsumi put on a smile, "my dear musume, I'm afraid I will have to end this pleasant evening. It seems I have an unexpected guest. Izumi will see you out." He went to Sophie and extended his hand to help her up. Said his goodbyes and left the room.

Izumi explained it would be best if they left from the rear entrance. Houston could tell there was something more going on. He put his hand on the small of Sophie's back and they followed Izumi. He asked them to wait inside the door for a moment while he gave instructions to the men and readied the limo.

Izumi had the men form a passageway so no one could see who was getting in the limo. Then he gave a nod to Houston, and he escorted his wife to the car. Izumi leaned in and apologized for the drama.

After the limo was out of sight, he went into the assembly room.

Kato led Mr. Zhao into the conference hall. Mr. Zhao bowed low and waited for the Kumicho to address him. The Kumicho did not invite him to the ceremonial table to drink sake.

"What do you mean by coming here?"

"I have an urgent request from the president of the Chinatown Tong, Kumicho."

"What would lead him to believe I would entertain a request from him."

Izumi was now standing by his Kumicho. Kato was standing behind Mr. Zhao.

"We are under attack; we don't know who our enemy is, or if it is one of our own betraying us. We have lost a large amount of merchandise, and many of our men are in jail. If this continues, we may not be able to recover. And it's not just us; the Triad have the same losses.

"By merchandise, you mean the women in your brothels, am I right?"

"Yes."

"What is that to me, Mr. Zhao? We do not peddle in flesh." He said without emotion.

"I am authorized to give you whatever you ask if you give us some information."

"Does it look like I need anything from the Tong?" He spits out.

"No, sir, not today, but someday you might need us, and we will owe you a favor."

The Kumicho sat in his chair on the dais, Mr. Zhao had him curious. "What information do you think I have that will help you."

"We have heard how you outwitted the government by getting your money back. A feat that only the great Kumicho could have accomplished. We also heard there was a woman who found your money, enabling you to retrieve it."

"If any of that is true, how will that help you?"

"We need this woman to find out who is doing this to us. We will pay her whatever she asks." He took a breath.

The Kumicho would never let these crude, undisciplined men get ahold of Ms. Star. But it may be of benefit to him to be owed a favor. He took a few moments to consider what to do.

"Mr. Zhao, if I had such an asset, I would never expose her to you. However, you are right; it could be beneficial for me to be owed a favor from your leader. That is, if I could trust you would honor your word."

"I swear on my life, we would."

"I will talk to this woman, if she wants to get you the information, she will only do it with Izumi as the middleman. You will never see or talk to her directly, do you understand?"

"Whatever you say, we will do it."

"I cannot promise she will do it, only that I will ask her."

He stood up. "Now leave me and don't come here again uninvited, or you will leave without your head." Katsumi nodded at Kato and waved off Mr. Zhao like a dog.

When Zhao left, Izumi turned to his Father and said, "If they ever find out who she is, they will take her, Father. I don't trust them."

"I know, and if they knew it was her doing this to them, they would kill her." He was very disturbed about this turn of events.

After they left the compound, Sophie asked, "What's happening, Houston?"

"I don't know, but it was evident he didn't want it known we were there." After saying that, he pointed his fingers to his ear to remind her the limo has mics and cameras. She nodded, and they made small talk on the way home.

It was Sunday morning, and Houston was glad to be in Church. The atmosphere of praise and worship washed away the lingering heaviness. Looking over at Sophie, he could sense she felt the same.

Only light pushes back the darkness. Houston and Sophie wanted to be light wherever God placed them, but they also needed to be rejuvenated. That's what Church did for them. They spent the day in Trenton with his family. The men watched football. But they all agreed there is nothing like sitting in the bleachers on the fifty-yard line. They reminisced about Thanksgiving Day.

On the way home, Houston asked Sophie about the Bible stories she's choosing for Mr. Katsumi.

"Your stories are terrific, Sophie, and I know your building a foundation. I get having him relate to the warrior David, but what direction are you going?"

"Katsumi's culture believes in many different deities. I want to show him there is only one true God. No power on earth or heaven can rival His."

"I had no idea you had memorized so much of the Bible."

"When I was a Sunday School teacher in Lake View, Suzie and I would act out many of these same stories. We tried to memorize as much of it as we could." She laughed at the memory.

"What do you have in mind for your next story?"

"I want to tell him of the Prophet Elijah on Mount Carmel."

"You're going to build on the truth that there is no other God. Then lead into the stories of Jesus and salvation."

"That's the plan. Once he understands there is no other God, then it is on him to decide whom he wishes to serve. Because contrary to what most people want to believe. Each of us serves a master. Whether it is God or someone or something else."

When they got home, they relaxed and ate a late snack of the leftovers Lily sent back with them. They decided to watch a movie on TV. Sophie laid her head on his shoulder and fell asleep halfway through.

Houston thanked the Lord for Sophie. He remembered when he was in eighth grade; his father gave him 'the talk'. He told him to save himself for the woman he wanted to spend the rest of his life with. Houston asked his father to tell him the story of how he fell in love with his mother. What he heard was an ongoing epic love story. Houston would daydream, from time to time, of loving someone like that and being loved like that in return. He even prayed about it. But he never understood it until Sophie.

He brushed away a strand of hair that fell across her face and put it behind her ear. He wrapped his arms around her, laid his cheek on the top of her head, and finished watching the movie. When it was over, he picked her up to carry her to bed. She wrapped her arms around his neck and whispered, "is the movie over?"

"Yes."

"Did I fall asleep?"

"Yes, sweetheart."

"I'm sorry."

"It' alright princess. Go back to sleep."

He tucked her in, kissing her forehead. God had answered his prayers.

The next morning Izumi found the gardener in the back of the compound. He noticed the beautiful sculptures Mr. Jo made of the shrubbery; he was a true artist. Izumi didn't know much about Mr. Jo. He showed up here one day last year and never left. All he knew was the Kumicho hired him and gave him the gardeners cottage on the compound.

Izumi walked up to him as he was repairing the coverings on some of the more delicate plants. He kept them protected for the winter. "Mr. Jo, may I have a moment of your time?" Izumi spoke up to get his attention.

Mr. Jo turned to see who called his name, setting down his tools and plastic and gave Izumi a deep bow.

"Mr. Izumi, what an honor." He directed him to the concrete bench nearby. "What can I do for you." He spoke Korean.

Izumi switched to Korean to make him feel comfortable since he spoke it fluently.

"Mr. Jo, I understand that you once belonged to the Triad."

"Yes, I came to the United States illegally as a young man, my family was dead, and I had nowhere to go. I ended up in Chinatown. There was no work for a Korean in Chinatown, but the gangs accepted my presence, not as an equal, but they let me do their grunt work. In time, the Triad allowed me to join. I became the runner, getting messages to and from other gangs, along with other menial jobs. I encountered your father at that time. He was the Saiko Komon for the previous Kumicho."

"How did a Triad gang member become Akuza?"

"The president of the Triad wanted a message sent to the Kumicho.

Everyone knew you didn't go to the compound without invitation; the others were afraid to do it. I had nothing to lose, and I knew it would get me noticed by the Triad leaders, maybe even get me a place to stay off the streets and alleys.

I was smart enough to locate your father outside the compound. I had seen him in Chinatown more than once. I staked out the restaurant where he often ate. The next time he came, I gave him the message. We met off and on after that, and one day we started a conversation; I considered him a friend.

Several years later he came to me with a problem. He was in love with a woman who was being abused by her husband. He couldn't take it anymore and asked me for a favor." He turned to Izumi. "You understand he was not afraid of your birth father. But it was not allowed for one Akuza to lay hands on another. He would have to get approval from his Kumicho, which he could not ask for or receive.

He asked me to make him disappear. I agreed. In exchange, he told me if I ever needed him, he would be there to repay me. He gave me a secure way to reach him."

Izumi wasn't sure how to take the revelation that Katsumi had his father murdered. He knew it was true that he was brutal to his mother and him on occasion. He barely knew his father, so his loss was of little consequence to him. "That was many years ago, Mr. Jo; you came here a year ago."

"Yes, that is true. I advanced in the Triad quickly after that. It soon came to their attention; I was a prodigy with numbers. When their accountant died, they put me in that position. I found discrepancies in the books handed in from the managers of the gambling houses and the opium dens. I pointed out who was skimming. From that point on, I had total control of the Triad books. I was able to put protections in place so that it couldn't happen again. My work won me much respect. The Triad Shan Chu (president or Dragon's head) boasted of me to the other gangs. It made him look more powerful, having such an asset. From that point on, no clan cheated him of the tribute due him.

By then, your mother had died, and Mr. Katsumi was the new Kumicho. I never saw him after that."

"It sounds like you were valued in the Triad, why would you leave that prestige to come here and be a gardener?"

"Mr. Izumi, you are still young. One day you may understand. Evil, cruelty, hate, it eats at a man's soul in time. I was growing weary of it all, but I would have never left if this one thing hadn't driven me over the edge."

"What was it, Mr. Jo?"

"I was called in to witness all punishments, as were the rest of the staff. It was supposed to be a deterrent to others. The president's second, a man about my age of 58, came in with his young wife, who was 16 years old. He had brought her in several times before. Her wealthy family in China had given her to him in marriage. They felt it would be advantageous for them. But she would not let him consummate the marriage. She would bite, kick, and scratch him. He would beat her, and of course, that was viewed as acceptable. But she still would not submit. That day he brought her in to get permission to kill her, so he would be free to remarry. The president gave his permission, and he immediately took out a knife and stabbed her to death. That was not typically how it was done, but the man was so angry with her that he went into a fit of rage. It was a bloody mess. The Shan Chu was not pleased." He dropped his head and took a moment. "It became clear to me; it is not right; to kill like that. None of it was right, but what could I do. I wanted peace. I wanted to be away from all of it.

I knew if I left, they would hunt for me; I needed protection. I went to work as usual and downloaded all the books onto three flash drives. I included all the information I had accumulated through the years about the other street gangs. I knew what businesses they ran, where their properties were, who ran the gambling houses, the opium dens, and the brothels. All that I learned on the streets when I was a messenger. Then I contacted your father. He told me where to meet him, and he brought me here. The next day he sanctioned my request to be Akuza and asked me what I wanted to do. I told him I wanted to have peace. I asked if I could be the groundskeeper to pay for my board. He agreed and gave me this home. I owe him my allegiance. I know if I ever leave these grounds and someone recognizes me, I would be a dead man. Even though I did not turn on them or use the information I had to harm them. I took it only for protection. My leaving was a great insult to the Shan Chu. Unforgivable."

"Why would you tell me this, Mr. Jo."

"I've been hiding those flash drives for the past year. I feel I need to pass them on to you. I need to unburden myself of them. Maybe they can be useful to the Kumicho." He got up and went to another concrete bench and tilted it slightly; it was cumbersome. He reached under it and pulled out a plastic baggy from a hole, with the flash drives in them. He brushed off the dirt and the bugs and brought them to Izumi, handing them to him.

"Mr. Jo, you think I am too young to understand wanting peace, but I am not. I also seek peace." He took the drives from Mr. Jo and stood. "Thank you for trusting me with your story. Please don't tell anyone of these."

"If your father asks, I will tell him. I owe him my allegiance, but no one else will ever know about them from these lips, that I promise." He got up and bowed low again, then got back to work. Izumi watched him for a while then went to his room to see what was on the drives.

Izumi thought the timing fortunate, maybe this was the answer to finding the missing girl.

CHAPTER EIGHT

A fter Houston went to work, Sophie stood in front of her whiteboard and assimilated the information. Any new information sent by Matt and Sissy was added to the board as it came in. Bully was sitting next to her; she was absentmindedly petting him.

When Houston got home, he looked for her, finding her in the mini command. He kissed her on the top of her head and patted Bully.

"How's it going, sweetheart. You have a plan yet?"

"Almost."

He'd learned one thing about his wife; she needed time alone to process information. He left her alone and went to make them some dinner.

After grilling chicken and putting together a salad, he let her know dinner was ready. After dinner, Houston brought up turning this over to the Task Force again.

"Sophie, when do you want to contact Director Cosby about bringing in the DC Task Force."

"I have come up with a plan. I'd like to share my idea, if you think it's workable, we'll decide."

"I'm all ears." They cleared the table after dinner and went outside to discuss it.

"With the information, Sissy's been able to extract from the hacked files, we have 12 more brothels. We also have names of women sold and their locations. It's a large number Houston, it will take coordination to get them all at once."

"How many?"

"With this one gang, we have 40 in just the one file." She paused as she collected her thoughts. "This is what I'm thinking. We need time to locate more leads on the domestics. But we should take down the brothels right away. I don't want them living one more day in those conditions."

"Is Dajao's name on the list?"

"No. After we take down these brothels, I want to apply one more element of pressure to the mix."

"What do you have in mind?"

"I want to put out an ultimatum. Either whoever has Dajao delivers her unharmed or we take their organizations apart piece by piece. The same message we gave to the Tong at the auto shop. It never made it to the leadership since they died at the scene."

He thought it over. "I understand where you're coming from with that. But are you risking someone getting nervous and killing Dajao to get rid of the problem?"

"That's the risk, do you think it's a bad idea?"

"It's something to pray about while we take down the brothels. The Captain's men reported two of the girls at Global were sold. They have their location."

"I'd like to let the Captain's department have this raid and get the collar. I know he will have to include the Gang Unit and ICE. But we'll need the help anyway."

"You said that before. You know the Captain was told to hand it over to the gang unit."

"Tell them I prefer to work with agencies I'm familiar with."

"In other words, if they want the collar, they have to do it your way?" Houston raised his eyebrow. Sophie knew exactly what it meant.

"Don't look at me like that. I want the Captain to get the collar. Besides, you know it's too late to bring in the DC Task Force on this."

Houston knew that much was true. "Alright, sweetheart," he relented. "I'll see if Fons and I can get off tomorrow. We'll meet with Captain Cartwright and Lieutenant Jenkins." He took his phone out to call Fons. Then he would call his Captain at the US Marshals office to ask for the time off to help with this operation.

Izumi wasn't surprised at the Triad information on the flash drives. He knew it would include all their leader's names, addresses, and info on their families. There were files on the names of the Mexican Cartels who supplied the drugs and the pickup location. It also showed the routes the clans use to smuggle women into the US. He had no idea how Mr. Jo got that information. There was a file that had addresses of brothels, gambling houses, and opium dens. It also had a record on the amount paid to politicians and police for bribes.

His surprise came when he saw the same information about the Tong and other street gangs in Chinatown. Now Izumi's dilemma was what to do with all this information. The Kumicho would never condone interfering with the business of another gang. It would start a war, but that wasn't the only reason. He had no moral compulsion to stop them, as long as it didn't affect the Akuza's profit or his men.

Izumi knew what Ms. Star would do with it, she wanted the human trafficking to stop, and she would go to any lengths to stop it. If he told his father what he had, he would insist it be destroyed. Izumi had the option of making a copy and give the original to his father, but that would be betraying his trust. He would have to think about what to do. He would provide Ms. Star the information on the brothels and the list of names and addresses of those in forced labor. His father had already told him to help her find the missing girl, so Ms. Star would end this.

At dinner he told the Kumicho, he had some information that would help Ms. Star. He asked if he should pass it on. The Kumicho said yes, then said he would like to talk with her about the Tong's request for information. He asked Izumi to see when she was available.

Izumi sent a text to Sophie requesting the meeting.

Houston, Fons, and Sophie pulled into the parking lot of the staging area at ICE headquarters. Captain Cartwright was to meet them there shortly. The raid was scheduled for 9 am. A mobile command vehicle was parked outside in a fenced area along with other tactical vehicles. The massive concrete building had no markings on the outside. When they walked in, the first thing they saw was a large open area with folding chairs stacked against the far wall. On the right was the Command Control Center. Halfway up, the twenty-foot ceiling were two 85-inch plasma monitors. A few feet below that were two rows, ten in each row, of 42-inch plasmas, divided into five sections. Below that were other electronics—portals for flash drives, sim cards, CDs, hard drives, and more. On each workstation was the keyboard and cordless mouse to operate it all. On the adjacent wall was one 85-inch screen with six 42-inch plasmas below that. Beside the other electronics were joysticks that looked more like an airplane tiller, used to operate the six drones that ICE had at their disposal.

Except for the fact the DC FBI Task Force had unlimited resources, this one was equally impressive.

ICE Special Agent in Charge, Leo Demonte stepped out of the conference room at the opposite end of the building. He called out and motioned for them to come in. A glass wall separated it from the rest of the staging area. Another 85-inch plasma was on the far wall. Agent Demonte introduced himself as he motioned them to take a seat at the twenty-foot oak conference table. Additional chairs were lined up against three concrete walls.

"Ms. Star, Agent Townsend, Agent Rodriguez, it's a pleasure to meet you. I've known Lieutenant Jenkins for years. He speaks highly of you."

Houston replied, "thank you, Agent Demonte. We appreciate your cooperation in this undertaking. Your facility is top-notch."

"Our team leaders will be here shortly. We would like to have the operation run on time," Demonte said.

Sophie heard the HVAC kick on from the exposed pipes in the ceiling.

"Ms. Star, your intel, has led to a significant number of successful missions for the NYPD. I appreciate your bringing us in on this. I've heard through the grapevine Director Cosby is a little annoyed you didn't do this through the FBI Task Force." Agent Demonte said as he motioned some of his team leaders into the conference room.

"My contract allows me to freelance when we're not on an official operation with them." The conference room was almost full now. Captain Cartwright came to her and said hello.

Agent Demonte closed the door. "The floor is yours, Ms. Star." He sat down at the conference table. In attendance were the Captain, Lieutenant Jenkins of SWAT, the NYPD SWAT team leaders, the ICE and Gang Unit field team leaders, and SAC Demonte.

"Actually, Agent Townsend has a handle on the tactical part of it, I'll hand that over to him." She turned to her husband and sat back down.

"Sirs, we have the names and addresses of 12 brothels that need to be taken down today." He turned to the plasma on the wall. He motioned the Tech to put up the information he handed him when they came in. "As you can see," he pointed to the screen, "we have dissected the city into sectors. Clumping brothels closest together into one sector. Each sector contains two brothels." Houston directed the next statement to SAC Demonte. "Sir, do we need to call in more teams, or do you think you have it covered?"

SAC Demonte conferred with Lieutenant Jenkins. "Between the SWAT teams and our own, we can handle this."

"Captain Cartwright, how many CSI units do you have working this?" Houston Asked

"Two. It's going to take time to get to all the properties. My patrol officers will relieve your men and secure the property until they can get to each one.

"Pictures and the name of each woman are to be sent back to the Command Center before any of them are removed from the property."

Houston turned it over to Fons, who was handling the drone pilots. They had requested to use the six drones and pilots that belong to ICE. "We will have one drone for every sector. This means each sector will share a drone between the two addresses. Before we begin the raids, they will surveil the target properties. We need a count of how many souls are in the buildings. We don't want anyone left behind."

Fons turned to Demonte. "Sir, if it's alright with you, I would like to have the pilots start their reconnaissance." He waited for approval and then gave the pilots permission to leave.

The meeting was turned over to Sophie.

"There's another matter we need to discuss." She directed this to SAC Demonte. "Do you have resources available to handle these women when they are rescued?"

He considered the question. An aide handed him a note. "Ma'am, because of the other raids, all but two of our shelters are maxed out. That means there are openings for 135 victims."

"Sir, we can't delay this because we don't have a place to take them. These women are being abused." There was no mistaking Sophies agitation that they hadn't dealt with this earlier.

"I understand that. I'll request the National Guard open their auditorium. They can set up cots and dividers for the women. The women can stay there until they are assigned a more appropriate facility. In the interim, we can have medical professionals there to treat them. And caseworkers to help with their other needs."

Sophie nodded her approval. "Sir, is it possible to have mental health professionals available? They will need help working through the trauma they have suffered."

"Yes. The caseworkers will facilitate those needs. And each woman will get an advocate who will help them apply for U Visa's. They must be willing to testify against their traffickers to qualify. I will recommend to DOJ they expedite their cases. Anyone under 18 will be put on a waiting list for asylum. It's a long process, but it will keep them from being deported. If anyone wants to go back to their home country, we will facilitate that too. In the meantime, they can learn English and a trade, so they are ready for the workforce. We will take good care of them, Ms. Star."

Sophie's opinion of Demonte went up a few notches. She had no idea ICE had so many resources.

"Captain, what do you think of having Ms. Turner earn her keep by putting out a request for aid for the women? They will need clothing, personal items, and internships to learn a trade." Sophie suggested.

"Are you giving her this story?"

"Yes, by rights, it's hers."

"I like the idea of getting the public involved." The Captain agreed.

"Sir, I know my parents' Church in Trenton would be willing to take some of the women, once they're triaged. It would give you more time to find permanent places for them. They may find other Churches willing to help. After the operation, I'll get ahold of them." Houston knew his parents would coordinate the effort.

"Also," Sophie added, "Director Cosby told me that this is one of the First Lady's targeted social issues. If she puts out a request for help, I'm sure victim advocates would be inundated with funds and supplies." She sat down and handed the meeting back to SAC Demonte.

"Ms. Star, I assume you have the no-knock warrants."

"I will have the electronic warrants in hand before we start the raids."

"Ok, let's get our men in position out of site at their assigned targets, and get this show on the road."

Sophie asked Captain Cartwright and Lieutenant Jenkins to stay back a moment.

"Captain," they were standing by the door, "there is one more thing."

"Of course, Ms. Star, go ahead." The two men gave her their attention.

She directed her comment to Captain Cartwright. "I'm afraid this might be the last operation we can work together. I was hoping we could see this through to the end, but it has gotten so much bigger than I expected. We are going to need the resources Director Cosby's Task Force can provide. And, as you know, Director Cosby has called me out on this. I wanted you to get this last collar before we turned it over." The Captain put his hand on her arm.

"Sophie, you owe us no explanation. What you have accomplished here is extraordinary. We're glad we could play a part in freeing all these women and put a dent in the gangs' coffers. It's why we do the job. But we've been around long enough to know there's politics in everything. The collars matter, it's how agencies get their funding, and its good PR. You should have taken all the credit, but you gave it to us. Thank you," Captain Cartwright responded.

Lieutenant Jenkins nodded his agreement.

SAC Demonte got everyone's attention. The rest of the teams had been waiting in the Command staging area. None of them knew what the mission was.

"Men, we are here today because we have an enormous task ahead of us today. ICE, in cooperation with the NYPD's SWAT, and the Gang Unit will be hitting 12 brothels, simultaneously. They mustn't have time to move the women out or warn other brothels. Agent Townsend and Agent Rodriguez will be running the Command Center for us. Ms. Star has the authority to change things at any time. Your team leaders will explain your part in the operation."

Lieutenant Jenkins took it from there.

"Each of the 12 teams will be comprised of five NYPD and five ICE and two Gang Unit members. You are to stay out of sight until every team is in place. We will have no-knock warrants for you. At Agents Townsend or Rodriguez's orders, each team will breach. You must get in and control the situation before anyone can make phone calls. Is that understood?" He watched all the heads nod.

"The drones will be our eyes outside before and during the operation. The Techs will disrupt the properties cameras with static interference. We can't disable the cameras for more than 90 seconds, or they will become suspicious. So you must be in position at that time. We want to start this operation at 9 am. Any questions?"

Sophie dialed the number for Ms. Martin, her contact at DOJ. While she listened to it ring, a contingent of Agents filling the staging area caught her eye. They were wearing windbreakers that read POLICE, in large white letters. Ms. Martin answered the phone and Sophie let her know she needed no-knock warrants within the hour. Sophie hadn't revealed the operation earlier for fear of a leak. Ms. Martin was not happy with the short notice and rebuked her. But Sophie knew Ms. Martin had access to judges 24/7 and would get the job done. Sophie had the warrants in twenty minutes.

By the time all the pieces were in place, the drones had picked up over 390 souls in the 12 brothels. There was no way to know who's who. ICE, the Gang Unit nor NYPD had handled a raid of this magnitude before. Captain Cartwright had patrol cars waiting as backup. Ambulances and buses for transport were also on standby.

Once word got back to SAC Demonte that the men were in place. He turned the command center over to Agents Townsend and Rodriguez.

Sophie had stepped away from everyone for a few minutes. She prayed the Lord would protect the men and women that were going to be in harm's way. And that no one would lose their lives during the raids.

Houston and Fons knew that Sophie prayed for every operation. They stood by and waited to get her nod before they gave the first order. Sophie moved to the monitors to watch it unfold.

"Teams one thru twelve, please give a roll call." Houston gave the first order.

"Team one, ready, sir."

"Team two, ready, sir." And on it went to Team twelve.

"Are you ready with interference." Houston turned to Fons, who was working with the Techs. "On your go, Agent Townsend."

"Teams, once the interference is up you'll have 90 seconds to get in place for the breach order, is that clear?"

The Teams all gave the click that meant they understood. They didn't want to lose the element of surprise.

"Alright, Agent Rodriguez, go with the interference."

"It's a go." He responded.

"All teams, your ninety seconds starts now."

They all watched the clock tick by. The drone cameras were already on the monitors. Now the team leaders' helmets cams and the officers' body cams were turned on. Only the team leaders' cameras were on the screens at this point. All footage would be downloaded to hard drives for viewing as training or for court if needed. Large numbers were placed on the monitors showing the sector and team it displayed. This allowed a quick response. The large plasmas were split into sections. The Tech that was running it could bring up any property to full screen if needed.

Six of the twelve addresses were homes in rundown sections of suburbs--two were in better neighborhoods. Four were in commercial zones that had legitimate businesses as a front. Those were more precarious because of the potential civilian casualties.

"Your ninety seconds is up now. Is everyone in place?"

They all acknowledged.

"Breach, Breach, Breach." The command was repeated.

On the screens, you could see them use their battering rams on the front doors. The team stormed in yelling commands. "POLICE! RAISE YOUR HANDS. GET DOWN ON THE GROUND," over and over, they repeated the commands. The men running the brothels were taken off guard.

Sophie saw a guard aim his gun at a team leader. The team leader already had his weapon at the ready and shot the offender. He ordered one of his men to secure him and check for a pulse. Then he continued to clear the rest of the home with his team.

Sophie heard shots at another site and listened to the team leader shout "MAN DOWN, MAN DOWN". He ordered someone to attend to his teammate as the others pinned down the shooter. The man laid his gun down after being wounded in the arm. They left someone to secure him and moved on. Overall the resistance was minimal. The element of surprise worked as predicted.

At more than one location, as soon as the front door was breached, suspects ran out the back, right into the arms of more Agents.

The drones were doing their job keeping watch in case anyone slipped out. One suspect climbed out a downstairs window. The drone caught it, and Agent Rodriguez let the

Team leader know. You could see men running to apprehend him. They kept the drone on the suspect since he had a good lead on the SWAT members chasing him.

There was one split-level home, the single level being the common area of the house. The second level above the garage had three bedrooms. They were VIP rooms. The rest of the house had single beds packed in with material or black plastic as dividers to give the illusion of privacy.

In one of the VIP rooms, a man was startled by the breach, he knew exactly what was happening. He grabbed his pants, zipping them up, but not buttoning them or buckling his belt, he slipped on his shoes, leaving his coat and shirt behind. The man had left his watch and wallet in his car parked a few blocks away. Too many of his things had been stolen on these visits. He crawled out the window onto the roof of the main house. The composition roof had missing and buckled sections, making it too difficult to get traction. So he sat and started scooting across the pitched roof. He realized there was no way down. So he laid himself flat on the roof, hoping to make himself invisible until everyone left.

The drone pilot was making its first sweep of the property. The pilot saw the man on the roof. Using the drone' mic, he said, "stay where you are. Sit up and raise your hands."

There was nowhere for him to go, so the man complied. "This was a dumb idea," he mumbled to himself. The drone picking up the comment on it's mic.

Fons sent men in to retrieve him from the roof, while others kept him at gunpoint from the ground.

Fons moved closer to the monitor. "He looks familiar, get a close up of him." The pilot maneuvers the drone around to get a good look.

Fons knew immediately who it was and waved Sophie over.

"That's Congressman Pfeiffer."

"What!"

"What do you want to do?"

"I don't believe in special treatment. But if it gets out, the raids will get lost in the scandal. That will interfere with my end game." Houston, SAC Demonte, and the Captain noticed the interaction.

"What's happening?" Houston asked.

"We just caught Congressman Pfeiffer on the roof."

"Captain, who can you trust to take him in on the down-low. Someone that will keep his mouth shut. We need the Congressman booked and allowed to call his attorney without being seen." She thought a moment. "Can you hold his booking info for a few days? I don't want a scandal to overshadow the raids."

"I'll take care of it." The Captain moved away and made some calls.

They went back to the action on the screens.

SWAT, the Gang Unit and ICE teams had the suspects in custody in all but three of the brothels. Those had basements that were more difficult to breach without casualties. They heard gunfire. The Tech put the property on the big screen. They heard an ICE Agent say the suspect was down.

There were only a few heart-stopping moments during the breaches before it was all over. All in all, things went according to plan.

Houston ordered a rundown of injuries and requested first responder help where needed. EMT's were close by to take care of the injured.

He sent ambulances to teams 4, 9, and 11 for women too ill to get on the bus. One of the business fronts needed multiple ambulances. The fire department rescue units were called out to help evaluate the condition of the women. Buses came to pick up the others and take them to the National Guard auditorium, where medical personnel were waiting to triage the ones not sent to the hospital. Food was ordered, and beds were set up for the women.

The johns and perpetrators were bussed to the closest NYPD precinct for booking. It made the processing more manageable.

Sophie asked Houston to send the pictures to the screen in the conference room.

"Well done, all teams stand by for your immediate Supervisors." Houston turned to SAC Demonte. "I'm handing the Command Center back to you, Sir." Houston moved aside.

Sophie went into the conference room and sat facing the large screen to wait for the women's photos to come in. She took the time to call Gail. She filled Gail in on all that transpired. She did not mention the Congressman or confidential work product.

Sophie made one more call to Director Cosby, filling him in on the results of the operation. She asked the Director to inform the First Lady about the plea Ms. Turner was going to make for assistance. The Director assured support from the First Lady would bring an overwhelming response. Sophie had no doubt that would be the case. He refrained from rebuking her for not turning the operation over to him.

Houston took that time to call his parents about housing some of the women. When his mom answered, he asked, "mom, can you get dad on the phone too?"

"Of course." He heard her call his father in from the yard. "We're here, son."

Houston told them they would hear the news shortly on TV. He wanted to know if they were willing to find housing for 128 women. It would take weeks before they could all be processed to more permanent housing. He explained they had assigned space for only 135. They were holding and treating the women temporarily at the National Guard facility.

"Did you say, 128 people Houston?" His mother asked.

"We raided another 12 brothels, and all the normal shelters are at capacity."

"Son, was this one of your Task Forces operations?" His father asked.

"It was not our Task Force, we teamed up with the Gang Unit, ICE and NYPD. You know we can't go public with our involvement." He knew he could trust his parents.

"How soon will these poor women need housing, Houston?" Lily spoke up.

"Probably a day or two, mom."

"What!" I need to get things moving. I'll get back with you shortly to let you know how many we can handle here. And I'll see about calling a few other Churches in town." She was in her element. Houston knew it was a done deal.

The Captain saw Sophie sitting in the conference room. Her body leaned forward, her arms on the table with her hands clasped together. He could see she was still holding out hope Dajao's photo would come up on the screen. He went in and sat down beside her.

"Has your girl shown up yet?"

"No, not yet." She leaned back on the chair, keeping her eyes on the screen.

"Don't worry, Sophie, we'll find her."

Sophie turned her head to look at him. Even at forty his smooth dark skin refused to show his age. "I'm sorry one of your men was injured, Don."

"I've checked on him, he'll be fine. He has a few broken ribs and a big bruise. The vest took the worst of it. These men go into this knowing the risk." He patted her hands still intertwined on the table in front of them.

"Did anyone die?"

He hated to tell her, she never wanted anyone hurt in her operations. Unfortunately, that was unrealistic.

"Yes, one offender died. Others are being treated at the hospital. Then they will be transferred to the infirmary at the jail."

Sophie didn't respond, she turned back to watch the pictures coming in again.

The Captain broke the silence. "We did a good thing here today, Sophie."

"I don't know, Don. It feels like a waste of time." She looked down for a moment. "We still don't have Dajao, and even if we take down a thousand brothels, there is still a thousand more. What good is it?" She lowered her head again for a moment and tried to keep from crying. The Captain didn't respond right away.

"Are you saying that these women's lives aren't as important as Dajao's?"

"Of course not." She turned to look at him.

"The women we freed today now have a chance at a decent life. That's worth everything."

A tear ran down her cheek. "I know, Don. I'm sorry."

They sat watching the screen. Sophie tried to lighten the mood and broke the silence. "Your bosses should be happy. You no doubt will be confiscating all the properties that the teams raided."

The Captain chuckled, "I'm sure there will be quite a tug of war between the Brass. All the agencies that participated will want to get their fair share."

Sophie smiled, "I'm sure. But I doubt the men on the ground care about that." She turned her head and nodded to the men that were filtering in after the raid. The noise level had increased as more of them came in.

"No, they don't, Sophie. The men that are out there risking their lives don't care about that one bit. They care about the lives they save."

Houston came in and greeted the Captain. Then sat next to Sophie taking her hand.

"Hey, sweetheart. Is Dajao one of the rescued?"

She turned to look at him. "It doesn't look like it. There haven't been any more photos come in the last five minutes."

"I'm sorry, Sophie." He kissed the back of her hand. She didn't reply.

Someone called the Captain's name, and he left the room.

SAC Demonte came into the conference room. "I don't think the men will leave until you address them, Ms. Star. You may not be aware, but all the teams know that you are the mastermind behind all the recent successful operations. Working on a Task Force with you means more to them than just a career boost."

She turned around and saw them all looking her direction. Houston patted her hand and helped her up.

Sophie stood in front of them. "Thank you for agreeing to put yourselves in harm's way to make this operation successful." She looked at Captain Cartwright. "You have given these women a chance at a real life. They owe that to you, the men in the field." She looked them in their faces. "Well done... well done."

Houston could see by the smiles that the men appreciated her kudos.

Houston, Sophie, and Fons went to the National Guard Facility to check on the women. It was almost 8:30 pm before they left to head home. Sophie had to see for herself that the women were taken care of before she would go.

Houston got a return call from his mom saying she found temporary housing for the 128 women that were overflow.

Houston had given her number to the Captain so he could let her know when they would be ready for transport.

While they were still there, Sophie saw the First Lady on the National Guard TV. Her plea for supplies and training for the women guaranteed they would get all the help they needed.

At the end of the day, the raid apprehended 62 offenders, 65 johns, and rescued 263 women.

CHAPTER NINE

When Sophie woke up the next morning, there was a note on her nightstand. Houston had taken Bully for a run. She got up and took a shower. By the time she was out of the bathroom, she could smell something cooking in the kitchen.

Houston was making waffles. She wrapped her arms around him from behind and gave him a big hug. "Waffles. I love waffles. They are my favorite."

He turned and kissed her. "I thought pancakes were your favorite," he laughed.

"They are, when you make pancakes."

"Can you finish up here so I can take my shower and change?" As he was walking to the bedroom, she heard him say. "I bought some blueberries on the way home to put on top."

Houston had fed Bully, so she let him out on the balcony. The news said there would be snow later in the week, but the skies were clear today. It had been a mild winter in New York.

While they were eating, Sophie brought up the text she received from Izumi yesterday.

"Mr. Katsumi wants to see me. I told Izumi I wasn't available until this evening."

"What does he want? It's only Wednesday, so it can't be dinner."

"Maybe he has some information on Dajao."

"When is Izumi coming for us?"

"He should be here by 6 pm."

After cleaning up breakfast, they discussed their

Christmas plans. They had permission to have a party at the Women's Domestic Violence Shelter. They spent the afternoon making plans.

Sophie decided to mention something that was bothering her while changing to meet Mr. Katsumi. "Houston, I'm not sure what to do about Mr. Katsumi." She sat down on the edge of the bed.

Houston came and sat next to her. "What is it?"

"I know it hurts Mr. Katsumi that I don't reciprocate the honor he has bestowed on me by calling me 'musume.'"

"Does it bother you that he calls you that?"

She looked up at him. "No. I'm sure he means it as a kindness. Does it bother you?"

"No, sweetheart. He's a lonely man who misses his wife and sees you as the daughter he never had."

"You know how much I loved my father...I could never call anyone else, father."

She laid her head on his shoulder; Houston put his arm around her. He had asked about her family many times. It was a difficult topic for her. The loss of her father took a heavy toll on her.

"You are under no obligation to reciprocate, sweetheart."

"I know. But I can see the hurt in Katsumi's eyes when I insist on calling him Mr. Katsumi after he calls me his daughter."

"Is there some other name you would be comfortable with?"

She lifted her head to look at him. "My father had many friends that were as close to him as brothers. I always called them uncle. I would feel comfortable with that. I'm just not sure it would be appropriate."

Houston stood and moved backed to the closet while saying, "You can ask Izumi on the way to the compound."

"That's a good idea." She finished getting ready.

On the drive to the compound, Izumi asked, "Ms. Star. I heard on the news yesterday; there were more raids. Was that you?"

"As I explained to Mr. Katsumi, I will take these syndicates apart piece by piece until I find Dajao," she said defensively.

"I understand, Ms. Star. I was sure it was you; did you find her?"

"No, she wasn't one of the victims recovered."

"I'm sorry. Have you considered that maybe Ms. Taru didn't survive the trip to the US? Many die on the way here; the conditions are harsh. I'm sure they would not record the names of those who don't make it, since they were never delivered."

The thought never crossed her mind; a sadness overwhelmed her. *What if Dajao never even made it this far?* Her eyes filled with tears. Izumi noticed and wanted to take back his words.

"My sister, I am sorry that distresses you." He would have taken her hand, but he felt it would be inappropriate.

She was able to compose herself after Houston put his arm around her. "I just never thought there was a possibility we wouldn't find her. That she never made it this far."

Izumi changed the subject. "I'm sure the Kumicho would be delighted if you had another story for us this evening after dinner."

"I wasn't aware this was a dinner invitation."

"Yes, of course, I'm sorry if I was not clear."

"No reason to apologize. It's a pleasant surprise, and I do have a story if the Kumicho chooses to ask." She had so much more she needed to tell him, to get him ready to hear the story of salvation.

"Izumi, I do have a question for you."

"Of course, Ms. Star. What is it?"

"Mr. Katsumi has honored me by calling me 'musume'. I appreciate the kindness, but I am afraid I insult him by not reciprocating by calling him 'father'."

"Ms. Star. Indeed he is hoping you will consider him more than a business acquaintance. But he would not wish you to be uncomfortable."

"When my father was alive, he had many friends that were close to my family. I used to call them uncle. I would be comfortable with that."

"Ms. Star, I am sure he would be very pleased."

Izumi escorted them into the smaller dining room, where Mr. Katsumi was waiting for them. He walked over to her when she entered, but Sophie was mesmerized by the view out the bay window overlooking the garden. *In the summer, it must look like a Thomas Kinkade painting,* she thought. There was just enough daylight to make the scene look surreal. She walked over to the bay window and stared out. Mr. Katsumi followed and stood by her; Izumi and Houston held back.

"The gardens are beautiful, are they not, musume?" He said proudly.

"Breathtaking, Ojisan," she said without thinking.

Houston and Izumi saw Mr. Katsumi's smile. The Japanese word she chose signifies an uncle who is not blood related. But it was the thought that he appreciated.

He took her hand and slipped it into the crook of his elbow. He insisted on showing the gardens to her. Houston and Izumi waited inside and watched this tender moment unfold before them. Mr. Katsumi was pointing out the sculptured bushes and what the designs represented. He showed her the rose garden; of course, there were no roses now. But the placement was perfect, along with the other flora and bushes. It was like walking in paradise. As the sunlight faded, the ground lights lit up the area. They walked to the gardener's cottage; the door open and a man stood there bowing low. Mr. Katsumi introduced Sophie to Mr. Jo as his daughter. They praised his work, putting a huge smile on his face. All the while, Katsumi never let Sophie's hand slip from his arm. When they came in, the server went to pull out a chair for her, but Katsumi waved him off and did it himself. The others sat down after Mr. Katsumi was seated.

"Nori, your sister thinks the gardens are beautiful." He stood and served his guests tea.

"As she should, watashi no Chichi (my father), you have made it a paradise." It was customary that everything good was always credited to the Kumicho, no matter who did the work.

"I thought you might enjoy a change in cuisine tonight. I prepared a traditional American meal. Fried Chicken and mashed potatoes."

"Thank you, Mr. Katsumi, that was very considerate of you, both Houston and I will enjoy it."

They enjoyed each other's company at the meal, and the men again tried to outwit each other. Sophie enjoyed their antics.

The server cleared the plates and put a new teapot on the table. After Mr. Katsumi served them all tea, he sat and asked her if she had a story for him tonight.

"It's my pleasure." She had already planned the story she would tell.

"You remember the story of the great warrior David, servant to King Saul. When King Saul died, God anointed David King. David loved God with his whole heart; God blessed him and his people. His son Solomon also served God and was blessed. But after them, there were many Kings in Israel, some who served God and some who did not. When the King turned from serving God, the people also turned away. God sent prophets to warn the Kings, saying. 'Take heed to yourselves, that your heart be not deceived and ye turn aside, to serve other gods, and worship them: and then the Lord's wrath be kindled against you, and he shut up the heaven, that there be no rain, and that the land yield not her fruit; and lest ye perish quickly from off the good land which the Lord giveth you.' (Deut. 11:16-17)

In those days, the people of Israel made yearly animal sacrifices to keep in right standing with God. The people would lay all their sins on an unblemished lamb and slaughter it. The blood would cover their sins for the year. The Kings that did not obey God tore down the altars for those sacrifices.

King Ahab was one of those kings. He did not keep God's commandments. The Prophet Elijah came and told the King that God would stop the rain because of his disobedience. And the rain stopped for three years. The drought devastated the King's land and people.

Then God spoke to Elijah and told him to go back and see King Ahab again, and he would send rain back to Israel. But when King Ahab saw him, he said, 'Is that you, you troubler of Israel?'

'I have not made trouble for Israel,' Elijah replied. 'But you and your father's family have. You have abandoned the Lord's commands and have followed Baal, a false god. Now summon the people from all over Israel to meet me on Mount Carmel. And bring the four hundred and fifty prophets of Baal.'

So, Ahab sent word throughout all Israel and assembled the prophets on Mount Carmel. Elijah went before the people and said, 'How long will you waver between two opinions? If the Lord is God, follow him; but if Baal is God, follow him.'

But the people said nothing. Then Elijah said to them, 'I am the only one of the Lord's prophets left, but Baal has four hundred and fifty prophets. Get two bulls for us. Let Baal's prophets choose one for themselves and let them cut it into pieces and put it on the wood but not set fire to it. I will prepare the other bull and put it on the wood but not set fire to it. Then you call on the name of your god, and I will call on the name of the Lord. The god who answers by fire — he is God.'

Then all the people said, 'What you say is good.'

So, they took the bull given them and prepared it, and they called on the name of Baal from morning till noon. 'Baal answer us!' they shouted. But there was no response; no one answered. And they danced around the altar they had made.

At noon Elijah began to taunt them. 'Shout louder!' he said. 'Surely he is a god! Perhaps he is deep in thought, or busy, or traveling. Maybe he is sleeping and must be awakened.' So, they shouted louder and slashed themselves with swords and spears, as was their custom, until their blood flowed. Midday passed, and they continued their frantic prophesying until the time for the evening sacrifice. But there was no response, no one answered, no one paid attention.

Then Elijah said to all the people, 'Come here to me.' They came to him, and he repaired the altar of the Lord, which had been torn down. Elijah took twelve stones; with the stones, he built an altar in the name of the Lord. He dug a trench around it large enough to hold 11 gallons of water. He arranged the wood, cut the bull into pieces, and laid it on the wood. Then he said to them, 'Fill four large jars with water and pour it on the offering and on the wood.'

'Do it again,' he said, and they did it again.

'Do it a third time,' he ordered, and they did it the third time. The water ran down around the altar and even filled the trench.

At the time of sacrifice, the Prophet Elijah stepped forward

143

and prayed. 'Lord, the God of Abraham, Isaac, and Israel, let it be known today that you are God in Israel and that I am your servant and have done all these things at your command. Answer me, Lord, answer me, so these people will know that you, Lord, are God and that you are turning their hearts back again.'

Then the fire of the Lord fell and burned up the sacrifice, the wood, the stones, and the soil, and also licked up the water in the trench.

When all the people saw this, they fell prostrate and cried, 'The Lord—he is God! The Lord—he is God!'

Then Elijah commanded them, 'Seize the prophets of Baal. Don't let anyone get away!' They seized them and Elijah had them brought down to the Kishon Valley and slaughtered there.

And Elijah said to Ahab, 'Go, eat and drink, for there is the sound of a heavy rain.' Ahab went off to eat and drink. But Elijah climbed to the top of Carmel, bent down to the ground and put his face between his knees.

'Go and look toward the sea,' he told his servant. And he went up and looked.

'There is nothing there,' he said.

Seven times Elijah said, 'Go back.'

The seventh time the servant reported, 'A cloud as small as a man's hand is rising from the sea.'

Elijah said, 'Go and tell Ahab, hitch up your chariot and go down before the rain stops you.'

Meanwhile, the sky grew black with clouds; the wind rose. A heavy rain started falling, and Ahab rode off to Jezreel. The power of the Lord came on Elijah and, tucking his cloak into his belt; he ran ahead of Ahab all the way to Jezreel. (paraphrased from 1 Kings 18:16-46 KJV)

The men clapped. "That was a powerful story, musume."

"It is a true story from the Bible; I am glad you enjoyed it."

Mr. Katsumi finally got to the reason for this midweek visit.

"Saturday night, I had an unexpected visitor. Mr. Zhao, he is the second in command of the Tong Clans in Chinatown. He had heard the rumors of my exploits against the government. He said he heard of a woman who had found the whereabouts of my funds, allowing me to retrieve them. He requests an audience with you. He wishes to find out who is doing such harm to their business and why. I told him he would never get an audience with you. However, through Izumi, I said, you may choose to respond to his request." He waited a moment before he continued. "I heard the news today. Have you found your girl yet?"

"I'm afraid not." She said softly.

"I am sorry, what do you want to do about the request?"

She thought for a moment. "I have run out of leads; I was considering putting more pressure on them with an ultimatum. This may be a way to do it without revealing myself."

"What do you have in mind?" He asked.

"I would say that I have found who is doing this, and the person has a message for them."

"And what is the message?" Katsumi put down his tea.

"You have twenty-four hours to give me Dajao Taru, alive and unharmed. Or I will take your organizations apart piece by piece." Sophie looked at Katsumi, "with today's success, they will believe me."

Mr. Katsumi stood and started pacing. He was not pleased with this. "Ms. Star, you are playing with fire. They will want to find you and force you to tell them who it is. They could do great harm to you."

"My husband wants to take me away from here and hide

me for a while. After the statement is delivered and the twenty-four hours are up, I will allow him to do that."

"Watashi no Chichi, if they don't deliver Dajao, Ms. Star will not stop her crusade. She may hide, but she will continue to destroy their business," Izumi told his father.

"Is this true?" Katsumi asked.

"I will not cower to these men who peddle in human flesh. Would a father want his child to bow down to such men?" She was not helping matters with her tone. Houston did not intervene. Sophie was capable of handling Katsumi.

"No, but sometimes if you don't bow, you break." He was equally as stubborn.

"Would you?" She stood and went to where he was looking out the window into the darkness. He hesitated to answer.

"I didn't think so, then why would you expect me to?" Sophie answered when he didn't.

He turned away from her.

"Then tell me what I should do. Leave those girls to be abused hour after hour? If one of them was your daughter, would you feel differently? I will consider changing my mind if there is a better way to stop this travesty." She moved in front of him and looked him in the eye.

He moved away and sat back down, motioning her to sit. "If they took my daughter, I would kill everyone who touched her. But these are not my daughters. And I cannot tell the Tong or the Triad how to run their business."

"Then give me an alternative," she said again.

They all sat for a long time. Finally, Katsumi spoke. "If you insist on giving them that ultimatum. Then you need to stay here where we can protect you. If they don't bring the girl to you, then your husband can take you away from here. I will do what I can to keep them from finding out who you are." Katsumi was oddly calm.

"May I have a private moment with my husband before I

decide?" Sophie requested.

"Please use the sitting room next door." Izumi escorted them to it.

He came back to talk to his father, "If I were to have access to information that could help her. Should I give it to her?" He asked.

"I cannot be seen as complicit in taking down a rival that has not harmed us. That would start a war," he responded. He was still the Kumicho and had a responsibility to his Council in Japan.

"You are not responsible for information that is not yours, and you did not pass on, father."

"That's true. If I know nothing of it. Who has it, where it came from, or to whom it goes. My hands are clean."

That was the confirmation Izumi needed to hand over the flash drive. He would wait for the right time.

"Houston, it may not be a bad idea to stay here for a day or two. No one would ever find us here, and there is plenty of protection. What do you think?" They sat on a black lacquered sofa. The seat and back were silk with geisha girls and blossoming cherry trees embroidered on it.

"I'm not opposed to the idea, I would need to let Fons know where we are, we can't go dark. Plus, we'll both need clothes, and we would have to do something with Bully."

"Fons could take him to Max for us. It will only be a few days at most."

"Do you feel safe here while I'm gone?"

"Yes, I'll be fine." They headed back to the small dining area; the door was open for them.

"Mr. Katsumi, if your offer for us to stay is still open, we would like to accept it," Sophie said as she walked over to him.

"The invitation is still open, musume." Katsumi smiled.

Houston added, "I will need to go to our condo and get some items for my wife and myself and take our dog to the sitter. With your permission, I would like to bring my car back here." Houston waited for his response.

"Izumi can take you to your home to get your things. But you are welcome to bring your dog here if you wish."

Houston looked at Sophie for her input, she smiled and said. "Mr. Katsumi, that is very gracious of you."

"I should be back in a few hours. With your permission, I'd feel better if Sophie waited here." He waited for Mr. Katsumi's agreement before he left with Izumi.

Izumi took Houston to a town car parked in the garage and drove it himself. It was the first time Houston had seen Izumi drive.

On the ride, Izumi started asking questions about the stories Sophie had told.

"Ms. Star says that the stories of God are true, Mr. Townsend. Do you believe that?"

"Please call me Houston. Yes, Izumi, there is a God in heaven, and he is the only true God." He told him of God's desire to reconnect with his creation, but they were spiritually dead because of Adam's sin. The animal sacrifices brought forgiveness, but not an intimate relationship. God wanted fellowship with his children. So He sent Jesus, His Son, to earth to be that ultimate sacrifice for sin and restore that relationship. He came as a man to his people Israel, who were God's chosen. But they rejected Him, even with all the prophets telling of His coming they wouldn't believe. He became the ultimate and final sacrifice. They took God's Son beat him, whipped him, and nailed Him to the Cross. He died willingly for you."

It was difficult for Izumi to believe that Jesus would die for him. Houston continued, "the blood shed on the Cross cleanses us from our sins. The grave could not hold Him. He rose from the dead on the third day, presented himself to his disciple, and told them to go and preach to all the world. Anyone who hears the truth and believes in His name can be born again. "

They reached the condo, Izumi pulled in front of the door. "Houston, when Sophie tells the stories from the Bible...I believe. Inside, I know it is true. All my life, I have longed to learn the true purpose of life. What must I do if I want your God to be my God?"

"You ask Him to forgive your sins. When Jesus shed His blood on the Cross, He promised forgiveness for all who ask."

"But I am an evil man. How can He forgive me?" Izumi asked, his head bowed in shame.

"He is no respecter of person. It is a gift; you can't earn it."

"What do I say."

"Just tell Him you believe He is the Son of God. Then ask forgiveness for your sins, ask Him to come into your heart and be your Lord and Savior. From that moment on, He will be with you. And when this life ends, you will spend eternity with Him in heaven."

Izumi bowed his head and repeated the prayer in Japanese. The language he felt best could express his feelings. At the end of it, Izumi began weeping. He wept for his sins, for the life he led, and all the years wasted without Jesus. Then the most amazing thing happened, he felt an actual weight of darkness lift off him, and the joy of the Lord replaced the darkness. He began laughing, a deep belly laugh. The laughter spread to Houston, and he too started laughing. When it lifted, Izumi was exhausted. But he knew he was a different man.

Houston had never witnessed a more remarkable salvation.

"Houston, what do I do now?" He asked.

"I will bring you a Bible when I come back tonight. I will find you one translated into Japanese as soon as possible. You need to learn all that you can, so you become strong in the Lord."

Houston reached over to lay his hand on Izumi's shoulder. "You are now my brother. I'll be back as soon as I can. Take care of Sophie until I get there."

"I will." Izumi left, and Houston went to the condo to get their things and call Fons.

Sophie and Katsumi were still talking in the small dining room when Izumi came back. He had asked her to tell him how she had gotten entangled with Nikko Morano. She told him the story.

When Izumi came in, Sophie turned to acknowledge him. Immediately she noticed something different about him. His countenance had changed. Katsumi turned to him, if he saw a difference in Izumi, he didn't say.

"Izumi, call Mr. Zhao, and have him come here in the morning."

"Yes, sir." Izumi went to Kato to have the message sent.

"Sir, I will show Ms. Star to her room with your permission." He wanted a chance to talk to her.

"No, I will show her." He got up, offered his hand to her, and led her to the private residence upstairs. Izumi followed them.

The upstairs residence was even more beautiful than the downstairs. Katsumi led her to a large suite. It had a private bath and a separate sitting area with a plush carpet that felt like walking on a cloud. He showed her the closet that held a mint green silk sleeping kimono. On it was elaborately embroidered branches of blooming cherry blossoms. There was also a black silk man's sleeping kimono. They were stunning.

"Mr. Katsumi, I would never dream of wearing anything so beautiful to bed. But thank you for offering."

He laughed at her. "My dear, they are only beautiful when someone wears them. Otherwise, it is just material."

Sophie thanked him for his kindness and his protection. He left, and Izumi followed.

She waited up for Houston. She decided to model the beautiful kimono to surprise Houston.

Houston hurried to get things together; he didn't like leaving Sophie there without him. He kept thanking the Lord for the miracle he witnessed tonight. Houston had never seen anyone saved and delivered in quite that way. He grabbed the extra Bible he had and put it in his bag. He gathered the clothes Sophie asked for and Bully's things before he called Fons.

"Fons, Sophie is going to give the Tong that ultimatum we talked about. Mr. Katsumi is going to have Izumi deliver it so we can try to keep her anonymous. He insists we stay there for the twenty-four hours of the demand. He feels they can protect her better there. I have to agree in this circumstance."

"Houston, are you sure your safe with them. We can give you both police protection."

"If we were in DC, I would agree, but here we already know there are moles in all the departments. There is little chance the Akuza would have a mole. But I didn't want to go off the grid without letting you know. I'm going to call Cosby too. Cover for me at work, OK."

"Alright, but at least connect with me a few times a day.

Let me know your safe."

"Fons, you can't believe what just happened. Izumi turned his life over to Christ."

"Did he tell you that?"

"No, I don't know that I would have believed it if I hadn't seen it myself. I witnessed with my own eyes when Izumi dropped me off here. The power of God came on him in a most unusual way. There is no denying it was real."

"Praise the Lord. I'll keep him in my prayers."

"Yes, I have no doubt the devil will fight for his soul. Can you locate a Japanese version of the Bible for me?"

"Of course. How can I get it to you?"

"I'll let you know."

Houston called Cosby; he told him what was going on. Cosby was not happy about it. When Houston explained that Sophie finally agreed to let the Task Force take over, he calmed down a bit.

"I don't condone you putting yourselves in jeopardy like this."

"Sir, right now, I believe that's the safest place for us."

He finished the conversation and made two trips to his vehicle to load up. His third trip was for Bully.

When Houston arrived at the compound, Kato directed him to drive his car into one of the garages to keep the vehicle out of sight. Kato helped him carry his belongings up to where Sophie was waiting in her suite. Bully was walking on the leash next to him.

Houston opened the door and put down her suitcase and

his bag. He asked Kato which room Izumi would be in. He told him it was the one on the other side of the stairs to the right.

Sophie squatted down and showered Bully with attention.

"What am I, chopped liver," Houston smiled.

She went over to him and gave him a big kiss. That's when he noticed what she was wearing.

"Wow, you look beautiful." He said with a big smile on his face.

"Thank you." She stepped back so he could see it better. "This is a sleeping kimono; there is one in there for you too."

"Is it green?" His eyebrows furrowed.

"No, it's black. I want to see you in it." She picked it up off the bed where she laid it for him.

After he got Bully's bed out and some water in his bowl, he tried it on.

She clapped her hands, "you look wonderful. I love these, but they are too beautiful to sleep in. I'm going to find my pj's. You didn't forget them, did you?"

At that point, he wished he had. "No, princess, they are in there," pointing to her suitcase.

After she got changed, she sat on the bed. "Now, you have to tell me about Izumi; I know something happened. His whole countenance has changed."

Houston told her the whole story as he changed, unloaded his clothes, and took out the extra Bible.

"I'd never laughed like that. I can't put it into words."

"Houston, God is so good, what a wonderful testimony of God's grace." Tears filled her eyes.

"I'm going to find his room and give him this Bible; I'll be right back."

CHAPTER TEN

In the morning, Bully was making noise by the door, he needed to go outside. Sophie checked her watch; it was early and she didn't want to disturb the house. Houston forgot to bring her robe so she put the kimono on over her pj's, slipped on a pair of ballet flats, and snuck out of the room. She found the back stairs that led to the kitchen and hurried down them. Sophie managed to get to the back gardens without disturbing anyone. She walked to one of the concrete benches and sat, holding the plastic doggie cleanup bag. She took Bully off the leash, so he could do his business.

Mr. Katsumi was in the small dining room overlooking the gardens. He was reading a newspaper from Japan that was sent to him each day. He put it down to pour more hot tea when he noticed movement in the garden. He smiled when he saw it was Sophie in a kimono, with her dog. He went to the gardens and said, good morning.

His voice startled her, and she stood up, startled. She laughed when she saw it was Mr. Katsumi. He motioned her to sit and sat next to her.

"Mr. Katsumi, I'm sorry if I disturbed you, Bully needed to come outside." She called Bully over to leash him; Katsumi stopped her; the dog was doing no harm.

"Mr. Katsumi, tell me about your wife. If it doesn't offend you that I ask."

A smile came to his face, "ah, my wife, Suki, she was incredibly beautiful, the most beautiful of anyone I have ever met. I grew up with her, our families were Akuza from the same clan in Japan. I think I always loved her. Her father was an Oyabun, mine was as Saiko Komon. When our clan moved to the USA, years later, and I became a Saiko Komon, I felt I had earned the right to ask her to marry me. The So-honbucho, Izumi Yuuto, was jealous of me. He heard me ask permission from the Kumicho to marry Suki. He went behind my back and offered the Kumicho a large gift if he gave Suki to him instead. The next day I found out Suki was to marry Yuuto. I was broken, but there was nothing I could do. Suki had no choice; her father insisted she marry him. But it was not her nature to surrender her mind. When Suki would not submit to Yuuto's every whim, he would beat her. He did not believe women had any rights, not even to question. Yuuto kept her isolated, and although her husband could afford many servants, Suki was made to do all the chores. He did many things to her, trying to get her to submit to him. Her only happiness was her son; Suki loved him dearly.

Our Kumicho was a very traditional Japanese leader. He ran things with an iron fist, and punishments were dealt out for the slightest offenses. He did not stop his So-Honbucho from beating his wife, he approved of such things. I watched him abuse her for ten years...I could stand it no more." Katsumi bowed his head. He was lost in a time long ago. "When he died, I received permission to marry her. Suki and Nori moved in with me.

Most marriages in Japan are arranged, some are happy, most exist together in peace. But Suki loved me, and I loved her very much, we were happy together. She begged me to leave the Akuza so we could have a better life. I promised her when I completed my contract, at the Kumicho's death, we would leave the Akuza and move away from here. It was not common, but if a member sent an extravagant gift to the Council in Japan, it could earn him permission to leave the Akuza. When she died before I could keep my promise, it broke my heart. I will never love another woman in the way I loved her.

My Kumicho died a few months later, but then I had no reason to leave."

Sophie sat quietly for a few minutes. "Unfortunately, a traditional Japanese story with a tragic end," she said very softly.

They sat there for a moment until the Butler came to tell them breakfast was ready.

She laughed, "I can't be seen like this, I must go change." She went to get Bully, but Katsumi said he would watch him.

Mr. Katsumi and Izumi were waiting for Sophie and Houston when they came down for breakfast. Bully was sitting next to Katsumi in the dining room that overlooked the garden. His head was on Katsumi's leg. They stood, and Katsumi pulled out her chair.

Katsumi had a traditional Japanese breakfast served. The meal included an omelet sitting over a piece of grilled fish, miso soup with tofu, and a rice bowl.

"Mr. Katsumi, this meal is delicious. if you continue feeding me like this, my husband may object to having to buy me larger clothes." She laughed as she sat back in her chair, full.

He simply smiled. Talking about his wife seemed to have sparked some sadness. He was absentmindedly stroking Bully. Katsumi was surprised when Bully sat up on his hind legs with his front paws up. He was trying to earn some scraps. Mr. Katsumi burst out laughing, he fed Bully his boneless fish and clapped his hands.

Houston would not show his disapproval since he was a guest. And what difference would it make, he knew Sophie did it all the time when she thought he wasn't looking. Houston was surprised at how much Mr. Katsumi liked the dog.

Kato came and whispered in Izumi's ear.

"Mr. Zhao will be here in an hour, sir," Izumi reported.

"Mr. Katsumi, I would like to hear what his response is, without being seen. Is that possible?" Sophie asked.

"Izumi will seat you behind the dividers at the ceremonial table on the dais. No one will see you."

They all stood to leave, Katsumi patted Sophie's hand and said he would speak with her later. Izumi asked to talk to Houston in the garden, Bully went with them. Sophie decided to go back to her room to read her Bible.

Houston and Izumi came to the concrete bench and sat down while Bully ran the grounds.

"I was up most of the night reading the Bible, there is so much I want to ask you." He turned his body to face Houston. "God is a Trinity, the Father, the Son, and the Holy Spirit, right?"

"Yes, they are separate, but they are one God. When Jesus returned to his Father in heaven, he said he promised to send the Holy Spirit to give us power."

"I believe all that I have read. What I would like to do is have you help me talk to the gardener; he needs to hear of Jesus. I do not feel I understand enough to tell him."

Houston waited on the bench while Izumi went to ask Mr. Jo to join them. Houston told Mr. Jo all that he had told Izumi the night before; Izumi translated it into Korean. Izumi then added his testimony and his experience of being born again. The Holy Spirit opened Mr. Jo's heart to the truth, and Mr. Jo believed. He bowed his head and gave his heart to the Lord. Izumi was so excited, he promised he would get him a Korean Bible. It had taken almost the entire hour.

Izumi directed Houston and Sophie to the table behind the screens.

The Kumicho motioned Kato to allow Mr. Zhao and a few of his men in. He watched as Mr. Zhao came and stood before him, they bowed low and waited to be spoken to. Katsumi stood in his power position, feet apart, hands clasped behind his back. He was wearing a Kiton K-50 suit made of the best sheep's wool. Izumi was standing behind the Kumicho to his right in a bodyguard stance, hands clasped in front. He was wearing his custom-made suit. Their appearance alone was intimidating.

Kato had stationed several of his elite enforcers in front of the platform. They faced the Tong on the assembly floor.

"Mr. Zhao, I have some news for you. I have gotten word from my asset that those who do you harm have a message."

"Kumicho, the police raided us again, almost all our brothels in New York have been shut down, and the properties confiscated. We need more than a message. We need it to stop!"

"Mr. Zhao, your problems are not my concern. You asked me to contact my asset. I have done that. If you do not wish to hear the message, this meeting is over."

Mr. Zhao again bowed. "I apologize, Kumicho. Please tell us the message." The Kumicho nodded to Izumi.

Izumi stepped forward, "this is how it was relayed to me. 'You have taken a girl that we want returned to us. We have tracked her to Chinatown. Return her to us unharmed, or we will take your empire apart piece by piece.'"

Mr. Zhao was stunned. "A girl? Who? Why has there been no demand before, and who would do this for one girl?"

"The girl's name is Dajao Taru. They intended to find her themselves. However, since you asked, they said they would give you twenty-four hours to release her. The demand says if you refuse to do so, they will continue to dismantle your operation until she is found or returned. They said when they are done, there will be nothing left. The message also stated if she is dead, there will be no mercy given to you." Izumi finished and stepped back.

Mr. Zhao turned to the Kumicho. "What if it is another gang who has her?" The Kumicho stepped forward again.

"Then I suggest you spread the message to them, so they can release her."

"You are Akuza. How can you condone this happening to a brother?" Mr. Zhao demanded.

The Kumicho moved closer to the edge of the platform, angry at that accusation. "I have nothing in it. Your lack of discipline and your choice of business has gotten you into this. Don't mistake the fact that I allow you to exist a sign of my approval, you are not my brother."

"You think you could take us down, Kumicho?" He made a slight move forward. Kato had him on the ground before he knew what happened. Mr. Zhao's men moved out of his way.

"I have no doubt, Mr. Zhao." He nodded to Kato to let him up.

Mr. Zhao straightened himself up and continued. "I apologize for my outburst; we are under a great deal of pressure." He bowed in respect.

Mr. Katsumi told the date and the Province in the Philippines from which Dajao was taken.

"She landed in Chinatown, that is all they know." He finished.

"This is impossible, how are we to find one girl? We need to talk to this woman; we will force her to give us the name of who is doing this."

The Kumicho moved even closer to the edge. "This woman is under my protection; you will not speak to her, nor will you interrogate her. Is that understood?"

Mr. Zhao's bravado melted away at the harshness of the Kumicho's words.

"Yes, my apologies. We thank you for giving us this message."

"You have twenty-four hours; Mr. Zhao, I wouldn't waste them here." He dismissed him with the wave of his hand.

Izumi escorted Houston and Sophie out, the Kumicho wanted to talk to him and Kato privately.

When they were alone, the Kumicho ordered Kato to bring fifty more elite enforcers to the compound. He ordered all his men to be on perimeter watch. The new men Kato was bringing in would be their relief. They would work 12 on and 12 off.

"If these men can't produce the girl, they will come back to try to force me to tell where Ms. Star is. They are desperate and not afraid to start a war. They have nothing left to lose."

Kato and Izumi left the Kumicho and went to prepare for wartime security around the compound.

Houston was with Sophie out in the gardens. He was telling her about the gardener when he saw the commotion going on. He understood they were preparing for a possible attempted breach.

Sophie asked, "Houston, what is the Lord doing in Mr. Katsumi?"

"I'm not sure, but before we can reach him with the gospel, the stone wall around his heart has to be down. Maybe that's what he's doing now." He took her hand as they walked Bully in the gardens.

The rest of the day, the Kumicho, conducted his business.

Sophie and Houston stayed in their room. They worked remotely with the DC Task Force. Lunch was brought to them in their bedroom, which indicated the downstairs was off-limits for a while.

Sophie told Sissy she had no direction left to take this. If the ultimatum didn't work, she wasn't sure what she would do next.

The Butler came to announce dinner would be ready in twenty minutes. Sophie changed, and they headed downstairs. They were told Bully was also invited.

They ate dinner in the formal dining room, and again it was the traditional twelve-course meal. The company was entertaining, and the meal was delicious. Mr. Katsumi asked her to tell a story.

Sophie told of the prophets who came to speak to God's people about a Savior. A sacrifice that would allow a personal relationship with their God again. They would no longer need a priest to intercede for them. But His chosen people turned from Him many times.

Then Sophie told the story of the captivity of Israel. She explained how the King who captured them, wanted the most intelligent and handsome of the captives to work in his court. Four captives were the brightest and made a good impression: Daniel and his friends Hananiah, Mishael, and Azariah. These four continually served the one true God of Israel.

Sophie took a breath and continued. "King Darius came to notice Daniel. He had distinguished himself above his other administrators. King Darius planned to put Daniel over the whole Kingdom. The other advisors became jealous and tricked the King into making a vain decree. It stated that for thirty days, no one could pray to any god other than the King. These men knew Daniel was faithful to his God and prayed to Him three times a day. Daniel was not afraid. He opened his windows and prayed to the one true God as he usually did. When the advisors saw him pray, they went to the King to accuse Daniel. The King had foolishly agreed that anyone who disobeyed the decree would be put in the lion's den to be eaten. Now the King realized what he had done. He loved Daniel and did not want him dead. But sadly, his decree could not be changed.

So the King gave the command, and they brought Daniel and cast him into the den of lions. But the King spoke, saying to Daniel, 'Your God, whom you serve continually, He will deliver you.' The King then sealed the den with his signet. (Dan 6:16 NKJV)

Now the King went to his palace and spent the night fasting, and no musicians were brought before him. He could not sleep. Then the King arose very early in the morning and went in haste to the den of lions. And when he came to the den, he cried out with a lamenting voice to Daniel. The King spoke, saying to Daniel, 'Daniel, servant of the living God, has your God, whom you serve continually, been able to deliver you from the lions?'

Then Daniel said to the King, O King, live forever! My God sent His angel and shut the lions' mouths, so that they have not hurt me, because I was found innocent before Him; and also, O King, I have done no wrong before you.' (Dan 6: 18-22 NKJV)

Houston was watching her audience. Izumi was soaking it up like it was water in the desert, his heart was so eager to learn more of the God he now served. Katsumi was taken in by the story of a powerful King. The story continued.

"Then the King took those who accused Daniel and threw them and their families into the lion's pit. Before they reached the floor the lions crushed their bones. After that, the King made a decree to go out to all the land that said. 'I make a decree that in every dominion of my kingdom men must tremble and fear before the God of Daniel. For He is the living God, and steadfast forever; His Kingdom is the one which shall not be destroyed, and His dominion shall endure to the end.

He delivers and rescues, and He works signs and wonders in heaven and on earth, who has delivered Daniel from the power of the lions.'

So Daniel prospered during the reign of King Darius. (Dan 6: 26-27 NKJV)

Sophie added the story of the other three captives who were rescued from the fire.

When she was done, they clapped as usual.

"Your stories are delightful. Thank you." Katsumi praised her.

"My stories are true; they come from the Word of God. Mr. Katsumi, I cannot take credit for them."

They continued to visit for another hour while sipping tea and eating green tea cookies. Then they all went to their rooms.

Izumi stayed up for hours reading his Bible. Houston had suggested he start in the New Testament. He explained how the Bible was arranged. His eagerness to learn was voracious.

After Houston took Bully for a walk, it was time for breakfast. Bully rushed to sit next to Katsumi, who was thrilled that the dog favored him. Bully laid his head on Katsumi's lap and had his fur stroked for his effort. Izumi was not at breakfast, Sophie felt it might be rude to ask where he was so she waited to see if her host would mention it. There was a large T-bone steak on a separate plate in front of Katsumi; she had an idea who it was for. When Bully did his trick to get scraps, Katsumi clapped and then gave Bully the steak. Bully was thrilled with his reward and sat under the table, enjoying it. Houston, on the other hand, was not so thrilled; it would take time to get Bully out of these bad habits.

As they were clearing off the table and fresh tea was served, Izumi appeared. He handed Katsumi a package and sat down. Houston asked Izumi to meet with Fons, while he was out doing Katsumi's errand. Fons had picked up a Japanese and a Korean Bible for the new converts. Houston had arranged a meeting place.

Mr. Katsumi had a big smile on his face. He handed Sophie the package with both hands and said, "I am pleased to give you this, musume."

It was wrapped in furoshiki, beautiful silk material. Sophie received it with both hands. "Thank you, this is most generous. But Ojisan, I have no gift for you." She took the time to admire the wrapping.

"Your gift to me is your presence, musume."

"I know in your culture it is rude to open a gift in front of the giver. But I can't wait, can I please open it."

Katsumi could not hide his pleasure in her eagerness to open it. He nodded.

She carefully untied the material. Inside were three of the most beautiful silk Japanese dresses she'd ever seen. She stood and lifted the first against her body. It was a long black gown, slit to the knee on each side, with long sleeves. The dress was embroidered with the traditional geisha scene and a standup collar. The buttons were made of material with braided loops clear down to the waist. He was clearly pleased with her exuberance.

"This is so beautiful, thank you." She leaned down and kissed his cheek spontaneously.

She realized what she had done, "I am so sorry, Mr. Katsumi, I realize no one is to touch you without invitation."

He touched her hand, "that doesn't apply to family, musume."

She lifted the other two dresses. The second dress was red,

165

knee-length. This one wrapped around the neck showing the shoulders and arms. The third was not a dress but a royal purple tunic. She thanked Katsumi again and then carefully folded them. She rewrapped them with the furoshiki.

He was clearly rewarded by her pleasure. They finished drinking their tea and visiting. Kato came in and whispered to Izumi.

Izumi relayed the information. "Kumicho, Mr. Zhao, will be here in an hour." His facial expression changed, as did Izumi's. Mr. Katsumi asked Kato if they were prepared; Kato explained all that was done. The Kumicho nodded his approval, and the men headed to the assembly room.

As they were leaving, Izumi handed Houston the package that held the Korean Bible. "Thank you so much for my new Bible, Houston. I must go with my Kumicho. Will you please go to Mr. Jo and give him this? Please explain to him where to start reading? He speaks and understands English well, he simply chooses not to." He then hurried to catch up with Katsumi and Kato.

Houston took Bully with him when he went to talk to Mr. Jo. Sophie went upstairs.

Katsumi was pacing on the platform, Kato and Izumi were standing close by.

"Kumicho, may I suggest we place a hidden sentry about 20 yards before the turn onto the access road. We need to have some warning if there is trouble coming. One of my men could go on a four-wheeler and take the trail through the woods, so no one knows he's there." Kato suggested.

"I agree, I don't trust the White Tiger Clan, you saw how aggressively they wanted to get their hands on Ms. Star. They may suspect you are hiding her here." Izumi added.

Katsumi stopped pacing and turned to them. "How many men do we have on the compound?"

"We have our regular 105, and, we have the additional fifty you requested yesterday," Kato reported.

"Do as you suggest. Up the number of men at the front gate to 30. If he comes with more than a simple escort, stop and disarm them then bring them to me. Have our men armed with their AK 47's. They need to see our firepower. But keep 25 men hidden in the house, we may need them."

"Yes, sir." Kato left to make it happen.

"Kumicho, do you think them so brazen they would try to take Ms. Star from your compound?" Izumi asked.

"I do. Arrogance and ignorance go hand in hand." He looked Izumi in the eyes, "they must never get their hands on her."

"Not as long as I am alive, watashi no Chichi."

Izumi left his father to help Kato prepare. He knew Ms. Star had no idea what danger she was in, but he also had no doubt Houston did.

Houston and Sophie were in place behind the screen when Kato came in with news. Kato's men were in place in front of the platform.

"Kumicho, our sentry has reported that Mr. Zhao has brought and envoy. It consists of eight black SUVs. The windows are dark, but he can see five men in each vehicle with machine guns. They have parked just before the access road. The two lead cars have continued on to the compound, but the others are waiting off the road."

"They plan on storming us if they don't get what they want," Kumicho stated. "I expected that. Send our men through the woods to overtake and disarm them, they won't be expecting it. Then I want them tied up and gagged and brought here. But keep them out of sight until I tell you," he ordered.

"Yes, sir." Kato left the room to take care of it.

At the front gate, the guards disarmed the men with Mr. Zhao and escorted them to the assembly room. When Mr. Zhao was brought in with his entourage, the Kumicho spoke.

"Explain yourself, Mr. Zhao, why is it you bring these men." He was referring to his entourage, not the men on the access road. "To a civil meeting. It assumes you mean us harm." The Kumicho was in his power stance.

Mr. Zhao and his men bowed low. "No, not at all, sir, but they are here to protect me. We still do not know who is out to harm us, so we are cautious. They can wait outside if you feel more comfortable."

"Your bodyguards are of no consequence to me, Mr. Zhao. But what is of consequence is that I do not see the girl. Did you not take the demand seriously?"

"We did, but we cannot find her. She is in none of our brothels or in any other Tong's or Triad's."

How he would have known if the Triad's had her he did not know unless they had joined forces against this unknown enemy. This would make Ms. Star's situation even more tenuous. The Kumicho considered the implications.

"We do not know if someone kept her for themself or if she died in transit. But we cannot be responsible for a girl we do not even know for sure exists." Zhao continued.

"Mr. Zhao, then our business is finished, and you and your men are free to go. Your future is in your own hands." He dismissed them, giving them a chance to leave peaceably.

"Not so Kumicho, you have it in your power to help us. And as an ally, we demand you do so." He was very haughty, thinking he could overpower the Kumicho with his hidden forces.

"As I explained to you before. You mistake my ambivalence to your existence as a sign of brotherhood; you could not be more mistaken. I owe you nothing."

"I am afraid I must insist that you release Ms. Star to me so we can find out what she knows."

Sophie made a small gasp; they knew her name. Luckily, no one heard. Houston put his finger to his lips.

"What makes you think Ms. Star is my asset?" Kumicho was a little surprised Mr. Zhao knew her name.

"The rumors of her abilities have been floating around for many months. It took me a while to put it together, but there is no one else it could be. And I believe you are keeping her here on your compound."

"What I do and who I entertain is none of your business. I will not allow my asset to be interrogated by anyone. You take my benevolence in passing on your request as a weakness, and now you try to strong-arm me. You overestimate your capabilities, Mr. Zhao."

"We do not wish a war with you, but she must give us the information we need, or we will take her by force."

"You think you can overtake my compound, Mr. Zhao, with eight men we have disarmed?"

"No, but I have a small army waiting in the wings that can," he asserted.

Kumicho nodded to Kato, who brought in the captured men. "Do you mean these men, Mr. Zhao."

He turned to see his men bound and gagged. He turned back to face the Kumicho, stunned. "Kumicho, you must understand we are desperate. We would never harm you or your men, but we must talk to Ms. Star."

"I am afraid the time for talk is over. You have declared war on the Akuza by your actions. You are ignorant and arrogant; those alone will take you down. But you also misjudge your supposed allies, the Triads. They will not back you if you come against me. We have had peace for years; they know the cost if they break it."

"What will you do to us?" He was bowing low in a humble position, knowing he was defeated as were all his men.

"Kato, hog tie them all, then pin a note to this one," he pointed to Mr. Zhao. "Put on the note. The next to come against the Akuza will be returned without their heads. Dump them in the middle of Chinatown so all can see and laugh at their humiliation."

Kato's hidden men came in and tied them up. They tied the men's hands and feet together, bowing their backs, mouths gagged. His men carried them out and put them in pickups to haul them to town. It was indeed a humiliation.

Houston and Sophie came out from behind the screens when everyone had gone.

"I'm so sorry I have put you in this position, Mr. Katsumi. Please forgive me." She stepped up to him to apologize.

He took her hand. "Putting them in their place is something that has to happen periodically. You happen to be the instrument by which it happened this time. I am not sorry." He took her to the ceremonial tables to sit with her.

"Musume, I am afraid you will have to let your husband take you away from here now. They know your name, and that you have been staying here, you are not safe. We can defend ourselves. But if something happened to you in the process, it would be a loss to me."

She looked at him, "I understand, I have caused you enough trouble. Houston has made an escape plan for us in case it was necessary."

"You have been no trouble; you have been a joy to my son and me. But it would be selfish of me to ask you to stay."

"I'm afraid a man as important as you will soon forget my

name, and I will never see you again." She was sincere as she stood to say goodbye.

He retook her hand. "It would be easier for me to forget my own existence, musume." He kissed her hand. "But you must go, take these men down if you can and find your girl. I will do what I can to protect you from here."

Houston thanked him for his protection and headed to the room to collect their things. Izumi went to speak with Kato.

Katsumi, Sophie, and Bully went to walk in the gardens for the last time. Sophie told him she had so many more stories she wanted to tell him. Katsumi told her there would be time once she was safe. When Houston had the SUV packed, he went to Izumi.

"What will you do now?" Houston asked.

"I have to stay; I am hoping God will continue to move on my father's heart. I will do my best to continue breaking down his walls. Although I know his heart will break at Ms. Star's leaving."

"You'll have to grow up fast in the Lord, Izumi, you have too many people depending on you. Mr. Jo needs your mentoring too, but you are still a baby yourself."

Izumi smiled, "Indeed, I am, but I will read the Bible every day, so I can grow fast."

Houston gave Izumi a man hug.

Sophie and Katsumi came around front. She hugged Izumi and whispered to him, she loved having a new brother. It brought a smile to his face, he slipped the three flash drives in her hand and told her to do what she needed to. She didn't give any indication he handed her anything. Mr. Katsumi's sadness at her departure was evident. Houston went over to shake his hand and thank him again. They got in the SUV and left the compound. Bully made himself comfortable in the back seat.

CHAPTER ELEVEN

Houston immediately called Fons, putting the cell on speaker so that Sophie could hear. "We have to leave town; the gangs are trying to locate Sophie. They believe she can lead them to the person destroying their business. They have no idea she's the one. They tried to make Katsumi give her up, but he overpowered them. We're going straight to Fort Hamilton Airfield. Will you go to our condo and take all the hard drives, secure everything, and set the alarm?"

"Houston, take a breath. Have you been on the internet? It's exploding with the pictures of the White Tiger's humiliation and the note the Kumicho pinned on Mr. Zhao? The stores and restaurants have closed. The tourists have left, expecting a huge retaliation."

"We didn't have a chance to see it. The Tongs virtually declared war on the Akuza by bringing armed men to the meeting. That was his response. I'll tell you more about it later; I need to call Cosby. Come as soon as you can. Thanks, Fons."

"No problem, I'll take care of everything and see you in DC."

His next call was to Cosby, "Sir, the Tong are after Sophie; we need protection."

"I saw the internet. I doubt the Tong will let it go without retaliating."

"The Kumicho wouldn't give her up; he is one shrewd military strategist. He was one step ahead of the Tong the whole time."

"Where are you now?"

"We're on the way to Fort Hamilton sir, we were on the other side of Manhattan, so we're about an hour and a half out." Houston kept checking his rear-view mirrors.

"I'll have a plane for you when you get there. The base will store your vehicle until you go home. I'll have military police there waiting for you at the gate."

"Thank you, sir."

"Get her back here safe, Agent Townsend. Is she alright?"

He looked over at his wife. She was looking out the window. "She's a little shaken, sir."

"We'll have protection on the ground when you get here." Cosby signed off.

Sophie's phone rang as Cosby was saying goodbye. She put it on speaker.

"Hello?"

"Sophie, why didn't you give me a heads up on what happened in Chinatown?" Gail demanded.

Houston rolled his eyes. "Gail, I told you after the last raid, I don't owe you anything else. I don't care for the way you disregard human suffering to get a story. If I find Dajao, I will give you the story, other than that we're done."

"That's not fair. You wouldn't have known any of this if I hadn't brought you in."

"And you wouldn't have had any story at all without my leads and connections. So, as I said, I owe you nothing."

"Well, then give me one of your contacts. I can take it from there," she insisted.

"Absolutely not! I would never trust you with my contacts. You'll have to get your own, weren't you an investigative reporter before you met me?"

"You have some nerve judging me, Ms. Star, you're a criminal," Gail blurted out.

Houston finally had enough. "Ms. Turner, you know nothing about my wife, so I'd appreciate it if you would keep your opinions to yourself."

"Is that your husband? You didn't tell me you had me on speaker."

"Gail, we have nothing further to discuss. As I said, when I find Dajao, I will give you a heads up." She didn't wait for Gail's response, she said goodbye and hung up.

"I'm sorry for getting in your conversation, but Ms. Turner had nothing to go on when you stepped in. She should be more grateful. Look at all the major attention she received from the stories. Ms. Turner gets the glory; you do the work." He was gripping the wheel a little too tight.

"Honey, you are my best friend, you always take my side, who does she have?"

"No you don't, you will not guilt me into feeling sorry for her."

She laughed and kissed him on his cheek. "My knight in shining armor."

They drove in silence for a while, then Sophie said, "I'd like to get a dog for Mr. Katsumi, do you think Titan will ever have pups again?" Titan was one of two police dogs that protected her when she was working with the DEA. They stayed with her during the dismantling of Nikko Morano's drug empire. The other dog's name was Bully. He is the father and the namesake of their own Bully Jr.

"I don't know, as soon as I have a chance, I'll ask. It's a great idea." He agreed, keeping his eyes on the road.

Katsumi, Izumi, and Kato spent the next few hours going

over plans to keep their compound safe from a breach. They put sentries on the roof and the access road. They had perimeter alarms activated and doubled the guards.

"By showing our enhanced security, I'm hoping to trick them into believing Ms. Star is still here. It will give them more time to get away." Katsumi explained. "Where do you think Houston will take her?"

"I don't know, sir; I didn't think it wise to ask," Izumi responded.

"Kato, how many fighting men do your spy's say the Tongs have?"

"The Tong have been badly depleted by the raids and arrests of the past few weeks. I am not convinced they could mount even a minimal assault. That is unless the Triad's get involved," Kato added.

"Kumicho, do you think we should invite Mr. Mato here to explain the humiliation? The internet is blasting the images. I believe he would be on your side if you took the time for him. He has always admired you and has wanted people to believe he was associated with you." Izumi suggested, feeling Mr. Mato, the Tongs, eminence grise (powerful decision maker behind the scenes), could calm things down.

"Let me think about it. Take care of the security for now." Katsumi went to his chair and sat down.

By the time they got to Fort Hamilton, there were four jeeps with military police. Houston's SUV was ushered through the gate. Four military vehicles surrounded his car, three Jeeps had a driver and a passenger with M4 carbines. The tail jeep had a machine gun mounted to the back.

Sophie was a little surprised. "I think Mr. Cosby has gone off the deep end on this, Houston."

After holding the flash drives in her hands on the trip, Sophie finally relinquished them to Houston for safekeeping.

"Izumi gave me these when we left."

"What's on them?"

"I have no idea. We should wait until we're on a secure network in Command before we open them." They were escorted to the plane and in the air in less than a half-hour.

"Houston, how are you going to mentor Izumi, he is all alone in a dark place. Then there is Mr. Jo. Do you have a plan?"

Houston had been thinking about it on the drive. "If I'm able to Skype with Izumi late every night after his duties. I can navigate him through the Bible. Then he can help Mr. Jo. It's not perfect, but at least he won't be so isolated."

"We need to do whatever we can."

"Sophie, I know I already told you of Izumi's conversion, but I can't stop thinking about it. I have never seen a conversion like that. After he repented and gave his life to Christ, the Spirit of God came on him, and he sobbed. He told me it felt like a heavy cloak of darkness physically lifted from him. After that, the joy of the Lord hit him, and he started laughing. Jesus knew he would need an experience that would carry him through what he's going to face alone."

"I love that testimony, but how long do you think he can stay with the Akuza?"

"I don't know what the Lord plans for him. For now, he doesn't want to leave his father; he's hoping he can continue what the Lord started in him."

They talked more about the new converts and how they may be able to help them.

When they touched down in DC, there were four more jeeps with armed military police. Sophie shook her head, but Houston didn't feel it was overkill. Sophie's a government asset hunted by Chinese gangs who traffics in flesh. A mix that made them extremely dangerous and Cosby extremely nervous.

Katsumi called Izumi into his private chambers. "I want to bring the Shan Chu (title of the Triad's leader) for dinner. Send him an invitation for tomorrow night. Then let the chef know to make a formal dinner. Invite the Shan Chu's whole family. He has three grown children, two boys that work with him, and a daughter who is in college. I've met his wife before. Make sure we have gifts for all of them." He hated entertaining most people. His guests spent the whole time trying to impress the Kumicho with how important they are. There was usually no stimulating conversation. But he needed to make sure the peace agreement with the Triad would hold.

"Kumicho, you feel entertaining the Shan Chu is of more value than smoothing things over with the Tong Leader?"

"Yes. The Tong can do us no harm unless they align with the Triad. I need to secure my relationship with the Triad's Shan Chu; confirm it will remain strong."

"Yes. sir, I will do it immediately."

When they walked into the Command Center, most of the team was waiting. After saying hello and letting Bully get his share of attention, they got down to business.

Houston gave the flash drives to Matt and Sissy. They needed to see what was on them. Matt put the files up on the plasmas. Sophie stood by Sissy.

"Sissy, this looks like it could be a file with brothels, and this file," she pointed to a spot on the screen, "could be domestics. Will you put that information up against what we already know, see if we have more brothels to raid? Kenny will you take this file," she pointed to one on the screen that said backtrack, "and see what's in it. Agent Timms this file might be addresses for Opium dens and gambling houses. Check it out; we might want to direct that to Homeland Security. I'll ask Director Cosby." She had the other files sent to her office so that she could look them over.

"Houston, can you work with the rest of the team on setting up the raids to recover the domestics? And can you see how many girls are still at Global Enterprises, we need to free them at the same time? I don't want anyone left behind."

He went to work with Timms; Fons hadn't arrived yet. About an hour later, Director Cosby asked to speak with Houston and Sophie in the conference room. Bully padded in behind them and sat by her side.

"I'm glad to see you both back here safe. I take objection to your careless disregard for Ms. Star's security, Agent Townsend." Cosby was leaning forward, forearms on the table, hands folded.

"Mr. Cosby, Houston has always been diligent with my security, I don't see where he's been careless." She objected to his criticism.

"Ms. Star, you are a government asset. We have a lot riding on you. When you take off the book actions, you don't have the resources you need to make the safest choices. Taking on Ms. Turner's hunt for this girl has put you in the crosshairs of some dangerous gangs. You were on your own with little to insulate you from them."

"I understand, but my agreement with you allows me to take on any case I choose, Mr. Cosby. I made that clear."

"Ms. Star, from now on, you and Agent Townsend, will have security with you 24/7. A military escort will take you to and from wherever you go. Another thing, I insist you stay on-site until this operation is complete."

Even Houston was taken back by those demands. "Sir, that's a little much."

"Agent Townsend, have you seen the internet in the last five hours?" He knew Houston had not, so he continued his statement.

"Then you better catch up to what's happening. Chinatown is shut down. The people are in fear of retaliation from the White Tigers for the Akuza's humiliation. There is a reward for anyone who can locate Ms. Star. They want her alive; we can be thankful for that. Her picture is everywhere. And the President and First Lady are down my throat for not protecting you sufficiently. They consider you and Ms. Star national treasures for rescuing so many women. Now you tell me again how you think I'm overreacting Agent Townsend." He had raised from his seat his hands on the table leaning towards them. Bully stood up and growled, taking his posture as a threat.

The growl startled the Director, and he realized he was letting his temper get away from him. He had just come from being reprimanded by the President; he was taking it out on them. That was his burden to carry, not theirs. He sat back down and took a breath.

"I apologize, sir, I had no idea things had escalated to that point," Houston said.

"Mr. Cosby, if my husband insists on your precautions, I will oblige him. But what I do when I'm not working with the Task Force, that's not up to you. If that's not acceptable, I can remove myself from the Task Force altogether."

"Make all the threats you want. But as long as you remain on this Task Force you will have the security I deem necessary, is that clear?" He wasn't backing down, but he dialed down his volume.

"I will accept your conditions, for now, sir," she relented.

"Thank you. Now tell me what new leads you have."

She told him Izumi gave her three flash drives. "It looks like accounting books. There is information on all the gangs in New York's Chinatown and a few in New Jersey." She explained they were going through the information. She would like to raid any brothels that had not been on their other lists. Sophie also told him her plan to rescue all those sold as forced labor. Sophie said there might be addresses of some Opium dens and gambling houses on the files too. She asked if they should be sent over to the Homeland Security to disseminate. Cosby agreed.

Sophie and Agent Smith were looking over the information that the drones sent back. They had requested ICE's drones in New York do some reconnaissance for them. It took six hours to surveil the 82 properties. Their own drones were being sent by helicopter to the ICE staging area. It would add four more to the mix for the raids. They would be run by the pilots that were now part of their Task Force.

The logistics to raid the properties had to be timed flawlessly. She asked Agent Timms to start working with ICE on housing and other necessities for the victims.

Sophie walked to Cosby's office to update him. Cassi buzzed her in right away. The Director stood to greet her and motion for her to sit down. He walked over to his coffee station.

"Would you like some coffee, Ms. Star?"

"No, thank you, sir. I'd prefer water if you have it." Cosby grabbed a bottle of water, and his coffee then sat behind his desk, handing her the water.

"Have the flash drives been productive, Ms. Star?"

"Yes, sir. Our new operation will encompass 82 properties, including Global Enterprises. Over 1000 souls, based on the drone's count, but the number will fluctuate. Of course, we don't know how many of those are johns or guards." She took the cap off her water and took a drink. "Director, I don't want the women ending up in a New Orleans Superdome situation.

I have Agent Timms working on temporary housing and necessities. I'd also like Ms. Martin to vet the women to see who is eligible for asylum or U Visa's." She took a breath and looked up at him. "I know you get weary of my requests, sir. But I care about what happens to these women. We could ask FEMA to help; they are very skilled at organizing and targeting needs..."

Director Cosby lifted his hand and stopped her. "Ms. Star...Sophie, you'll be surprised to know, I care about these women too. I'll ask the First Lady to make another public appeal. Her request for clothing, medical specialists, and educational assistance should cover the needs. She has a lot of influence, as you have already seen. She'll make sure these women are taken care of, and I'll help Agent Timms find safe places. I promise you that."

"Thank you."

"But we are not giving away the collars on these raids, Ms. Star."

"I understand, sir. But since this operation is so massive and in New York, we will need to include the help of law enforcement there. Besides our SRT's, I would like to bring in ICE and the NYPD's SWAT teams, who are already familiar with how we work."

"Alright, let me know when you need a conference to go over the plan, and I'll arrange it."

"Thank you, sir."

"I'm sorry I had to be so blunt with you. But if anything happens to you on my watch, the President is the one I will have to answer to." Cosby sat back in his chair and looked directly at her.

"I understand. Thank you."

When she had a moment alone with Houston, she asked,

"you don't think all this security is necessary, do you?"

"I do. What the Director told us was accurate. So yes, it's absolutely necessary."

"Well, he didn't seem to mind if I left the Task Force, so I can't be that important."

"You don't get it, Sophie. It would be better for him if you left the Task Force than if you got injured. It would be a major failure on his record if that happened on his watch. But your leaving would be on you, not him."

"Alright, sweetheart, but I will need things from the house."

"I'll get them for you. I need things too," he said.

Sophie spent the rest of the afternoon in her office, working on a safe plan to have the raids happen simultaneously. Bully left her side to find Houston. He needed a bathroom break.

Matt gave Sophie a list of the law enforcement agencies they've worked with and were confident had no moles.

Sophie stepped back into the tactical command hub. "Houston, we're going to need six hundred thirty-four officers minimum to do this. I was thinking ten for each brothel and six for each home. What do you think?" He had just walked back in the door with Bully and took his leash off. Bully decided he needed attention from the team and went from station to station for back rubs.

"That sounds doable for the raids. But we will need more when you include backup. We will also need buses, ambulances, and staging areas. It's a big undertaking."

"If you handle getting the men and equipment, I can put together a plan on the logistics."

"I'll take care of it." Houston moved to his desk to make calls.

"Kenny, I need a map with the location of all the brothels and homes. Make the brothels red the homes with domestic's green. I'll need your help to find the best spots for the mobile command vehicles and divide the targets into sectors." Sophie walked over to his station.

"Yes, ma'am." He quit petting Bully and got back to his keyboard. Bully decided it was time for another nap and went back to his bed.

Sophie took a break to go down to the cafeteria to get lunch for her and Houston. As soon as she left the door, an armed guard was by her side.

Houston left the Command Center to get their things from the house. He asked to use a government vehicle but was told he had a driver, Cosby's orders. Later, when Sophie took Bully for a walk, she had four armed guards with her. She thought it was a waste of time for those good men, but she complied.

By dinner, she had a plan formulated. She called Cosby, asking if the heads of the agencies involved could meet in two hours. Cosby called the locals, and Denny contacted SAC Demonte, Lieutenant Jenkins, and Captain Cartwright. Requesting they be available to meet at the ICE staging area for a video conference in two hours. He requested the team leaders be there too.

Houston packed what was needed for their stay at headquarters and was in the car when Fons called to say he was at the airbase. Houston asked the driver to stop at the airbase to picked him up. After the team took the time to greet Fons, Sophie told them she was ready with her plan.

184

"Houston, can you and Fons meet with me for a minute?"

They went into her office, and she laid out what she needed. "I have a checklist here of everything that needs doing before the teams hit the ground. Now I know you already planned to have backup and hostage negotiators. But can we go over this list and see if I missed anything."

"Sure, read it off," Houston said, making himself comfortable on the couch.

"Dogs to help clear each location.

All those rescued will have their names and photos sent into the DC Command Center.

All personal electronics, including cell phones, are to be left at the ICE staging area. With the number of personnel on this raid, we need to ensure there are no leaks," she added.

"After the raid, we will need officers to secure the premises until a CSI unit can get to it. Since there are only 10 CSI teams, it could take hours to get to all the properties.

We'll have to split the 82 sites, between you." She nodded to Houston and Fons. "No site is released until you approve it."

"Sophie, we should have our team take a video of the sites before releasing them to the uniformed officers. We need to have a record before CSI takes evidence. With this many properties, evidence could go missing. We need proof of how these women lived," Fons included.

"Perfect, I'll put that on the list. Anything else?"

"When you take Command make sure everyone is clear what you expect of them. Some of these men haven't worked with you before. This operation is big, and there are a lot of moving parts. We can't assume they know what you expect. We can't afford any missteps."

"Thanks, Houston, that's good advice." They spoke some more about the logistics.

"Can you send Sissy and Matt in for me?"

Houston passed on the message and went to make sure

everything was moving forward.

Matt and Sissy came in, "is it possible to take Kenny's maps and overlay it with the number of the team that will take it down. I'd also like it color-coded by whether it's a brothel or domestic. Is there a way to show when a target is cleared?"

"We can do that," Matt answered.

"I noticed all the security. Is that for Sophie?" Fons asked.

"Yeah, she's upset about it. But there's a reward offered by the Tong, for anyone who locates her."

"I know, I saw it online on the way here."

"Hey, how was your date with Carol, Saturday?"

Fons got a big smile on his face. "She's terrific, Houston, so much fun. She's smart too. I can talk to her about anything. And she's gorgeous."

Houston just laughed and put his hand on Fons's shoulder. "I can't wait until we double date again. I love watching you make a fool of yourself."

"Like you have room to talk." He jabbed Houston with his elbow and smiled.

"Fons, can you get the drones up again and maintain surveillance? We need a continuing soul count; it's going to fluctuate. The pilot did one run already."

"I'll get right on it." Fons moved to where the drone pilots were doing preflight checks. He would be handling four of the drones they sent to New York. The other six drones will be operated from the ICE Command Center.

The conference room wasn't big enough for everyone, so they moved into the Command Hub. 1st Lieutenant Denison came in. He would be running rough shot over all the DC FBI, SRT and the New York SRT for the raid.

Denison was leaving with his men right after the meeting. He took the time to greet Ms. Star and Agent Townsend. The Lieutenant was injured in the last Task Force operation and was now back to work. He worked with the team many times and considered them friends.

Agent Smith put the video up from the ICE Command Center in New York. All requested department heads and team leaders were visible on the screens.

Sophie stood and got everyone's attention. "Sirs, my goal is to have this operation start at 2 pm tomorrow. I will lay out the general plan; others will get into the details. I want to breach all 44 domestic residences and 37 brothels, simultaneously. We also have women held at Global Enterprises we need to retrieve. Ms. Martin has secured no-knock warrants for all the premises. No one other than yourselves is to know what the operation is until a half hour before we breach.

The rest of your teams will think it's an Interagency Terrorist Task Force drill. Agent Townsend will explain how the teams are assigned. ICE will have two mobile command units strategically placed nearby — one for the domestics and one for the brothels. Agent Smith will break down the map for you shortly. All available drones will be operating during the entire operation. The DC pilots will supervise the drones from here with the pilots help in the ICE Command Center. He will speak on what he has found so far concerning numbers of souls at each location. All cell phones must be left at the staging areas; we want everyone using Task Force comms. I will not take a chance that someone might tip off the gangs that were coming." She turned to Houston. "Please give them the rundown of the sector assignments, Agent Townsend."

Houston gave them a detailed explanation of how the teams will be structured.

Agent Smith put the areas map and the targets on the plasmas, breaking it down into minute detail. The drone lead pilot addressed the number of souls and any obstacles that were visible from the air. He had blueprints of the properties. Because properties with basements added risk, there would be backup close by if needed.

After everyone completed their briefings, Sophie asked if there were any questions. Hands went up.

"Do we know how many of the people in the brothels are guards?"

"No, sir, it is impossible to tell," she replied.

"We're going in with a skeleton crew, so why not more men?"

She turned to Houston to answer that. "Sir, our main concern here is a leak, as it is, we have over six hundred officers and agents working this. We don't want to lose the element of surprise. With that going for us, ten men should be sufficient for the brothels. But to be safe, we will have vetted uniformed officers on standby. We also have negotiators available if they're needed."

"Where are we taking these victims? All the temporary housing in New York is full." Lieutenant Jenkins asked.

Houston turned to Mr. Cosby to answer that question. Matt had read Director Cosby in on what he was able to find.

"We have three temporary family housing apartment buildings on the military bases here. That will hold a total of three hundred fifty women. And in New York, the National Guard auditorium is available. It will work for a temporary holding facility. All the women who were there previously have found more permanent housing. The closed Army barracks in Trenton, New Jersey, will be repurposed into private rooms, with common kitchen and bathroom areas. We will be asking churches and private citizens to volunteer their time and supplies to renovate the barracks. We have transportation lined up to those locations. We will use the National Guardsmen for protection. And FEMA will temporarily run the facility. In time we will find a non-profit to take over until every woman has found a permanent residence."

"What about the ICE facilities?" A man Sophie didn't recognize in New York, asked the question.

"ICE is already overburdened in their holding facilities. The First Lady will put out a request for necessities."

Cosby answered more questions then made a few closing remarks.

"Almost everyone here has worked with this Task Force before. Agent Townsend and Agent Rodriguez will supervise the operation from here. But make no mistake, Ms. star is in charge. She makes the final calls. Is that clear?"
When no one commented he moved on.

"Ok, any of you who want to watch the operation, if you're not in the field, are welcome to do so. Let's keep focused. We have a lot of balls to keep in the air. You are dismissed."

Sophie stopped Houston before he went to the Command Center.

"Are you going to ask your folks to supervise the renovations of the barracks in Trenton?"

"Already have."

"What? When?"

"When Matt told me it was available. My parents loved the idea."

"Jack and Lily should get a medal. They are the epitome of what a Christion should be."

"They would rather get their reward in heaven," Houston told her. He gave her a quick kiss and headed back to work.

Sophie went to Agent Smith to make sure the streaming from New York will be in real-time. She didn't want any delays. She was concerned it could cost a life.

Agent Smith told her there was a one-second delay. It was the best they could do, even with their super high-speed security cable.

The Command Center had been upgraded twice since its first operation. They had added twenty more plasma screens. They also acquired four drones, instead of borrowing from the military. The drone operators had separate workstations and screens. These new additions meant they had to add members to the team to keep up.

Sophie knew one of the reasons the Task Force is so successful was that the members personalities melded well. So when it was time for added personnel, she decided they should be voted on by everyone.

The list of people wanting to join the Task Force was long and expanding every day. The new hires included two new Techs, one woman, one man, and four drone pilots two women and two men. The drone pilots supported other stations when not operating drones. The men still outnumber women, but they were gaining ground.

CHAPTER TWELVE

By 8 am, the team was making sure the pre-mission checklist was complete. Sophie was still in her office; she had spent time in prayer last night and read her Bible. She finished getting ready and cleaned up the office.

About 12:30 pm, agency heads started filtering in to view the operation firsthand. Director Cosby had spent most the morning with the team at the ICE Command Center in New York. He wanted to view the operation in New York with SAC Demonte.

At 1 pm, Sophie came out. She requested all team leaders to be on tac one and all other agents and officers on tac two. She had Agent Smith open both channels so she could speak to the teams. Agent Smith put up the visual connection with the ICE center.

"Good morning team, for those who don't know me, I am Ms. Star. I am the one in charge of this operation. You know by now; this is not an Interagency Terrorist Drill but an FBI Task Force raid in cooperation with ICE and NYPD. Your team leader will explain your objective today, and then you will commute to within striking distance of your target. Your best protection is the element of surprise; with that in mind, we will simultaneously hit all targets. We will disable the surveillance cameras on the properties for 90 seconds. The blackout will allow you to get into breach positions. If you encounter strong resistance, do not put yourselves in jeopardy. Surround the premises, so they have nowhere to go and wait for back up. If you run into a hostage situation, we will send out a hostage negotiator. We have drones and dogs available to help locate victims. The operation is not over until your checklist is complete. Agent Townsend or Agent Rodriguez will go over those with you after the raid. They are the only ones that can relieve you. I will be back online to give the order for the operation to begin. Don't take unnecessary risks. I want everyone to go home tonight. Command out."

All unnecessary chatter stopped on the comms and in Command. Everyone was watching the clock. At precisely 2 pm, Sophie got on the speaker and started the operation. All the team were in place by fifteen minutes after two. Sophie gave the 90-second order. The Techs disabled the cameras, and the 90 seconds on the clock began. A team leader called the first 'breach' once the clock ran out. After that, 'breach' rang out like dominoes. With the helmet cameras on each team leader and the comms, you could hear and see most of what was going on. Smith, Timms, and the two new Techs oversaw the flood of activities on the screens streaming from the ICE Command Center.

Command heard shots ring out, "This is Team 22. Command were under fire. What are your orders?"

"Do you feel you can safely take the premises?" Sophie questioned.

"No, they have at least eight men in there with AK 47's," he replied.

She turned to Houston to take it over. "Team 22 back off, we will have backup officers there in less than five minutes," Houston ordered. Timms called in the address to the standby units for that sector. Fons sent a drone to that location to help secure the premises.

"Yes, Sir, backing off."

Most of the breaches were going smoothly.

"Command, this is team 76 we have a hostage situation, the

homeowner has a weapon on the domestic. We have given him space and backed out of the room. He said he would kill her if we don't let him leave."

"We will have a negotiator there and back up," Sophie responded. Houston sent out the word for help at that address.

The map was beginning to show some forward movement. The teams were taking offenders and johns into custody. The colors on the screen were steadily changing. By 3 pm, 66 of the targets were blue, which meant everyone was safe, and the guards and johns were in custody. Houston and Fons were working with those teams to complete the checklist. Ambulances and buses were on the way.

They heard more shots, "Command, this is team 19. Ma'am, we have resistance from offenders in the basement. The upper floor is secure."

Sophie turned to Houston, "Stay where you are, don't breach we will send backup. Do you have the women out of the premises?" Houston asked.

"We don't know if there are more in the basement, we have 22 secure outside."

Fons checked the address from the earlier drone surveillance to find soul count at that location.

" Ms. Star, there are still 18 souls in that basement. I'll send a drone to determine where the people are standing," Fons responded.

The drone flew over the target.

"Team 19, the drone is showing 18 souls in the basement. It looks like three are a distance away from the rest, they are most likely the guards. We will send the images to you."

"Understood."

The blue colors were growing on the map. Uniformed officers from NYPD backed up team 22. With their help, they managed to take the premises without further shots fired.

Fons and Houston were busy finalizing checklists with the

teams. For those teams, it was a waiting game. They had to wait for busses to transport their victims and their prisoners. They also had to wait their turn for drones and dogs to make sure the properties were clear.

"Command, this is team 14; we cannot locate our victims. The property owner swears he has no idea what we're talking about."

"I will have a drone fly over ASAP." Came Sophie's reply. Fons ordered the support needed.

"Ma'am, the upstairs is clear, but we can't penetrate the basement walls. They must have gypsum boards lining the walls." The drone pilot reported.

Sophie turned to Fons, "please send in a dog."

Fons relayed the order.

Things kept progressing. Team 76 had a negotiator on-site and was working through the process of talking the homeowner down.

"Team 14, I need an update." Sophie requested.

"The dog is still working ma'am. I'll let you know as soon as we've located the victims."

It was 5:30 pm, and most teams were finishing checklists. Only three teams were still active. Team 76, the hostage situation, was still unresolved. Team 14, with the dog searching for the hidden room, was still active. And Team 19, the basement standoff was still a standoff.

As part of the checklist, every woman's name and a photo were sent to the Command Center. Agent Smith put them live on one and of the plasmas.

Team 19 had backup and was ending the standoff in the basement. Shots rang out randomly at the door from inside. The team's tech slipped a camera under the door to locate the gang members before they breached. They were getting ready to use a flashbang. It would be uncomfortable for the women, but they needed to get inside safely. Sophie approved it after talking to the Team leader to see if there was another solution. The men pulled down their protective face masks and put in ear protection, waiting for orders.

They heard the SRT unit order the grenade tossed in as soon as they breached the door. The noise was deafening; the command center turned off all the comms for the few seconds of the initial blast. They could see the men and women in the basement, protecting their ears as SRT invaded the basement. The guards dropped their weapons, and the SRT team took control. While some of the team extricated the women, others cuffed the guards.

"Which team had Global Enterprises, Fons?" Sophie asked.

"Team 82, Ms. Star."

"I see it's blue, do we have names coming in from there yet?"

"No, ma'am."

The Command hubs were clearing out of Agency brass now that the activity was mostly over. They were still dealing with the hostage situation. But the dog found the hidden room, and Team 14 secured the women and took the homeowner into custody. CSI had already started working a couple of the brothel properties. Names and photos were still coming in. Fons and Houston were clearing teams so that the uniform officers could relieve them. The uniform officers would stay at the property until CSI could make it there and finish their work. New York had a limited number of CSI units working. It would be many hours before they would release all the premises.

Team 76 finally reported that the hostage was released,

and the homeowner was in custody. It was 6:15 pm, every target was blue, there was a cheer when the last property turned.

Sophie let Bully out of the office since most of the visitors were gone.

"Sophie, look!" Matt hollered.

Sophie turned to the plasma. On the screen came the name Dajao Taru. Houston threw his arms around her.

"You did it, princess, you found her. God answered our prayers." He whispered as he lifted her and did a 360.

Loud applause and hollers rang through the room. The few ranking officers still there asked what was going on. Agent Smith explained they located the missing girl that started this operation.

Sophie, was still hugging Houston, "Sweetheart, I have to see her and her sister, can you make that happen?"

"I'll make it happen." He let her down and smiled at her.

"Matt, where was she?"

"Global Enterprises."

Sophie turned to Houston, distressed. "We were only a few yards away and didn't know it."

"Sweetheart, if we did, these other women would still be enslaved."

She realized what he was saying and knew it was true. She took the time to thank the Lord for his goodness.

It was 8 pm when the last team was released. The teams were still on the comms, filtering back into the ICE Command Center. They all wanted to keep in the loop with the progress of the other teams. None of them had been part of an operation of this magnitude; it would be a boost for their careers.

Sophie's face came on the plasmas, "All teams, this operation is officially completed. The young girl that started this, has been located and freed. Beyond that, your outstanding work has freed 900 women from a life no one should suffer. You should all be proud. In addition, you took down 189 gang members and 252 johns. You did all this while only wounding six offenders. Unfortunately, two of your teammates also needed medical care; I understand they will be fine and back to work soon. It is my pleasure to work with such professional and brave men and women. Thank you." Sophie could see the men who filled the Command Center in New York on one of the screens, as they exploded in a cheer. She smiled and turned it over to Director Cosby to say the final words.

Director Cosby returned to DC and the Command Center's hard drives were secure in his safe. Finally, Houston sent everyone home to meet up again in the morning.

Only Fons, Houston, and Sophie stayed. Fons offered to go off-site to bring them some dinner; they were tired of the cafeteria food. Sophie sat next to Houston on the couch in her office and snuggled up close to him.

"We found her, Houston, thank the Lord." She whispered to him.

"God was good to us." He turned to her and kissed her. "You did great today."

"Thank you, but it's the team that makes for a successful operation. Our new members did a great job."

"Yes, they did."

Fons came back with the food, and they ate in the conference room. Sophie asked him about his date with Carol

Saturday.

"Why didn't you tell me she was a National Ice-Skating Champion." Fons scowled at Sophie. She laughed.

"When are you going out again?"

"I wasn't sure when we would complete this mission, so I haven't set one up yet."

"When will she be in DC?"

"She said she was going to be here tonight."

"Good, I'll see if I can order brunch for the team tomorrow." She excused herself and gave Carol a call. It was an excuse to get her side of the date.

"Sophie?" Carol answered on the first ring.

"Yes, hi Carol. I'm sorry to call so late, but I had to hear about your date."

Carol laughed, "he was trying so hard to make sure I didn't fall and get hurt. It was so sweet. When he finally realized I was doing better on the skates than he was, he asked me if I'd been on ice skates before. I hated to tell him the truth and bruise his ego, but I didn't want to lie to him." She chuckled some more.

"His ego could use a little bruising." Sophie joined in the laughter.

"I had to pick him up off the ice a few times, but we had loads of fun. Then he took me out to dinner. I haven't heard from him since, so I'm wondering if he was a little upset about the ice-skating thing after all."

"No, not at all, he loved it. He and Houston are on a job right now. We're all in DC. Which is another reason I called. Can you put together a brunch for fifteen tomorrow? I know it's short notice, I'll have Fons pick it up if that encourages you to say yes."

"I don't need any encouragement I am happy to do it. It

won't be fancy, but I know what you like. Have Fons meet me at the usual place at 11 am."

"Thank you, Carol, it's a reward for a job well done." She didn't elaborate.

"Will you ever tell me what you really do for a living?"

"I'm an accountant, Houston and Fons are bodyguards. You already know that."

"If you say so." She wasn't buying it.

"Thanks, Carol, when they're done with this job, I'll get in touch. We'll all go out together again."

"That would be lovely. I'll talk to you soon."

They said their goodbyes and she went back to the conference room.

"Fons, can you pick up brunch for the team tomorrow at 11 am?" She waited for a beat, "If not, I can send someone else." She teased him.

"I will be happy to do you a favor, Ms. Star. No matter how challenging." He tried to keep a straight face.

They enjoyed each other's company while they started to relax and wind down from the day's events. Sophie snuck Bully some scraps from her dinner.

After Fons left, Sophie and Houston headed to her office to go to bed. They designed the office, knowing overnight stays were inevitable. She had a full-size bathroom and a pull-out couch. The large glass panels that separated her office from the Command Hub had mini blinds for privacy. The Command Center also had a breakroom with a kitchen and a full bath.

When she finally laid her head on the pillow, she was asleep as soon as she closed her eyes. The quest to find Dajao Taru was finally over.

Sophie opened her eyes when Houston and Bully stepped

into her office. They were sopping wet, dripping water all over her office floor. She jumped out of bed and ran into the bathroom to grab some towels.

Houston spoke as she was coming out of the bathroom. "It's a monsoon out there."

Sophie tossed a towel to Houston and knelt in front of Bully and started drying his fur. He was licking her cheek in appreciation.

"Bad Houston," she said to Bully, "taking my sweet puppy out in this weather."

Houston was taking his wet coat off, hanging it on the coat rack.

He addressed Bully, "hey bro, how about you back me up here. You were the one wanting to go outside." Bully looked up at him without a glimmer of guilt for his betrayal. "I get it. You're kissing up to the one who feeds you table scraps."

Sophie laughed. "Thank the Lord it didn't come down like this yesterday. It would have hindered our operation. How long were you out there?"

Houston went into the bathroom to change into dry clothes, answering her through the door.

"I only intended to give Bully a chance to go to the bathroom, but it wasn't raining, so we went for a long walk. We were on the way back when the heavens opened, and an icy rain came down."

When she finished drying Bully, she went to Houston and kissed him. She used a towel to dry his hair.

Mr. Katsumi played the gracious host to the Shan Chu and his family. He had gifts for them and made sure the formal dinner was exquisite. He complimented them and received their adulation with graciousness. Katsumi thought the children rude and entitled. But they were of a generation that had no manners or understanding of traditions.

He had Izumi take the others on a tour of the house. Katsumi needed to speak privately to the Shan Chu.

"Mr. Tian, I am sure Mr. Mato, and Mr. Zhao of the White Tiger's and other Tong leaders have filled your head with talk of retaliation. Maybe even war against me. But I would like to explain to you what happened. As the head of the Triad, you deserve an explanation."

"You are right, Mr. Katsumi. I have had many visitors from the Tong Clans and some of my own Triad Clans. We have suffered great losses as well. Many of the Tong want us to align with us to retaliate. They say you are no longer an ally to the Chinese and have turned your back on us. By doing so, you have made yourself our enemy."

"Do you believe that?"

"If I did, I would not be here, Mr. Katsumi. But the Tong do not understand the cost of doing business in America. There are not enough corrupt police to pay off to keep us exempt from raids. All we can do is find a few willing to give us a heads up when trouble is coming." He paused and took a sip of the sake, Mr. Katsumi poured him, "it's not like in our home countries, is it Mr. Katsumi?"

"No, indeed, Mr. Tian. You have the wisdom of one who has lived a long life." Katsumi refilled his cup. "Out of respect, I would like to explain to you what happened."

Mr. Tian nodded as he sat back in his chair. "Mr. Zhao had come onto my compound intending to take what he wanted by force. He planned to remove a guest under my protection. You understand I could not let that go unchallenged. According to our laws, I could have killed them all, but I restrained myself and only put them in their place. Do you not agree, I was within my rights?"

"Yes, Mr. Katsumi, I do, but the issue is that you would

201

protect this woman and keep her from them. As the injured parties, they have the right to the information on their assailant. Ms. Star is the only one who knows who it is. If she will not tell willingly, they have the right to *encourage* her to tell. My question is why you would protect her. I would understand if it were one of your advisors or even one of your soldiers or a wife."

Izumi came into the room; Katsumi could see he had some news.

"Will you please excuse me for a moment, Mr. Tian?" He motioned for the servant to attend him.

"Kumicho, 37 brothels and an unknown number of private homes with domestic slaves, have been raided.

"Tong's?"

" Both Tong and Triad. It will hit the news shortly."

"Ms. Star has a death wish," Katsumi responded.

"Ms. Star is fearless," Izumi countered.

Mr. Katsumi went back to the table but remained standing. He needed to cut this short. He didn't want the news to break while the guests were here. "Mr. Tian, I have no compulsion to answer your question. It is enough to say that the woman you are referring to is a personal asset to me. She chooses who she wants to work for and who she answers too. But if she were to reveal her client's names, they would likely kill her. Why would she put herself in jeopardy? I know if she were to betray us, we would not let her live. I have always sought peace with you, but I do not have to explain my actions. And make no mistake, I owe my loyalty to no one, other than the Akuza."

"That may be the case, but I am afraid the Tong, in particular, are not willing to let her be. They insist on getting that information."

"What is it you want from me, Mr. Tian?"

"I am here to appeal to your sense of brotherhood and have you release her to me. I will make sure she is not harmed as long as she gives us the information we need?"

"Or what?"

"Or...I am afraid I cannot guarantee that I can deter the Tong or even my clans from coming after her. Even here at your compound."

The Kumicho was furious but could not let on. "Mr. Tian, Ms. Star, is no longer my guest. She went on to take another client. She may be back here in a week. I will let you know when she arrives. If she does not tell me who hired her, then we can discuss other options."

"A week is a long time. I cannot say the Tong will stop looking for her in the meantime." Mr. Tian stood.

"I understand, Mr. Tian." He motioned him to the sitting room where his family was waiting. "Thank you for honoring me with your presence tonight. I will get a message to you as soon as Ms. Star arrives."

Izumi escorted the family out, then went to see his father." Kumicho, what did he have to say?"

"He is demanding we turn Ms. Star over for interrogation if she doesn't tell me who hired her."

"You know she won't give up Ms. Turner, but it's Ms. Star who is doing the damage."

"I know that, and once they hear of the new raids, they will be at my doorstep again. I told them I would let them know when Ms. Star returns."

"Kumicho. Would you give them Ms. Star?" Izumi was careful with his reaction.

"No, Izumi. I won't turn her over to them, but not because I care about her. It doesn't matter how much I care for Ms. Star. She is not Akuza. I explained to her that I could not go to war to protect her or any woman not related." He walked into the dining room and sat down.

"If I turned her over, I would appear weak. They would think I trembled under their demand." Katsumi poured himself some more sake and continued. "The rumbles of war between the Chinese gangs and the Akuza has been brewing for years now. As the older leaders die off, the younger men who have no memory of the cost of war are rising in the ranks. They have not lived through it or seen the loss and suffering war brings. They are bloodthirsty and undisciplined.

If I don't give her up, they will use it as an excuse to break our peace. Sometimes the only way to keep the peace is to go to war. Do you understand that concept, Izumi?"

"Yes, sir. There are times that you go to war to prevent future war."

"Yes, and if necessary, we will do that, and win. Then we can have peace again."

Izumi considered his father's answer. What his father said was true. If the Tong or the Triad gangs tries to go to war, Akuza will win. But if they aligned themselves together, Izumi worried the battle would not be so easy to win. Would his father give up Ms. Star for the survival of the Akuza in that situation? He knew the answer to that. The Kumicho made it clear. He would give up Ms. Star to protect the Akuza. He had one loyalty, and that was to the organization. Katsumi had proven it before. He refused to go against his own Kumicho when he was Saiko Komon and watched as Suki's first husband beat her. The woman he loved with his whole heart. Izumi would hate to betray his father, but as long as he had breath, he would find a way to protect his sister.

Izumi's thoughts were interrupted by the voice of his father.

"Izumi, bring in Kato. We must prepare for war."

Bully was asleep on his bed in the corner, exhausted from his little trek this morning. Sophie could see the team through her window as she worked on the files Izumi gave her. Houston was with them, finishing up their After-Action Reports.

She found that the Triad had a very sophisticated cyber theft ring working. It appeared they would steal thousands of viable credit card numbers. Then they cloned cards. Maxed them out with cash withdrawals and online purchases in the first 72 hours and then dumped them. The merchandise purchased as gifts were sent to addresses other than the cardholder's homes. Many companies offer this service, particularly for weddings. Gang members then stake out the address and steal the packages off the porch, without the unsuspecting recipient knowing anything. For the big items, they would have them held at the transportation center for customer pick up. When the claims come in for fraudulent purchases, it ends with a recipient who has no idea what happened. She had to admit it was well thought out. *I guess even thieves must keep up with the times,* she thought.

She decided to ask Director Cosby what Agency should receive the information.

Houston came into her office. "Hey sweetheart, I have Halina Taru on a plane to DC. Dajao was one of the groups that was sent up here. She will reconnect with her sister at the hospital early this afternoon." Sophie got up and gave him a big hug.

"Thank you, Houston. When can we go see her?"

"The hospital will release Dajao in the morning. They needed to pump fluids into her. She was dehydrated and malnourished. I'm arranging a room for her and her sister at a Doubletree Hotel close to the hospital."

"I want to talk to Ms. Martin about getting them asylum. I don't want there to be any chance they will have to go back."

"I was praying last night about it. I wondered if Yon Moon could be her guardian until her sister is out of College and can afford to take care of her?"

"I can see the benefit there; she would be able to relate to Yon Moon."

"Mom says she and Han Kang-Dae are doing very well. Yon Moon shows up every visiting day at the prison to see her son and says he spends his time studying to be a lawyer. Yon Moon says there are Christian groups that have helped his spiritual growth," Houston said.

Yon Min-ji became a Christian after being caught and arrested for counterfeiting US currency. The DC Task Force's last big operation.

"It's a great idea, but we don't know if Halina will want the help, Halina may insist on taking care of Dajao. And we haven't asked Yon Moon yet." Houston recognized he was getting ahead of himself.

Sophie brought up a concern. "I promised Gail when I found Dajao; she could have an interview. But I don't know that exposing her to the media is a good idea. She could be too fragile."

"I agree; she has been through enough. If she doesn't want to talk to Ms. Turner, we keep her away from her."

Fons headed out to get the brunch from Carol. When he returned, Sophie noticed he was smiling.

"Get that smile off your face, Mister." She teased him.

"Ain't gonna happen, ma'am."

Sophie set the brunch up on the conference room table and asked everyone to come and eat.

They were midway through brunch when the President and the First Lady showed up. Everyone stopped what they were doing and stood to greet them.

The President addressed the team. "Sorry to interrupt your lunch. The First Lady and I just wanted to let you know, the work that you have done here is outstanding. I haven't gotten the last count yet but with all the raids included it appears more than fifteen hundred women were rescued, some of them as young as twelve..." He took a moment to compose himself again. The thought of tender age girls sold as sex slaves was hard to accept. "Over three hundred offenders from different gangs are arrested, along with a few hundred johns. If that doesn't slow them down for a while, I don't know what will. Excellent work. I might have to create a new medal for this kind of achievement," he laughed. He moved to where Ms. Star and Houston were standing. "I heard you found your girl, Ms. Star."

"Yes, sir, we did."

The First Lady came over and hugged Sophie. "Thank you for this, Ms. Star. I promise you we will take good care of them. I'll see to it."

"I appreciate that, Mrs. Madden. I won't worry about them if they're in your hands."

The First lady took Sophie's hand in both of hers, then hugged her again.

"Would you care to join us for brunch, ma'am?" Houston offered.

"Thank you for the offer, Agent Townsend. But the President and I are on the way to the temporary housing complex. The women they're transporting from New York will be here soon. We want to make sure they have everything they need."

Director Cosby had instructed all the information left on the drives to go to Homeland Security to disseminate to the different Agencies.

Sissy and Matt were filtering out all repeats and anything to do with brothels or domestics, leaving gambling dens, money laundering, loan sharking, and cybercrimes to send.

Sophie held the file with the names of members of the Triads and the Tongs, thinking she might need it, particularly those in command positions. Sophie put it on a separate flash drive to keep with her. At some point, she planned on sending it to the MAG (multiple agency gang unit). For now, she felt she needed to keep the information confidential.

She also held onto the information from the 'Backtrack file.' That file showed the routes used to get women and drugs into the country.

She planned on asking Director Cosby if the Task Force should be the ones to disrupt the routes. It would hinder the gangs from rebuilding for a more extended period. That's what Houston said he wanted, and she intended to help him do it.

Sophie stepped over to where Houston was working and asked if he had time to talk to her. He finished what he was doing and went to her office.

"I wanted you to see this, Houston." Sophie was sitting at her desk with the computer opened. He moved over to stand behind her.

"What is it, sweetheart?"

"There is a file that shows the traffickers' routes to bring in drugs and women from all over the world. This information is what you need to make a more permanent dent in their business. It's what you wanted."

Houston sat in the chair next to her and moved the computer over to scroll down the information. "This is great, Sophie, it could do some long-term damage."

"That's what I was thinking. We could take this to Cosby

and get an approval for the Task Force to handle it," she said.

He closed the computer and looked at her. "I know you want to do this for me because of what I said after the raid, on the night of the Global Enterprise stakeout." He took her hand, "but I only care that it happens. It doesn't have to be us that does it. Cosby gets his directives from the President. The policy is that the Task Force takes cases that the other Agencies are not equipped to handle. Several Agencies, including MAG, the FBI, and the DEA can handle this."

"That's true, but I know if we ask he'll approve it."

"We have other issues to deal with. There are still a lot of dangerous men looking for you. And the team needs some downtime. The Task Force has run one big operation after another."

Sophie put her hand on Houston's cheek. "Are you sure? I want you to know I'll back you up anytime."

Houston leaned over and kissed her. "I know you would and I love you for it. But I'm comfortable with turning it over. Send it to Homeland Security with the other information. They'll make sure it gets to the right Agency."

CHAPTER THIRTEEN

Houston let Sophie know it was time for them to go to the Doubletree Hotel, to meet Dajao. After grabbing her purse and coat she decided to take Bully with them, she knew he would comfort Dajao and break down some barriers. Even though Sophie felt she knew Dajao well, to Dajao and Halina, they were strangers.

After security checked with the front desk to get the room number, they took the elevator to the second floor.

Houston knocked. Halina opened it a crack, "yes."

"Hello, my name is Sophie Townsend, and this is my husband, Houston. Can we come in?"

She moved away from the door so they could enter. Halina noticed the bodyguards.

"Are you the ones that requested we come here?" Halina asked.

Dajao was sitting in a protective posture on the bed. Her knees bent to her chest and her arms wrapped around them. Bully instinctively went to her and put his head on the side of the bed closest to her. Dajao smiled and started running her hands over his soft fur.

"Yes. Please let me explain." Halina pointed to the chairs and they all sat. Sophie told her that Gail Turner approached her. The reporter Halina had told that Dajao was missing. "Gail asked me for help and with the support of law enforcement we were able to find Dajao, along with almost fifteen hundred other women."

Halina's eyes went wide when she heard that. A little voice came from the bed and said in broken English.

"Thank you for me." Dajao looked so frail.

"Dajao, is it alright if I come and sit by you?" Dajao nodded her head. Houston stayed where he was. He thought she might be uncomfortable around men. Halina was still standing, arms folded. Dajao patted the bed so Bully would come up by her.

"Dajao, a lot of people looked for you. Can you tell us what happened from the beginning?"

She took a deep breath and nodded her head. Her sister got on the bed and put her arm around her. Dajao spoke in Tagalog, and Halina translated.

"I didn't want to stay with my uncle anymore. I was afraid he would keep hitting me or worse. My sister said she would send for me to come live with her, but I never heard from her. A man in town said he would take me to New York and get me a job as a domestic." Halina paused as she listened to Dajao speak. Then she interpreted again. "I agreed because I knew Halina was there. I thought I would be able to find her."

It was obvious Halina felt guilty she hadn't been able to get a Visa for Dajao, but she continued translating Dajao's story. "When I went to the dock to get on the boat, they tied me up and put me in the fish holding tank. The tank was beneath the boat and there were many other people. We had no food and no water for days. The stench was unbearable. When we finally landed, they took me to Chinatown. They sorted out the women and took us to a building with cages.

Sophie figured it must have been the Global Enterprises since she said she never left there. Sophie asked how come they never moved her anywhere else.

Dajao spoke to them in broken English. "My Nanay took me church, I ask Jesus," she patted her heart. "Nanay say if I in trouble call Him," she pointed up. "He helps me. They take bag, but Bible in coat pocket. They not see. I pray Jesus make me invisible. I pray and pray and read Bible. Every day, girls come and go, I stay. I never go. When girls there, food come, but not me. Girls share to me. When no girls no food. I am invisible. Angels hide me."

Dajao's story was fascinating. Sophie didn't doubt for a moment the events happened as she said. God indeed had made her invisible. He kept her safe until she was rescued. She praised God for his greatness.

"Are you all right, what did the doctors say?"

Halina answered. "They say she is dehydrated and malnourished. They gave her antibiotics, liquids, and vitamins intravenously. The Doctor said not to feed her anything too heavy while her body is readjusting."

"Halina, what do you plan on doing from here?" Houston asked.

"I don't know what our options are. I can't let my sister go back to our uncle in the Philippines. Our parents died a few years ago, and he was our only living relative." Halina said.

"Can you take care of her and finish school?" Houston asked.

"The college won't allow me to have her in my dorm room. I have a work-study job that gives me a small amount to live on. But it wouldn't be enough to pay for an apartment. If I quit school to get a better paying job, I will lose my visa, and we both will have to go back."

"Would you be open to a suggestion?" He asked. Halina nodded.

"My parents live in Trenton, New Jersey. Many of the women rescued have been sent to a barracks at the recently closed military base there. My parent's church is housing others. There is a woman named Yon Moon. She has asylum here from North Korea. God answered her prayers by delivering her from the darkness in her country. If she were willing to take Dajao in until you finished school, would you

213

be alright with that? You could stay at my family's home whenever you had a break or to visit her on any weekend. She would be well taken care of."

"Did she offer?" Halina asked.

"I haven't approached her yet. I needed to know if you were comfortable with the idea," he responded.

Halina spoke to Dajao for a long time in Tagalog. Houston waited patiently for them to finish.

Halina turned to Houston. "My sister and I appreciate the generosity of your family. If you are sure it would not be too much trouble, we are happy to accept." It was the first smile they saw on Halina's face.

Houston left the room to call his mother. His mother said she would have to contact Yon Moon and get an interpreter before she called him back. Although Yon Moon could understand English, something this important needed an interpreter.

He went back into the room. "It will take a while to get a return call. In the meantime, could we take you to the restaurant downstairs for dinner?"

After dinner, his mother called back. Yon Moon and the interpreter were at his mother's house on speaker; Lily was on the kitchen line.

"Houston, Yon Moon is here with her interpreter."

"Yon Moon, how are you doing in Trenton?"

"I very fine, Mr. Houston."

"I have a question, are you aware of all the young women who have been rescued from the brothels?"

The interpreter spoke, then her answer came, "Yes, I help the church."

"There is a young girl, 14. Her name is Dajao, she's a

Christian, who is one of those women. I'm trying to find her a place to stay until her sister gets out of college. Would you be interested in taking her in?"

He could hear the interpreter, then a voice so excited talking in Korean. He had no idea what was happening. "Yon Moon?"

"I here, I here. I pray and pray, plead to God, send me one girl to mother back to well." She started crying.

"Is that a yes?" Houston was not surprised now at the direction the Lord gave him.

"Yes, Yes. When girl come?"

"Maybe tomorrow," he replied. "I have to make arrangements."

"Thank you, Mr. Houston, I take very good care of her, I promise."

"I know you will." He said goodbye to her and asked his mom to stay on the line.

"Honey, she's beside herself with joy." His mom interjected.

"Mom, I'm afraid I volunteered you to her sister. I offered your home as a place to stay when she has time off from college. She'll want to be near her sister."

"You know very well I enjoy having guests. I'm fine with that."

"I need to see if dad can pick them up at the Newark Liberty International Airport when they leave here. Halina will need to get back to college, and Dajao will need a ride to Trenton. If he can do it."

"Of course, dear, I'll go with him. He and Kang-Dae are working at the military base, making repairs at the barracks. Right now, they are making sure all the plumbing is working. Others are dividing the barracks into small private rooms. I'm sure there are hundreds there working today, the First Lady put out a call for volunteers. Kang-Dae is such a good young man, he loves your father, and your father always takes time for him."

"I don't think either of you understands the term retirement." Houston laughed.

"We're doing what we love best, working for the Lord," she replied.

"I'll let the girls know what's happening, and then I'll text you with their flight number and arrival time. I love you, mom."

"Thank you, son. I love you too."

Houston headed back to the room to tell them the good news. Sophie had one more subject that needed addressing.

"Halina, the reporter you first talked to, Ms. Turner, wants to interview Dajao for her news station. I told her I would agree to tell her where your sister is if she wants to talk to her."

Halina explained what I said to Dajao, then they decided.

"My sister feels by telling her story it would bring Glory to Jesus for protecting her, she is willing to talk to her."

"I agree, I will have her come to Trenton a few days after Dajao gets settled. I'll give her Houston's parents' address. That way, his mom can make sure Ms. Turner doesn't push Dajao to hard."

"Thank you."

Before they left, Houston gave Halina three hundred dollars to take care of incidentals. He knew she came stone broke.

Houston had Halina and Dajao on a flight leaving DC late the next morning. He didn't want them rushed.

"I'll have a car pick you up in the morning, Halina."

Halina stood and hugged them both. "Thank you so much for finding my sister and giving her a place to stay." She turned to look at Dajao. "I should have never left her. I knew how mean my uncle was. I should have done something."

"Halina, none of this is your fault. And God had his hand over her. Now you both have a chance at a good future." Sophie comforted her.

Dajao never moved from the bed where she had been petting Bully. She hugged Bully, said goodbye, and smiled at them.

The teams were wrapping up their reports. Others were downloading all the audio/visual from the operation to go in Cosby's safe. By six o'clock, Fons had collected all the hard drives and taken them back to Director Cosby's office.

Fons stuck his head in Sophie's office. "Sophie, we're ready to close down the Command Center. Is there anything else you need before we send everyone home?" Fons asked.

Sophie stepped out of her office to say goodbye. They all gathered closer together. "Houston, has Director Cosby given us a timeline of when to expect another operation?"

"He never knows for sure, but he thinks we will have a few months between each assignment."

"Thank you." She turned to her teammates, "I hope you all have a wonderful Christmas. If you are in New York Christmas Eve, Houston and I will be having an open house starting at 7 pm. We will love it if you and your families stop by. I know you all have family commitments; I just want to be sure you know you are welcome."

"Ms. Star, my wife wants to know if you are going to the shelter again, to bring gifts to the children?" Kenny Smith asked.

"Yes, Kenny, we have permission to be there early afternoon Christmas Eve to host a party."

"We would like to buy gifts for one of the families." He responded.

"That's a wonderful gesture, Kenny. Houston will call you with a family's information, including ages and sizes. We don't have that information yet. Thank your wife for us."

The others insisted on being a part too. Houston and Sophie were excited to have the team's support for the families.

The team said their goodbyes and left.

Fons stayed behind to ask if they needed anything before he left.

"In a hurry to get to a hot date?" Houston teased.

"You bet." Fons laughed.

"Find out when Carol is going back to New York for me, Fons?" Sophie added.

Fons answered while he was heading for the door. "Sure, I'll ask her."

"Houston, do you think we could go out to dinner tonight?"

"As long as we have an escort, I don't see why not."

"Before we go, I'd like to talk to Director Cosby," Sophie said.

They headed to his office. Cassi stood and greeted them.

"Agent Townsend, Ms. Star, congratulations on another successful operation."

"Thank you, Cassi. Is Director Cosby in, we would like a moment of his time," Houston responded.

"I'll check. One moment please." She moved into the Director's office. She was back in a few seconds to open the door and usher them in.

Cosby offered them coffee and a chair. They declined the coffee but accepted the invitation to sit.

"Mr. Cosby, now that the task force completed this operation, can we dispense with the escorts?" Sophie asked.

"Ms. Star, you are not out of danger, I'm sorry the security is permanent."

"Permanent! You mean until the Chinatown threat is over, right?"

"No, Ms. Star, the President, wants protection for you going forward."

She was shocked, but she noticed Houston was not.

She turned to him, "did you know about this?"

"No, but I'm not surprised."

"I won't have my life disrupted like that, Mr. Cosby."

Director Cosby hesitated before he replied. "After the Chinatown incident is over, I will address it with the President again. That's all I can promise."

Sophie looked at him for a long time, "I guess that will have to do, for now."

"I am sorry, Sophie, I know this isn't what you want. The President is leaning on the side of caution."

She calmed down, "I know it isn't your fault, and I must seem like a spoiled child. It's just that I am very protective of my freedom."

"I understand that, Ms. Star. And I will pass that on to the President at the appropriate time."

Houston and Sophie stood to leave.

"Director, if you and your wife are in New York Christmas Eve, we would love it if you stop by. Houston and I are hosting an open house starting at 7 pm."

"Sophie, that is a generous invitation, and normally we would love to. But Trish and I are spending time in Montana with our Son. He's back from his first tour of duty in Afghanistan. We are meeting him at his home there."

"He's in the same unit as President Madden's son, isn't he?" Houston asked.

"Yes, they joined on the buddy plan. They've been friends since high school."

Sophie turned to look at him. "I had no idea."

"I don't tell people this, but the President and I grew up together. We were friends in grade school. We're still close. Our wives spend a lot of time together."

"Have a nice time with your family, Director."

"Thank you, Sophie."

They said their goodbyes and headed out.

Houston called for their escorts and driver so he could pack out their belongings. The driver asked where they wanted to go. Houston said they want to drop off Bully and their belongings at the house. Then they would like to go to the Italian restaurant they like.

The restaurant was busy, but they had a reservation, so they were seated immediately. Their security stayed outside. It was the first time Houston and Sophie relaxed and enjoyed a night out for what seemed like a long time.

Sophie appreciated the fact that Director Cosby agreed they could move back to their DC home. With the caveat, that they have plain clothes military police guards outside their home. It wasn't ideal, but she soon got over it. She walked into her living room and sat on her very own couch with pillows that swallowed her up.

"I was thinking of video conferencing Izumi tonight. I want to spend some time with him. He must have lots of questions about what he's reading." Houston broke into her revelry.

"That's a great idea. I'll lie here and soak up the ambiance."

Houston laughed at her melodramatics.

The strategy meeting with Izumi and Kato was grueling. Katsumi decided it was worth the loss in revenue to close his gambling houses in Chinatown. At least until the threat of war was over. The money laundering business fronts would have to close too. But they could deal with that. As far as his loan sharks, they could work off the cuff. They would lose some business, but their coffers were well padded, they could take the hit. He wanted his presence in Chinatown to become minimal until this was over.

Only a few Akuza shop owners lived in Chinatown above their businesses. Akuza gave them protection for a percent of their business. The families would have to relocate, and board their businesses up. The rest of his men with families lived on the outskirts of Chinatown.

Katsumi ordered Kato to have all the single men, in a 50-mile radius, ages 18 to 40 report to the compound. They needed to increase their numbers.

"Have you checked our stockpile of weapons and ammunition, Kato?" Katsumi asked.

"Yes, sir, we are well armed."

"Do you have any idea how many more men will come on our order?"

Izumi answered. "Sir, if we don't include men outside our local area, we should have three hundred that come."

"Have the Chef order two weeks' worth of food for the compound." He turned to Kato.

"Will the barracks hold them?"

"We will make it work, sir," Kato answered.

Katsumi dismissed Kato but directed Izumi to stay."

"Have you heard from your sister?" Katsumi asked.

"No, sir," Izumi responded.

"Have we heard anything from the Triads or the Tong since the news of the raids became public?"

"No, sir. Total silence." Izumi responded, knowing what that meant.

"Silence is not good, Izumi."

Houston waited until late in the night to call Izumi. He knew the Kumicho required Izumi's presence at his side until he retired to his room, which was usually late in the evening.

"Houston, I am so happy you called. Did you find the girl you were looking for? I have been praying for your success. The raids are big news here."

"Yes, I am glad to report we did find her. And thank you for those flash drives. Without them, many women would still be in bondage."

"No one must ever know where they came from."

"I understand, you can trust us."

"I know, of that, I have no doubt. I miss our talks. I'm almost through the New Testament. However, I'm having trouble understanding Revelations."

"Izumi, if you want, you could skip Revelations until we can be together and go through it chapter by chapter. Go to the Old Testament. It will give you lots of insight into who God is and how He operates."

"I will do that. I read in Acts about the Holy Spirit; I want to know more about Him."

They talked for well over two hours.

"Hello?"

"Mr. Zhao, is that reward for information on Ms. Star still good?"

"Yes, who is this?"

He gave his name, "I just saw her at an Italian Restaurant in DC. I took a picture on my phone; I'll send it to you. But I want the reward first."

"Do you know where she is now?" Zhao asked.

"Yes, I followed her and her husband when they left. I have their address."

"Send the address and the picture first, I need proof, then I will send the money," he promised.

"She has bodyguards."

"That's to be expected," Zhao responded.

The informant agreed to the arrangement and sent the information.

Houston and Sophie slept in the next morning. Neither of them was in a hurry to leave their comfortable bed with its soft down comforter. Eventually Bully got impatient. He insisted on getting someone's attention to let him outside. He jumped on the soft bed and started licking Sophie's face.

Sophie refused to budge. "Houston, is the doggy door locked?"

"Of course."

"Take your dog out, please he won't leave me alone." Her voice muffled by the pillow she put over her face.

"My dog? It's your face he's licking."

"Houston!"

"Alright..."Houston tossed off his covers and swung his feet over the side of the bed. "Come on, Bully. I'll feed you and take you out. But you have to back me up next time Sophie yells at me. Got it! No more kissing up because she feeds you food off her plate."

Bully looked up at him, his tail wagging, giving him a 'no promises' look.

After breakfast, Houston and Sophie decided to go to National Harbor to see 'Icy Village'. They bundled up and put Bully's service vest on him. After training as a working police dog last year, he received certification following in his parent's footsteps. They spent the day looking at the most beautiful sculptures made from ice, such a shame they would melt away. It warmed up enough to snow. It made the 'Icy Village' look like they were inside a snow globe.

When they got home, Fons came down to say hello. They decided to grill steaks on the covered back patio. Houston and Fons went to the store to grab what they needed. Bully wanted nothing to do with the snow, so he headed to his warm bed in the kitchen's corner and took a nap.

After dinner Sophie said she would clean up, so the men spent the rest of the night watching a game Houston had recorded earlier.

While the men were watching sports, Sophie went to the den and called Izumi. She knew they served dinner after eight at the compound.

"Sophie?" He answered, pleased.

"Yes, Izumi, I am so glad to hear your voice," she smiled.

"I spoke with Houston late last night. He said you are safe and for me not to worry."

"I am. How is Mr. Katsumi?"

"Very lonely and sad since you left."

"I thought I might call after your dinner time and tell him a story. What do you think?"

"He would be delighted."

"Call me when you feel the time is right."

They said goodbye, and she spent the time going over the story she would tell.

It was 8:45 pm when she got the text they were finished with dinner.

Sophie got on her computer and Face Timed Izumi, who had the laptop set up in front of his father.

Sophie saw Katsumi's face when the call connected. "Hello, Mr. Katsumi."

Mr. Katsumi was surprised to hear her voice. "Musume?"

"Yes, how are you? I miss our time together."

She could see a big smile come to his face. "I'm afraid I have little time to miss my wayward daughter." He said, smiling.

"Well then, if you're too busy for me, I can call you back later." She couldn't resist teasing him.

"That would make me ungracious. I will take time for you."

"Great. Do you have time for a story?"

"If you wish to tell me one, I would not object."

Sophie started her story. "From the time of the first lamb sacrifice offered to God to cover the people's sins; Prophets foretold of a coming Redeemer. A perfect lamb without spot or wrinkle sacrificed once for all humanity. The Prophets foretold the Redeemer would be born of a virgin.

For almost five hundred years God did not speak to his people. He went silent.

225

Then an Angel appeared to a young woman. The Angel told her she would bear a son who would be the Redeemer.

The young woman named Mary became afraid. She asked, 'how can this be? I have never been with a man'. But the Angel said that the Spirit of God would overshadow her, and she would conceive. And the child would be called the Son of God.

Mary was promised to Joseph. When Mary told him what happened, he didn't know what to do. He was confused, unsure if he should marry her.

Then the Angel of the Lord appeared to him in a dream. The Angel told him that this child was from God, and the child would bring salvation to His people."

Sophie went on with the story, telling about King Herod's census. The census required all people to be counted in their home country. So Joseph traveled with his pregnant wife to his home country of Bethlehem.

Mary gave birth to Jesus while in Bethlehem, fulfilling the prophecy that the Redeemer would be born there. Then she told of the Wise Men.

"In the East in a faraway country were Wise Men who studied the Hebrew scriptures and the stars. A new star appeared in the heavens. They believed it would lead them to the King of the Jews. They followed it as far as Jerusalem.

The Wise Men asked to speak to King Herod and asked him where they might find the King of the Jews. Herod didn't know, but he pretended to want to worship the child King too. So he asked for the Wise men to come back once they found this King."

Sophie explained to Katsumi that this was a wicked King. He was afraid he would lose his throne to baby Jesus because of the prophecies. Herod intended to kill him.

"The Wise Men found Jesus by following the star to Bethlehem. They gave Him gifts of gold, frankincense, and myrrh. An Angel appeared to the Wise Men in a dream and told them not to go back to King Herod because the King wanted to kill the child. So they left and went home another way.

After the Wise Men left, an Angel also appeared to Joseph in a dream. He warned him of Herod's intention. So Joseph took his family to Egypt to be safe.

When King Herod realized the Wise Men had betrayed him, he was outraged. He ordered all the boys two years old and under in Bethlehem and its surrounding areas killed.

King Herod was a wicked man," Sophie said. "But God knows all things, and no man could stop God's plan to save his people from their sins." (Luke 1:29-35, Matt 1:20, Matt 2: 1-16)

Sophie could tell Katsumi, and Izumi enjoyed the story by the smile on their faces. They continued to visit for another hour. Before they said goodbye, Bully came into the den.

"Bully, say hello to your best friend." She brought the laptop down so Katsumi could see him. He barked, hello. Katsumi laughed and replied, "good boy."

Katsumi hated to say goodbye. "Is my daughter going to dishearten her brother by keeping silent again?" She knew his pride wouldn't allow him to say he missed her.

"I would never want to hurt my brother; I will do my best to be more considerate." Sophie prayed nothing would hinder her from telling him the final chapters in the story of redemption.

"That would make him very happy," Katsumi responded.

"Indeed, it would," Izumi added with a smile.

After they said their goodbyes, she went into the living room. She kissed Houston on the cheek and said good night to Fons. They were still in a football fog; she headed to the bedroom.

When Sophie hung up, Izumi could see how her call had brought Katsumi joy. They were getting ready to head up to the private residence when Kato came in to talk to them.

"Sir, I am concerned that we have not heard from the Tong or the Triad after the raid on their brothels."

"What do you think it means, Kato," Izumi asked.

"I don't know. I dispatched one of our men to bring back what he hears on the streets of Chinatown. Things are too quiet."

"Let me know as soon as you hear," Katsumi commanded.

"Yes, sir."

CHAPTER FOURTEEN

Houston was in the kitchen cooking breakfast by the time Sophie was up and dressed. She noticed Bully was too busy eating the food set out for him to greet her.

"Sometimes, I wonder if Bully would trade me in for two bags of treats." She said to no one in particular.

"I think he would trade us both for that," he laughed. Sophie patted Bully's back as she walked by.

"Mmmmm…French Toast and bananas, my favorite." Sophie took a deep breath. Then wrapped her arms around Houston from behind and laid her head on his back.

"I thought waffles were your favorite," he chuckled.

"They are, when you make waffles, today you're making French toast, so they're my favorite." She responded, not moving her head.

"You are a fickle princess, my dear." He said as he turned to return her hug and kiss her.

Sophie set the table and let Bully out. As they sat down to eat, she said, "Houston, I'd like to get back to New York. I have a lot to do before Christmas."

"I know, sweetheart, but it's not safe. You're lucky the Director let us leave the Command Center. He wasn't joking when he said he had orders from the President to keep you safe."

Sophie picked at the bananas left on her plate. "I want to be home for Christmas, Houston."

"Ok, then we need to come up with a plan to get that

bounty off your head."

She dropped the subject for now, and they cleaned up from breakfast.

Houston had wanted to extend the back patio since they bought the house. Fons came downstairs to see what he was doing today. Houston volunteered him to help on the project.

They were drawing out the new addition and taking note of what they needed. Sophie worked on her Christmas shopping online. She would have to spend the extra money on shipping, but she could get twice as much done by doing it this way.

Houston walked into the kitchen. "Hey, Soph, Fons and I are going to Home Depot to get materials. Since Fons is with me, both our security will stay here." Both had security assigned to them.

"Let me feed you some lunch, before you go."

Sophie was surprised by how much the two men accomplished in one day. She had them take a break and fed them one of Carol's prepared meals.

After they ate Houston said, "we need to go back to Home Depot, sweetheart. We need a few more things so we can finish up tomorrow."

Houston turned off the floodlights they set up after it got dark. He told the security he was leaving, kissed Sophie goodbye and set the alarm.

"And men say women always travel in twos." She teased them.

Sophie got a text from Izumi. They finished dinner and were expecting her call.

"Hello, musume. I am pleased to hear from you. Do you have a story for me tonight?" Katsumi asked.

"I do if it pleases you."

As Sophie started her story, Kato came in and interrupted. Katsumi excused himself from in front of the computer for a moment.

A black SUV with tinted windows slowly drove through the quiet neighborhood. It stopped down the street around the corner. Two men got out of the vehicle and met up with a third man that they dropped off hours earlier. They found him crouched behind some bushes in a neighbor's yard.

"There are two guards. They sweep the perimeter every fifteen minutes. Her husband and another man left five minutes ago. They've been working outside all day."

They discussed the best way to enter the house. They were all dressed in black with ski masks. In the dark, they were almost invisible. They waited until security made their next sweep of the perimeter. Once the guards were back at their stations, the three men pulled down their ski masks. They snuck along the property's boundary line to the garage. One of the men cupped his hands and boosted the other two up to get on the roof. So far, no one heard them.

The two men crossed the garage's roof while the third man went to get the SUV ready to pick them up with their package. They planned to take Sophie out the front door after disabling the man guarding it. They were able to reach the small balcony off the back of Fons' apartment. The men leapt over the railing and picked the lock.

"Katsumi, I apologize, but this is urgent. I have news about Ms. Star."

"What is it?"

"They know where she is. Ms. Star is in DC."

He went back to the computer; he didn't want to scare her. "Musume, is Houston home?"

"No, he and Fons left for the hardware store. Is everything..." she started to ask when Bully made a low guttural sound.

"Bully stop, what's the matter with you?"

"Sophie, go lock the door to the den. Someone's in your home," Katsumi ordered.

"Ojisan, we have security around the house; you have no need to worry," Sophie responded.

"Just do it, please!"

Although Sophie felt it was unnecessary, she went to the door to lock it as a gesture of respect.

Bully was growling louder now. His hackles were up, and he was scratching at the door feverously.

Izumi called Houston and told him someone was in his house.

Katsumi could hear someone trying to break down the door to the den.

The door splintered, and two men grabbed Sophie. She tried fighting them off, but they were too strong. She started screaming to get her guard's attention, but she barely got a sound out, before one man put a cloth in her mouth, and a black hood over her head, then zip-tied her hands. Sophie struggled to get loose, to no avail. Bully was attacking one of the men viciously. The man finally let go of Sophie long enough to hit

Bully hard on the head with the butt of his gun. Bully yelped then hit the floor unconscious. Katsumi was yelling at the men. His voice coming from the computer, telling them that he will hunt them down if they harm her. If they heard him, they didn't show it.

The security guards outside heard a commotion in the house and were using the code to get in.

Katsumi could hear a struggle going on in the hallway; men were yelling. He heard someone yell, "let her go." A shot rang out, more demands were yelled. Katsumi and Izumi couldn't tell what was happening. But they could see Bully gain consciousness and run to aid Sophie. It was an agonizing few minutes. Katsumi was pacing yelling at the computer.

Bully attacked the man left holding Sophie by jumping on his back. Bully knocked him off balance and set his jaw around the man's arm, biting and shaking his head. One security officer took control of the intruder Bully had contained, while the other took Sophie out of harm's way and freed her.

Houston and Fons came running in as the offenders were put in cuffs. The man who was shot was lying on the ground; he wasn't moving. Sophie ran to Bully to make sure he was alright. Houston maneuvered around the chaos to get to Sophie. He helped her to the sofa. Bully followed and laid down on her lap.

Fons was dealing with the FBI and local police who arrived at the same time. An ambulance came for the perp unconscious on the floor.

Sophie was stroking Bully's fur; she could still feel his heart racing. She realized Katsumi must still be on the computer, so she asked Houston to go and let him know she wasn't injured.

When he walked into the den, he saw Katsumi on the computer screen. "Izumi, thank you for the call."

"Is she alright, Houston!?" Katsumi anxiously waited for the answer.

"Yes, she's pretty shaken up."

"Bully took a hard hit to his head, Houston," Izumi said. "He might need to be checked out. He did a valiant job protecting her." Izumi gave him the rundown.

"Thank you for being here for her. I need to talk to you about what you know, but I don't want to leave her alone. I'll call you later."

He shut down the computer and went back to his wife.

Sophie insisted they take Bully to the animal urgent care clinic.

The Vet looked at Bully; he had a mild concussion. They gave him oxygen and corticosteroids. The Vet suggested Bully stay overnight for observation. Sophie hated to leave him but knew it was best.

Fons stayed at the house and helped with the investigation. The police investigator told him the men had broken into his apartment upstairs. They had identified the men, but Fons already knew who sent them.

Police canvassed the neighbors. The neighbor two houses down told the officer a black SUV had parked on the street next to their home. It was gone now. It left little doubt it was the getaway car. The driver got away.

The lead FBI agent was speaking to Fons, "it's a good thing the security detail was here. If they had been able to kidnap Ms. Star, it could have ended badly."

Director Cosby called to get the details from the Agents he sent. He then asked for Agent Townsend, when told he was gone he spoke with Agent Rodriguez. Fons filled him in on everything he knew regarding the attempted kidnapping.

"I'm going to order them back to the Command Center. I should have never let them go back home."

When Houston finally had Sophie home, and everyone had left. He took her in his arms and held her close. She broke down.

"I'm sorry I wasn't here to protect you, sweetheart."

"Houston, of course they waited until you left. They would have been fools to try taking me when you are here to protect me." She patted his chest, "you would have beaten them to a pulp."

He gave a faint smile. His wife was trying to make him feel better, but this guilt would stay with him a while.

"Will I ever be safe?" She asked, wiping away tears.

"I've got you; you're safe now." He knew she would never be safe until they could find a way to get this bounty off her head. But right now, what she needed was for him to hold her until she felt safe.

He spent the night praying for a way out of this. When he got off his knees, he knew what needed to happen. Sophie needed to talk with the gangs face to face. He knew what needed to happen; now he had to figure out how to do it without getting them both killed.

Houston didn't remember climbing in bed and falling asleep, but he woke up when Sophie wiggled out of his arms to get up.

"Go back to sleep, sweetheart, I'll wake you when breakfast is ready." Sophie kissed him and got up.

As Houston sat down for breakfast, he said, "Sophie, you're going to have to talk to the Tong and Triad. You need to convince them as long as they leave you alone, this is over."

The look on her face said it all. She did not want to face those men. He moved to where she was sitting, squatted down in front of her, taking her hands.

"If you don't want to do this, I will figure out another way. You don't have to do it, Sophie."

Sophie looked at the concern in his face and kissed his cheek. "No, you're right. I don't want this following us for the rest of our lives. I can do it."

Houston knew they didn't dare reveal themselves by going to the gangs directly. They needed a buffer. They needed a place that would be safe for this meeting. He knew of only one place.

"The safest way is for Mr. Katsumi to host the gathering. With his protection, you would be safe," Houston said.

"You're right. It's the only way to reach them all at once."

"We'll call Mr. Katsumi after we pick up Bully from the clinic."

Mr. Katsumi was still upset over the incident the night before. If they had gotten their hands on Sophie, there would have been nothing he could have done about it. He didn't like the feeling of being helpless. He called Izumi in.

"I have tried to come up with a way to keep Ms. Star from her enemies. I'm not convinced there is a way short of her giving them the information. Would you agree?"

"Watashi no Chichi, you know very well she will never do that. But what if she did talk to them and convinced them it was in their best interest to leave it alone."

"She is impressive, but that would be impossible even for her."

At that point, Kato came in, he said there was a call for him and asked if he wanted to take it.

"Who is it?"

"Mr. Townsend, sir." Katsumi took the phone. He put the call on speaker so that Izumi could hear.

"Mr. Townsend, how is Sophie?" Izumi asked.

"I'm right here, I'm alright, thanks to you and Bully. I can't thank you enough, locking the door gave the guards enough time to figure out that there was someone in the house."

"Musume, we must find a way to end this. They will not stop until they talk to you," Katsumi stated.

"That's what we called to talk to you about. You're right, Sophie must speak with them. Would you be willing to provide a safe place for her to do that?" Houston asked.

"Of course. It would be best. When do you wish to do this?"

"As soon as possible," Houston replied.

"Who do you want to talk to?"

"I think we should address all the heads of the Tong, the Triad, and any of the other gangs involved. Get it out there all at once," Houston suggested.

"I agree," Izumi said.

"I can get word to all the gangs. We will give them forty-eight hours' notice and set the time for an assembly here at the compound. But you cannot drive here; there are men on the roads watching for you to come. Take a helicopter; I have a landing pad on the roof," Katsumi insisted.

"Mr. Katsumi, I have one more favor to ask. Sophie has security, three of them, would you be offended if they came with us. It is not a slight on your ability to protect her. It will be extra hands if we need them." He knew Cosby would not allow her to go anywhere without personal security.

"I am not offended, Mr. Townsend, I understand your need to protect your wife. How soon can you come?"

"We could be there this evening if that isn't imposing on your hospitality." Houston wanted her out of DC.

"You and your wife are no imposition to me. Come as soon

237

as you can," Katsumi responded.

They packed their things. Houston told Fons the plan. Fons insisted on being one of the security men. There was no one Houston trusted more than Fons and had no intention of leaving him behind. His next call was to Cosby.

"Have you lost your mind! Addressing those men will only make things worse," Cosby blurted out.

"I don't think so, sir. If she can convince them this is over unless they pursue it, it could work. Only when they have warred against each other has their livelihoods been so impacted. Sophie must make them believe her client can do worse if they pursue him. Of course, there is no client, but they don't know that."

"Do you think she can do it?"

"She can, sir."

"Are you convinced the Akuza won't turn her over to them." Cosby wasn't as confident as Houston seemed to be.

"Sir, he will protect her, and we will bring our security detail with us."

"How and when?"

"We will leave here shortly to take a flight to the base in New York, then take a helicopter to his compound. We should be there tonight. The meeting is set for the day after tomorrow."

"Have security give us a wellness update every three hours, or I will send in the SRT to get you out." Houston knew he meant it.

Houston and Sophie landed on the roof helipad as it was getting dark. Kato immediately escorted them to Katsumi.

Bully ran to Katsumi, who bent down to pat him on the head and tell him how brave he was.

Mr. Katsumi went to meet Sophie as she was coming to the door. He kissed her cheek and took her hand, then acknowledged Houston. "Your husband was wise to trust your safety to me. You are safe here I will make sure of it." Fons and the FBI Agents assigned to them stood outside the door with Kato's men.

"I can't thank you enough. I hope I can convince the gangs it is in their best interest to leave me alone..." Sophie looked down at her hands. "I was frightened last night."

He could feel her hand tremble a little talking about it. It hurt his heart to see her afraid.

"We will find a way to make you safe again, musume."

The butler came in to announce dinner was ready. He continued to hold her hand and directed them to the small dining room. Katsumi made sure there was a large steak there for Bully. He gladly did his trick, sitting up with his front paws in the air, to get his treat. How could Houston object after Bully had done such a valiant job protecting his wife. At supper, the mood started to lighten, and afterward, Katsumi asked her for a story.

Sophie started where she left off before the attempted kidnapping.

"After Jesus was born and Joseph hid him in Egypt, it came to pass that King Herod died. When the news reached Joseph, he took his family back to Nazareth.

When Jesus turned 33 years old, he went to the Jordon river to be baptized by John the Baptist. When John baptized him, the heavens opened, and the Spirit of God descended like a dove and rested on Jesus. Then a voice came from Heaven that said, 'this is My beloved Son, in whom I am well pleased.'" (Matt.3:16-17)

Sophie continued, "from there, Jesus went into the

wilderness to fast and pray. At the end of forty days, he was hungry. Lucifer, the Angel who God cast out of Heaven, came to tempt Jesus.

Satan said to him, 'If You are the Son of God, command that these stones become bread.'

But Jesus answered and said. 'It is written, Man shall not live by bread alone, but by every word that proceeds from the mouth of God.'

Then the devil took Him up into the holy city, set Him on the temple's pinnacle, and said to Him. 'If You are the Son of God, throw Yourself down. For it is written: He shall give His angels charge over you, and, in their hands, they shall bear you up, lest you dash your foot against a stone.'

Jesus said to him, 'It is written again, you shall not tempt the Lord your God.'

Again, the devil took Him up on an exceedingly high mountain. And there showed Him all the kingdoms of the world and their glory. And he said to Him, 'All these things I will give You if You will fall down and worship me.'

Then Jesus said to him, 'away with you, Satan! For it is written, you shall worship the Lord your God, and Him only you shall serve.'

Then the devil left Him, and behold, angels came and ministered to Him." (Matt 4:1-11)

Sophie took a sip of her tea and continued. "Jesus did not sin as Adam and Eve did but was perfect in all his ways. Adam gave in to his fleshly nature, but Jesus did not. He loved His Father more than his own flesh and would not sin against Him.

After this, He began his ministry; He knew his time on earth was short. The world needed to know that God had sent the promised Redeemer to give them eternal life."

Sophie told of the miracles Jesus performed. How He healed the sick, opened blind eyes, and cast out demons.

"Jesus even raised one man from the dead, but many still

would not believe. The Jews were looking for a warrior Redeemer. They wanted someone to defeat the Romans and make them rulers of the world. But Jesus did not come for that reason. He came to save them from eternal separation from God. He came to be the ultimate and final sacrifice for sin and restore man's relationship with his Creator.

One day Jesus will return with His saints and take back this earthly kingdom from the evil one. For now, Satan is the 'prince of the power of the air'. But his time will come to an end."

"Mr. Katsumi," she said, "it would take many, many dinners to tell of all that Jesus did and the miracles he performed."

Houston could see that the story touched Katsumi. The combination of all he's heard had to be weighing on his spirit.

Katsumi asked, "do you believe there is an 'evil one'?"

"I do, Ojisan. I believe every word in the Bible. Satan's presence is evident all around us in this world." Sophie answered while lifting her cup of tea. "I am sure you have seen evil."

"Indeed, I have seen evil, my whole life. The only good I have seen was in Suki…" he put his hand on hers. "And now you, musume."

"Ojisan, the only good in me, is because of Jesus." Katsumi patted her hand and smiled in response.

After visiting for another hour or so, Katsumi finally got up and led her to her quarters. Izumi offered the barracks to house Sophie's personal security.

Izumi asked Houston if they could speak. They took Bully for a walk in the garden.

"Izumi, do you think Sophie can persuade the gangs that this is over?" Houston asked.

"If she can persuade them no more harm will come to their businesses; and give a good explanation for all the destruction. Then, maybe," Izumi said.

"It was the same thought that came to me. I know God will give her the words to say."

"I agree."

Houston asked what Izumi was studying. Mr. Jo saw them in the garden and opened the door to say hello. They invited him to join them. Houston treated their time together as a Sunday School class. He instructed them on the Bible and how to walk a Christian life. They stayed in the garden for several hours. Then they prayed together.

Houston asked Izumi to take him to the barracks so that he could talk to his security. Izumi escorted him to it, then left for his quarters.

Fons was in the game room watching TV. "Fons, I'm sorry you're out here, I should have insisted they set up a room for you at the house."

"Are you kidding, look at this place, it's nicer than any barracks I've ever seen. And besides, I can get a scoop on what's happening."

"Thanks, Fons, during the assembly I want our men with us on the platform. And I want a chopper pilot on standby in case we have to leave immediately."

"I hear ya. I'll make sure it happens."

.

When Houston got back to the room, he saw that Sophie had fallen asleep waiting for him. She had dolled herself up in one of those sleeping kimonos and put her hair up with those chopstick things. He felt bad he hadn't come earlier to appreciate her effort. He woke her up; he couldn't let it go unappreciated.

"Sweetheart, I'm back," he whispered in her ear.

She stirred; it took her a few seconds to get fully awake. "Honey, where were you."

He explained what he was doing. She was glad he spent the time with Izumi and Mr. Jo.

He pulled her up off the bed to get a good look at her. "You are the most beautiful woman in the world."

"See, that's why I love you, you stretch the truth so convincingly," she laughed.

"No, princess, you look stunning. Was this all for me," he smiled.

"Who else, there is no one else's opinion I care about but yours."

He never wanted to imagine life without her. This plan had to work.

CHAPTER FIFTEEN

In the morning, Sophie snuck down the stairs to the garden to let Bully do his business. She threw the ball for him a few times.

Katsumi was in the dining room, sitting at the bay window, overlooking the garden. He was reading his Japanese paper and drinking tea, as was his custom. He looked up and saw them in the garden. There was something about the scene that made him feel like he had a family. Then a sadness washed over him. Regrets. He should have spent more time with Suki, when she was alive, with Nori when he was growing up. Instead, he put all his energies into the Akuza and serving a Kumicho that could care less if he lived or died. Now he wished he could do it all again, differently.

At breakfast, Bully sat next to Katsumi. As if on cue Bully did his trick and delighted Katsumi, who rewarded him with another steak.

After breakfast Sophie went upstairs to connect with Sissy remotely. She wanted to know if they had found anything else on the flash drive that might be helpful.

"You know Sophie; we have the addresses of all of the gang's gambling houses. Maybe you could use that as leverage to call them off?"

"That's a good idea, send the information and the names and addresses of their loan sharks too. I already have all the leader's names, their family's names, and home addresses on a flash drive."

Houston came in before the butler brought lunch up. They discussed the information Sissy sent and the best way to leverage it.

"What if we give the info on one gambling house and one loan shark in Chinatown to Captain Cartwright. Do you think he would standby to raid them in case the negotiation doesn't go well?"

"That could work, Sophie. We could text him if we need him to raid them. It would prove more damage can be done if they don't agree to end the hunt." Houston headed into the bathroom to take a shower and change.

"Will you call Captain Cartwright and fill him in on what we need?"

"When I'm out of the shower."

"The Captain said he would remain on standby until he hears from us." Houston told her. He then sent a text to Fons, asking him to come to their room.

Sophie told Houston and Fons what she was going to say to the assembly.

"I'm trying to incorporate as much truth as possible. It's easier to keep straight." Sophie said.

"That's true. Your story follows Dajao's story, to some extent." Houston sat on the bed to put his socks on.

"If you give a name, it will have to be one of the victims. They have the names of all their women. If she is not on their list, they will know it." Fons sat on the chair positioned at an angle to the settee.

"They already know her name is Dajao, from when you gave them the ultimatum. It would be wise for her to change her name after this. We don't want anything to ever come back on her. And we will have to cancel the interview with Ms. Turner. If the stories don't match, it would be a disaster." Houston got up from the edge of the bed and went to sit next to Sophie.

"Sophie, your story is believable. This will work." Fons said.

They finished discussing how things might play out, and Fons when back to the barracks. He didn't want to miss dinner. "I'm eating better here than at home." He added on the way out the door.

The butler let them know it was time for dinner. Sophie started looking for something to wear. She found the dresses Katsumi had given to her. They had never made it to their New York condo to unpack. She felt the long black one would be most appropriate. "You look beautiful, princess," Houston said as he put his arms around her.

"I will be sad the day your rose color glasses wear out," she laughed.

"Don't worry princess, I have a box full." He pulled her to him and kissed her.

When they came into the dining room, the two men stood and greeted them.

"Musume, you honor me by wearing my gift," he smiled.

"Your gift is beautiful; it should be worn." She thanked him again.

"A dress is only beautiful if the one in it makes it so."

He pulled out her chair and held it for her. Bully followed him to his chair and laid his head on his lap. Katsumi stroked him through the meal as became his custom.

After a lively dinner discussion, the plates cleared, and fresh tea brought. Katsumi asked Sophie to tell a story.

She summarized the story from last night and went from there.

"Jesus spoke this parable to the crowds." She said, "A man planted a vineyard. He put a wall around it, dug a pit for the winepress, and built a watchtower. Then he rented the vineyard to some farmers and moved to another place. At harvest time he sent a servant to the tenants to collect from them some of the fruit of the vineyard. But they seized him, beat him and sent him away empty-handed. Then he sent another servant to them; they struck this man on the head and treated him shamefully. He sent still another, and that one they killed. He sent many others; some of them they beat, others they killed.

He had one left to send, a son, whom he loved. He sent him last of all, saying, 'They will respect my son.' But the tenants said to one another, 'This is the heir. Come, let's kill him, and the inheritance will be ours.' So, they took him and killed him, and threw him out of the vineyard. What then will the owner of the vineyard do? He will come and kill those tenants and give the vineyard to others." (Matt 21: 33-40)

Sophie stopped to sip some tea. "The Jewish priests knew Jesus' parable was about them and became angry. They wanted to arrest Him, but they knew the people believed in Him, and they were afraid of the crowd. So, they sought to find a disciple who might betray him.

She told one more story. "There was a King that arranged a wedding for his son. But when the feast was ready, the guest did not come. So he sent his servant out to tell the invited guest that the feast was ready. But still, they would not come. Then he said to his servants, 'The wedding is ready, but those who were invited were not worthy. Therefore go into the highways, and as many as you find, invite to the wedding. So those servants went out into the highways and gathered together all whom they found, both bad and good. And the wedding hall was filled with guests.'"(Matt 22:1-10)

She ended her story with a final comment. "That's what God did for us. When His chosen people, the Jews, turned away again, and again, He opened a door for the rest of humanity. Anyone can now become His son or daughter. If they choose."

Katsumi and Izumi praised her story. Katsumi asked, "so you say that now your God no longer calls the Jews his people?"

Houston answered, "the Jews will always be His people, and one day they will be reconciled with Him again. But they refused to believe Jesus was the Son of God and their Redeemer. Their rejection gave an opportunity for others. " Katsumi nodded his understanding.

Katsumi's attention diverted to another issue. "Musume, do you have a strategy to end this demand for your client's name?"

"Mr. Katsumi, I do. I hope it will satisfy them. I don't know what will happen next if it doesn't. Do you think they would try to take me by force, here at your compound?"

He looked at Houston and Izumi. "No, they will ask me to hand you over."

It didn't appear that Houston picked up on the comment, but Izumi did. The Kumicho never fully answered the question. He never said he would not turn her over. Even though he told Izumi, it would make him look weak if he did, and had prepared for war. The Kumicho would always look out for the organization's survival first. No matter the cost.

"Do you have any suggestions on what I should say to end this?"

He thought for a moment. "If you could convince them that their pursuit will only bring more destruction. It may deter them."

"That was our thought. You know I will never give up Ms. Turner's name. Nor would it be smart to tell them of my part in all this..." She paused for a moment, "I do have a story that may convince them."

"I hope so, musume."

They ended the evening there.

Houston and Sophie took Bully for a walk in the garden. Mr. Jo came out to say hello; Houston asked him to remember them in prayer.

Mr. Katsumi couldn't sleep that night. He paced his floor, worrying about Sophie and this threat to her life. Finally, he stopped, looked up and said, "if You are truly the God, Sophie speaks of. And all the things she says of you are true; please make them listen to her tomorrow. If she is Your daughter, protect her, for I know I cannot."

A peace came over him, something he had never felt before. He finally went to bed and fell asleep.

When Sophie woke up, fear started to torment her. She knew she couldn't allow herself to let it take her over. She got down on her knees by her bed and prayed until she felt it lift.

Houston and Sophie went to breakfast and asked Katsumi how this would all play out.

Katsumi said, "Izumi will bring you through the private door to the dais, behind the dividers. You need to stay there until I call for you." He turned to Houston. "You and one of your men will guard the door on the inside. My men will guard it from the other side." He continued, "Kato's men will have their backs against the dais facing the assembly. They will keep an eye out for trouble."

Houston said, "if the assembly turns on Sophie, I will take her to the roof." Katsumi agreed.

"I'll have my helicopter on standby."

Houston stayed with the men, but Sophie went to her room. She needed to decide on what to wear. Sophie didn't want to look intimidating or give them any hint she was the one they're looking for. She wanted them to think of her as they think of most women, of no consequence. That way, she might be able to outwit them. She finally decided on the tunic Katsumi had given her and black silk pants. She wore her hair in a chignon with decorative hair sticks.

Houston came in, "You look great." He wrapped his arms around her.

"Thanks, sweetheart." She laid her head on his chest and closed her eyes for a moment.

"Titan is pregnant again; she's due in a week. I asked if we could buy one of the puppies for a gift. He said as soon as they're weaned and have some basic obedience training, we could have one. I told him we would like a male puppy that looked as much like Bully as possible."

"I'm so glad. I can't wait to give Mr. Katsumi a puppy."
Sophie knew Houston was trying to take her mind off the meeting.

It was time for Houston to escort Sophie downstairs. They waited outside the private entrance to the assembly room. Houston took her hands and prayed with her; he could see the concern in her eyes.

When everyone had arrived in the assembly hall, Kato let the Kumicho know. He walked out of his private study and stopped next to Sophie, he patted her hand, then walked through the door onto the dais. Houston, Fons and Sophie followed but stayed out of sight.

The Kumicho stood close to the front edge of the dais, legs spread apart, hands behind his back, confident and intimidating.

"I am accused by some, of not being an ally to you because I choose to keep my asset from your hands. Although, I do not acknowledge that accusation. I have decided to respect the request of the Shan Chu." He acknowledged him in the crowd with a bow of his head in his direction. "I have ordered my asset to answer your questions."

The Kumicho turned to her and asked her to reveal herself from behind the screen. Sophie walked to where the Kumicho stood; her knees were shaking. All she saw was a room filled with hardened, brutal men. She was facing down a Goliath. But instead of a sling and a stone, her weapon was faith and a story.

Katsumi addressed her, "I command you to answer these men." His stern aggressive tone shocked her.

Katsumi could see the hurt in her eyes at his perceived betrayal; it cut deep in his heart. But he could not worry about that now. Those assembled needed to believe he had no emotional connection. Or they would take matters in their own hands. He knew Houston and Izumi understood that, though Sophie did not.

She looked away from him and stepped to address the assembly.

"I have been ordered by the Kumicho to come here. Since no one defies an order from a man as powerful as the Kumicho,

I am now standing before you. What is it you want?"

At first, no one spoke. Then Mr. Zhao of the White Tigers moved a few feet closer to the dais. "Ms. Star, we believe you have information about the man who has decimated our businesses. We demand to know who it is."

"Mr. Zhao, if I gave up my clients' names, how long do you think I would be alive?"

"Ms. Star, how long do you think you'll be alive if you don't?" He threatened her. Murmurs of agreement rose in the assembly.

The Shan Chu stepped forward, "Ms. Star, I apologize for Mr. Zhao's remark. I am a man of authority, like the Kumicho, we understand your predicament. But you do realize the harm that your client has done to us, needs addressing. First, tell us a little about why he hired you."

"My client and his partner were young men when they came into this country. They went into business together and became extremely well connected and extraordinarily wealthy. The connections came about because the men were willing to do things that their clients could not do for themselves. The business was so profitable that they wanted to guarantee a permanent bond that would last past their lifetimes. They wanted it to continue to the next generation without internal conflict.

My client's wife was pregnant with a daughter; his partner had a ten-year-old son. A large sum of money transferred to my client. A payment in expectations that when his daughter was fourteen, she would be given to his son in marriage. He accepted those terms. When his wife was told, she was furious. She would not allow her daughter to be sold, so she ran. My client looked for them for fourteen years. A month ago, he finally found where they had been hiding. His wife had died, and his daughter was living with an uncle. He sent an emissary to bring her home. But when he got there, he found the uncle had sold her. They traced her to the docks; the girl had been placed on a fishing boat. They tracked it to Chinatown, and that was where the trail ended.

He had heard of my abilities and hired me to find her. After I determine what had happened to her, I tried to find her name linked to a specific organization. I started asking questions of anyone who might know what happened to the people on that boat. My inquiries to her whereabouts were ignored, and my life threatened. I explained to my client what I thought needed be done next, so people would take me seriously and answer my questions. That's when the brothels started getting raided. When I knew you were listening," she swept her arm out over the crowd, "I told you the destruction would stop if you released the girl to me unharmed. You did not comply with my request." She stopped for a moment to look at their faces.

"My client still hoped his daughter had not been violated. You failed to give her up, so the search for his daughter continued as I told you it would.

She was located and fortunately had not yet been put into one of the brothels. I'm afraid to think about what my client might have done if that had been the case.

He is willing to be done with it now that he has her back if you leave him alone. He only has one demand, that you do not harm me in any way. As you may expect, he is in my debt for finding his daughter." She ended there to see the response.

One of the other leaders spoke up, "he suggests that we do not retaliate after all he has done to us and our business?"

"Yes, he says you still have a lot more to lose. He told me to say, 'do not think I can't take down the rest of your enterprises as I did the brothels'."

Shan Chu spoke up again, "is that a threat, Ms. Star?"

"I am only a messenger, Shan Chu. It is for you to determine if it is a threat."

Mr. Zhao stepped forward again, "I demand you tell us his

name."

She turned to Houston and nodded, he took out his cell phone and sent the text.

"He told me he would give you another demonstration of his reach into your world if you did not heed his warning."

She stepped away to give time for Captain Cartwright to make his arrests.

The leaders were speaking among themselves. Thirty minutes later, several of their cells went off.

Mr. Zhao's face turned red. "you have torn one of my gambling houses to shreds and had my men arrested." he yelled.

Another said, "one of my loan sharks is in jail."

"I have done nothing; I am here with you. My client will continue his vendetta against you until you have made a truce with him. As you can see, his contacts are unlimited."

A few men tried to rush the dais, but the guards took them down to the ground. The Kumicho stepped forward.

"Gentlemen, I will not have this in my house. You wanted to talk with Ms. Star, now you have. Do you doubt her story is truthful?"

No one answered. "Then, you must determine if the client is as powerful and his reach is as long as she claims."

The Shan Chu turned to the assembled crime lords. "The damage to our businesses has been crippling. Some of you have lost all your girls, and nearly half of your men are in prison. Do you have the resources to fight this man? And at what cost? You would certainly lose more businesses and more men. How long will it take you to recover after that?"

They spoke among themselves for a while.

"Ms. Star, how do we know he will stop if we agree not to search for him?"

"My client is an honorable man, had you not taken his daughter, you would have never heard from him in the first place. He has no interest in who you are or what you do. He will keep his word, with one caveat. He told me to tell you. If I die from anything other than natural causes, he will eliminate every one of you here. He will burn down your homes with your families in them. If you doubt he knows who you are, I have a list he gave me with all your names and your family's' names and addresses. You are welcome to see it if you like. And don't think moving would help. He found you once; he would find you again."

That statement fired up the group. They were angry at the threat and yelling at Sophie. She wondered if she had gone one step too far, but they had to have an incentive big enough to leave her and Houston alone.

The Kumicho came forward again and raised his hand for silence. He opened his hand for her to give him the list, she pulled it out of her pocket and gave it to the Kumicho. He read it.

"She indeed has a list with your names and addresses on it. I would not doubt this man's capacity to do what he threatens."

Mr. Zhao spoke up again, "And you, Kumicho, you would allow this man to take down your brothers?"

"I have told you before we are not brothers, I allow your existence because you do me no harm. But your lack of discipline makes your clans too unstable. I would never align with you."

"You think you are better than us because you are Japanese, you think us to be beneath you." One clan leader yelled out.

"What I feel about you is not the issue here. You must decide if you believe Ms. Star." He turned and gestured to Sophie, "and the threat."

The leaders spent the better part of an hour talking among themselves. The Shan Chu being the mediator. He finally turned to the Kumicho.

"Kumicho, will you be the witness to this arbitration? And will you stand by us if Ms. Star's client comes against us again with no cause, and fight on our behalf?"

He hated to agree and be held to such a possibility, but he had no choice to make this work.

"I will."

"Then, Ms. Star, you can tell your client, as long as he does not come against us again, we will not seek him out or harm you in any way."

"And you will remove the bounty from my head?"

"Yes."

"Then, I will tell him it's finished."

The Kumicho dismissed the assembly, and the men filtered out.

Everyone left the assembly room except, Katsumi, Izumi, Houston, and Sophie. Katsumi directed them to the ceremonial table to sit.

"Sophie, it appears they are willing to cancel the bounty. But you have to know it will take some time for the information to reach the street," Izumi said.

"I understand. Do you think it's over? Do you think they will keep their word?" She asked.

"They asked me to be a witness, and they understand what that means. Not only do I have to stand by them if you renege on it, but I have to stand by you, if they renege on it," Katsumi explained.

She relaxed, "thank you, Mr. Katsumi, I could have never convinced them to negotiate a truce without you."

"Sophie, I'm sorry I spoke to you so sharply in front of the assembly. They had to believe I had no personal attachment to you," he took her hand in his. "You must never go after them again; if you break this agreement, there will be no stopping them," he added.

"I agree, I have no plans to break this agreement."

"Please, stay and have dinner with us, musume."

CHAPTER SIXTEEN

Bully came to dinner with them, so Katsumi could see him again before they left. Bully was going to miss his treats. The weight of the assembly was still heavy on their minds as they sat down. By mid-dinner, the mood lightened, and they had a lively exchange.

"Musume, will you honor us with another story tonight?"

"Of course, this is the climax to the stories I have been telling you. I told you of the many miracles Jesus performed. And that the priests and the leaders of the Jews were afraid. Many believed Jesus was the Son of God.

One of Jesus's disciples was Judas Iscariot. He believed Jesus was here to establish His throne on earth and to tear down the Roman Empire. But Jesus was teaching about redemption, about laying down His life for the salvation of the world. Judas was losing faith that Jesus really was the redeemer he'd been waiting for.

Satan used Judas's displeasure and doubt to lure him into the hand of the Chief Priests and elders. He knew they wanted Jesus dead, so he agreed to betray Him for 30 pieces of silver.

Jesus was with the disciples, praying in the garden called Gethsemane. Judas came with the Chief Priests and soldiers. To make sure they arrested the right man, Judas betrayed Jesus with a kiss on the cheek. The Priests then had the soldiers arrest Jesus.

The soldiers took Jesus to Caiaphas, the High Priest, and

questioned Him. 'Are You the Christ, the Son of the Blessed One?' They asked. Jesus said, 'I am; and you shall see the Son of Man sitting at the right hand of Power and coming with the clouds of Heaven.' Tearing his clothes, the high priest said, 'what further need do we have of witnesses? You have heard the blasphemy; how does it seem to you?' And they all condemned Him to be deserving of death. Then the guards took him and beat Him. (Matt 26:47-66)

In the morning, the Chief Priests, elders, and Sanhedrin decided to take Jesus to Pilate.

Pilate was the governor of Judea. He asked Jesus, 'Are you the King of the Jews?'

'You have said so.' Jesus answered.

The Chief Priests accused him of many things. So again, Pilate asked him, 'Aren't you going to answer? See how many things they are accusing you of.'

But Jesus still made no reply, and Pilate was amazed.

Now it was the custom at the festival to release a prisoner whom the people requested. 'Do you want me to release the King of the Jews?' Asked Pilate knowing it was out of self-interest that the Chief Priests handed Jesus over to him. But the Chief Priests stirred up the crowd to have Pilate release Barabbas instead.

'What shall I do, then, with the one you call the King of the Jews?' Pilate asked them.

'Crucify him!' they shouted.

'Why? What crime has he committed?' asked Pilate.

But they shouted all the louder, 'Crucify him!'

Wanting to satisfy the crowd, Pilate released the other prisoner to them. He had Jesus flogged and handed him over to be crucified.

Then the governor's soldiers took Jesus. They stripped him and put a scarlet robe on him, and then twisted together a crown of thorns and set it on his head. After that, they took him

260

away to crucify him. Jesus carried his cross to a hill called Golgotha. When he could carry it no longer, they forced a bystander to help him.

They laid Him down on the cross and nailed His hands and His feet to it. Then they lifted the cross up with ropes and placed it in the hole to stand it up.

It was now about noon. Darkness came over the whole land until three in the afternoon, for the sun stopped shining. Jesus cried out, saying, 'my God, my God, why have you forsaken me?'

Then Jesus shouted again, 'Father, forgive them, they know not what they do.'

At that moment, the curtain of the temple was torn in two. Jesus called out with a loud voice, 'Father, into your hands, I commit my spirit.' When he had said this, he breathed his last." Sophie stopped to give Katsumi time to absorb what she had said.

Sophie told of the righteous man who belonged to the Council. He did not agree to this action and went to Pilate and asked for the body to bury it in a tomb carved in the rocks. Some women, who were believers, followed to see where he would be buried. They watched as they placed Him in the tomb and rolled the heavy stone in place to seal it.

"On the first day of the week," Sophie continued, "the same women took the spices they had prepared to anoint his body and went to the tomb. They found the stone rolled away from the tomb. When they entered, they did not find the body of Jesus. Then two men in clothes that gleamed like lightning stood beside them. The men said to them, 'Why do you look for the living among the dead? He is not here; he has risen!"

Sophie stopped to take a drink of tea. "The women ran and told the disciples what happened. Peter and some of the others went to see for themselves.

Later, Jesus himself stood among them and said to them,

'Peace be with you.'

They were frightened thinking he was a ghost. So Jesus said, 'Look at my hands and my feet. It is I myself! Touch me and see; a ghost does not have flesh and bones, as you see I have.'

He said to them, 'This is what I told you while I was still with you. Everything must be fulfilled that is written about me in the Law of Moses, the Prophets, and the Psalms.'

Jesus said, 'This is what is written. The Messiah will suffer and rise from the dead on the third day. And repentance and forgiveness of sins will be preached in His name to all nations, beginning at Jerusalem. You are witnesses of these things. He told them to go and tell the world that whoever believes and is baptized will be saved. But whoever does not believe will be condemned.'

He stayed with them for many days and performed many signs. So many, that if they would have written them in books, the whole world could not contain it.

While he was blessing them, he left them and was taken up into heaven." (Matt chapters 27 and 28 and Mark 16:9-19)

Sophie was finished; it was the end of the story. This time Katsumi's face did not seem pleased. He did not smile. Sophie didn't know what to think.

"Ojisan, are you alright?" She asked.

"You say Jesus was the Son of God, why did His Father allow this?"

Houston answered, "Jesus gave His life willingly. He could have called ten thousand Angels, but he chose not to. Jesus had to fulfill the law. When the knowledge of good and evil, sin, came into this world, it became necessary to have laws. Punishment is the response to sin. The punishment for sin is spiritual death. But the law also allowed for redemption. Jesus became our redemption and took our punishment on Himself, that we could live.

God turned his back on His Son, at the moment all the sins of the world laid on Jesus's shoulders. God is holy and cannot look on sin. Now Jesus intercedes with His Father for us. His blood covers our sins when we ask forgiveness."

Katsumi didn't say anything else for a long time. He kept stroking Bully's soft fur.

"I believe your story about Jesus, but I am Akuza, this is the only life I know. I cannot split my allegiance. I have already pledged myself." He got up and left the room.

The others were stunned by the exchange.

Izumi finally spoke. "Please, stay tonight, don't leave under these conditions. He will want to explain himself in the morning."

"Izumi, Katsumi he is under conviction, I don't believe he is rejecting God. I believe he is trying to reconcile his desire to believe, with his commitment to the Akuza, an organization that has been his whole life. If what we told him is true, then his whole life has been for naught—all his sacrifices to serve Akuza worthless. We need to continue to pray for him. There is a battle for his soul going on." Houston said.

Houston and Sophie agreed it would be best to stay the night.

In the morning, Houston was on the phone with Director Cosby. He explained what happened in the assembly. He asked him to stop Homeland Security from moving on the information they had supplied. Cosby said they would figure out a way to use it that didn't implicate Sophie's 'client'. Her life depended on her not breaking the truce.

Sophie called Gail to let her know she could not interview Dajao.

"You have no right to do this, Ms. Star. Dajao's sister came to me. I promised my editors I would complete this story." The tone of her voice left no doubt she was furious.

"I am sorry, but if she tells her story, it will put her in great danger. I cannot explain the whole situation to you; you'll just have to take my word for it." Sophie responded as she took the leash from the back of the chair. Bully started dancing around, excited to go outside.

"Trust you! After you cut me out of my own story..." Sophie stopped her there and said.

"I am sorry, Gail, but it can't happen..." she thought for a moment. "However, I could arrange it that you speak to some of the other rescued women. You could make a series out of it."

"How many?" Gail asked.

"How many would satisfy you?"

"Six. Any more and it would become redundant."

"Alright, Gail, I will contact Captain Cartwright and ask him to do this for you."

"Good. I'll expect to hear from the Captain today."

Sophie ended the conversation there and called Captain Cartwright with the request. He agreed, although he was not pleased about it.

Sophie left Houston upstairs and took Bully for a walk in the garden. Katsumi was at the table having his tea and reading his paper. Afterward, she went inside. Katsumi stood to greet her.

"I must apologize for my rude behavior last night."

"You owe me no explanation, Ojisan." She was hoping he'd insist on telling her what he was feeling.

He smiled and led her to the table to sit with him. "Your story last night about the sacrifice of the Son of God; I want to believe it. But if I do, then my whole life has been a waste. And worse than that," he bowed his head. "it means I allowed Suki to be abused by her husband in obedience to a Kumicho and an organization for nothing. I cannot live with that."

She took his hand, "Ojisan, when you give your life over to Christ; He gives you peace, you have to let go of the past. It was all you knew, now you know better."

"No! I cannot turn my back on my life. A life I sacrificed everything for. I belong to Akuza. I have no life outside of this."

"God's word says that when we are born again, old things pass away, all things become new. Your past will not haunt you when you give it to Jesus."

Katsumi never responded. He just sat there. Sophie sat with him; Bully had his head on Katsumi's lap. Soon Houston and Izumi came in for breakfast. It broke the silence.

"Mr. Katsumi, good morning," Houston said.

"Good morning Mr. Townsend. I must apologize for leaving without properly saying goodnight to you."

"I was not offended, Mr. Katsumi, you have been a perfect host. Unfortunately, it's time for us to leave you to enjoy your home's beauty without intruders."

Breakfast was served, the highlight for Mr. Katsumi was Bully doing his trick for scraps. After breakfast, Houston gathered their things and headed up to the helipad. Their security was waiting for them.

Before she left, Sophie went to Mr. Katsumi, "Ojisan, now that my mission is over, does that mean I will not see you again."

Katsumi put his hand on her cheek. "I hope with all my heart that is not so. Will you continue to come to Saturday dinner?"

"Yes, of course, as long as the invitation is open." She gave him a quick hug and then, with Houston's help, stepped to the helicopter.

Katsumi and Izumi stood on the roof until the helicopter

left.

It seemed like forever since she had been home in their New York condo. Christmas was almost here, and she had no decorations up. Sophie tried to get Houston to take a few days off to shop with her, but he and Fons had to work. Sissy was on a job in Seattle and Carol had catering contracts until Christmas Eve.

Sophie didn't want to go alone, she had security, but they were working, they couldn't *shop* with her. She sat at the table, drinking her coffee. Then it came to her, Izumi, she would convince Izumi to take her.

"Brother, how are you today?" She said.

"I am not sure, sister, what is it you are sweetening me up to ask?" He could tell she wanted something.

"I don't have anyone to take me shopping; everyone is working. Please come with me; I don't want to go alone."

"Alone? You have security, do you not? That is hardly alone."

"It's not the same and you know it. Please come."

He couldn't hold out any longer. "Alright, I will do it under duress. I will pick you up in an hour." He had to get permission from the Kumicho to leave the compound.

He went to the assembly room where his father was talking to Kato.

"Kumicho, may I leave the compound?"

"Why do you wish to leave, do you have business I need to know about?"

"No, sir, your daughter, wishes to go shopping and does not want to go alone," he said.

"Alone! Houston has no security for her?" He stood from his seat.

"Yes, of course he does. But he is working and no one will watch out for Sophie like family."

"I see...she is right to be careful. The termination of the bounty has not had time to filter to everyone yet. Though Houston has provided security, as you said, no one will protect her like family. Maybe you should spend this week with her to ensure her safety. You may leave the compound."

"As you wish." Izumi left pleased he was given more freedom than he asked for. He would accept yes for an answer. He took his Mercedes and went to pick Sophie up.

Izumi called Houston on the way.

"Hello?"

"Houston, it is Izumi."

"Is there trouble?" Houston asked.

"No. No, Houston. Sophie wishes to go shopping at a mall and asked me to accompany her. I wanted to make sure you felt it was safe for her to be so exposed."

"I would feel better if you were with her, but can you take time to do it?"

"The Kumicho permitted me to leave the compound to give her extra security. So, yes, I am free."

"If you can be with her, I see no reason for me to worry." Houston paused for a moment. "And while you are shopping, will you see if anything catches her eye. I have bought her a few things, but she hasn't mentioned anything she wants."

Izumi laughed. "I can do a little espionage for you, Houston."

"Thanks. I have to get back to work. I'll talk to you soon."

Sophie asked to go to the Manhattan Mall because it had a

Nordstrom store. Izumi drove. Her security followed in a black SUV. She was reading off her list of things she still had to do before Christmas.

"Sophie, there is no way you can get that done in one day," he said.

"I know..." she turned her face to him, "that's why I need your help. Picking out the men's gifts will go much faster with you helping." She paused again, "I may need you for more than just today."

Izumi laughed. "You think I have nothing better to do than be your shopping companion?"

"Well...not exactly." Sophie smiled, "but Houston and Fons are working. You don't want me to go by myself, do you?"

Izumi knew she was trying to guilt him into doing what she wanted, and he was happy to oblige. "My sister, you are lucky my father had ordered me to protect you, or I would be obliged to say no." She could tell he was just playing hard to get. She laughed and went on reading her list.

"Sophie, if you want me to help, you must feed me."

Sophie looked at her watch. They had been shopping for hours. "I'm sorry, Nori. But I don't' want to spend an hour in a restaurant. Let's eat at the food court."

Shopping with Sophie was fun. They critiqued some of the ridiculous items people bought. They laughed, watching children beg their parents for toys they saw on commercials. Izumi had to take packages to the car three times. When they passed a music store, he was surprised when she wanted to go in. She sat down at a beautiful baby grand and played masterfully.

He finally got her out of the Mall for dinner. On the way home, she insisted they stop at a Home Depot to get a tree. Her condo association did not allow living Christmas trees.

They agreed on a 12-foot tree with multicolor lights already attached. It wouldn't fit in Izumi's sedan, so he insisted on paying extra for it to be delivered tonight.

"Now, you have to come up and help me decorate. I can't do it by myself," she said.

"Sister, do you think a man, such as I, has nothing better to do?" He laughed and he agreed to come help.

The tree arrived as they were putting up the final garland on the fireplace. She worked on wrapping gifts as Izumi tried to put together the tree. It was a little more complicated than advertised. They spent a great deal of time laughing instead of accomplishing anything.

When Houston finally made it home, he noticed all the packages and the decorations up. What he couldn't see was Izumi, he was tangled up in the tree he was struggling to put together. But he could hear the laughter. Sophie saw him come in and went to greet him with a kiss.

"Sweetheart, you have to help Izumi, the tree has outwitted him," she laughed.

"I beg to differ. I am the master of this tree." Izumi retorted.

"I can see that" Houston laughed.

Houston changed out of his suit. It took time to put the wayward tree together. It probably wouldn't have taken so long if they hadn't spent most of the time taking breaks to eat.

When they finished putting the tree together, Houston and Izumi went to the balcony and talked about what Izumi was reading in the Word. Sophie went back to wrapping packages.

After their Bible study Izumi asked. "Houston, you asked if I found anything that caught your wife's eye, to tell you."

"Did you?"

"Yes. I notice you don't have a piano, but your wife is an amazing pianist."

"She told me when she was young, a friend offered to give her lessons. Her father was thrilled and encouraged her to continue with it when she got older. His mother was a concert pianist, and he hoped she might have the same aptitude. But I have never heard her play, nor has she given me any indication she wished to. You heard her play?"

"When we were at the Mall we passed by a music store. She went in and sat at a piano and played. She seemed lost in memories. She stopped when she realized a crowd had gathered to hear her."

"Thank you, Izumi. I'd like to know the store and the piano she played."

Izumi gave him the information.

The next day Sophie called Izumi again and asked him to shop with her. This time he didn't even try to act reticent. He said yes and headed over to pick her up.

They went to Macy's first then to the Mall of America. She stopped at an expensive jewelry store and saw a watch she wanted to buy Mr. Katsumi. She asked Izumi's opinion.

"Sophie, it doesn't matter what you buy him he will love it. He doesn't have a watch because the organization runs at his pleasure, so time to him is of no consequence. But that is a beautiful gift."

They went to the Christian bookstore next. While Izumi looked around by himself, she found some items she wanted to buy for him.

"Nori, If I buy Mr. Katsumi a Bible, would he accept it?"

"Yes. It would be best to get him one in Japanese."

The next stop was a men's fine clothing store. She wanted

to get a new suit for Houston, and his father.

"Sophie, I insist you do not buy from these stores. I will have suits made for them from my tailor with silk I have sent here from Japan."

"Izumi, I can't possibly allow you to do that. It would be too much."

"I insist. Houston is my best friend and mentor. I want to do it. I'll have suits made in their sizes off the rack; then they will need to come to have it fitted after Christmas."

She finally relented, and they finished shopping for the day. She asked him to come up and help her wrap the gifts.

When Houston got home, he saw the wrapping strewn all over the house.

"Did you manage to get any on the gifts?" He laughed.

"Your welcome to take over," Izumi said.

"No, no, you're doing a great job." He patted him on the back.

After dinner, they decorated the tree. Houston lifted Sophie so she could put the star on the top. Izumi had taken many pictures in the last few days. He always wanted to remember this. It was the life he dreamed of.

Izumi and Houston spent time together talking about the Lord before he went home. Houston asked Izumi to pass on what he was learning to Mr. Jo. Izumi was growing spiritually; spending time away from the compound in the presence of believers was good for him.

When Izumi made it back to the compound, Katsumi was waiting for him. He could see that his father was lonely and missed the company at dinner. The Kumicho didn't mingle with his men; it was indecorous. Other than Izumi, he only spoke with Kato or Mr. Jo.

Katsumi wanted to make sure Sophie was coming to dinner on Saturday.

The next few days flew by with Izumi's help; she managed to get ready for Christmas. She wanted to buy one more thing for Katsumi. Izumi told her about some fruit candy his mother use to order from Japan for Katsumi. Sophie spent hours online trying to get some here by Christmas Eve.

By the time Izumi came to pick them up Saturday, she was ready for a break. They brought Bully at his request.

Dinner was delightful, they were happy to see each other, and the men outdid themselves with their wit. Katsumi did not ask for a story tonight. Sophie wasn't surprised. Instead, Katsumi kept the conversation going for hours to extend their visit. He made sure Bully's steak was ready for his trick. After the final tea Bully went to the door, he needed to go outside. Katsumi stepped to the door to accompany him to the garden and asked Sophie to join him. He offered his arm to her and she wrapped her arm in the crook of his elbow, and they walked around the garden for a long time.

"Ojisan, will you please come to my house for Christmas Eve. Please, Ojisan, it won't be the same without you."

He stopped and turned to her. "Musume, it is not fitting for me to leave the compound. My life belongs to Akuza; they demand I am always protected. The death of a Kumicho throws the organization into turmoil until a new one is inducted. And if one is assassinated, it means war."

"I'm sorry. I was asking too much. I apologize."

Houston and Izumi visited in the dining room while they walked.

That night Katsumi couldn't sleep; he wanted to accept Sophie's invitation.

It was 2 am when he finally made his decision. He called Kato in from the barracks.

"Kato, I will be going to Ms. Star's home on Dec. 24th. I want you to make it happen."

"Sir, you know that is not possible, the Kumicho cannot leave the compound's protection."

"I am the Kumicho, and if I want it, you will make it happen. Do you understand?"

"Yes, sir."

On the 23rd, Houston came home and needed to get Sophie out of the condo. He made reservations for 6 pm at her favorite restaurant. He had a special delivery coming; the super was going to oversee its delivery.

When they got home, she walked in, and he got the reaction he was hoping for. Shock, she gave a big gasp.

"How did you know I've been longing for a piano?" She threw her arms around his neck and gave him a big kiss. "It's the one I've been looking at on the internet. A 'baby grand.'"

"A little birdie told me." He was so proud of himself.

"Is the birdies name Izumi?" She asked.

"I will never tell. Play for me, princess. How is it you never asked for a piano. We could have gotten one for you anytime."

"Since the day I met you, our lives have been a whirlwind, I guess it never came up."

"It will take me a lifetime to learn all about you. And I'm looking forward to every second of it." He held her close.

"This is the best gift, Houston. I don't have anything for you that comes close to this."

"Sweetheart, every day you're with me is a better gift than this."

She cupped her hands on his face, "you are such a romantic

ham, and I adore you for it," she laughed as she kissed him again.

CHAPTER SEVENTEEN

Carol and Fons came with Houston and Sophie to the Domestic Violence Shelter. One SUV was filled with presents the other with food. Each member of the Task Force took responsibility for a family at the shelter. They were very generous in their giving. Carol had food prepared for a Christmas dinner for them tomorrow at the shelter and a dinner for them tonight. Fons wore a Santa Suit and passed out gifts for them to put under the tree. After they ate, Houston read the story of the birth of Christ to everyone.

It was an enjoyable experience. The families were so grateful, and the children were happy seeing all the gifts under the tree.

Carol helped Sophie get the condo ready for the open house. Sophie had invited all their friends to stop in on the way to their final holiday destinations.

Friends started coming early, at 6 pm. Matt, Sissy, Kenny, his wife and daughter, and Denny who brought a date; all came at once. The building super came up and friends from the DEA and SWAT. Captain Cartwright came and stayed for a while; he didn't bring a date. Sophie was disappointed and made sure to tell him so. Don just laughed, promising to do better. In spite of his lighthearted response, Sophie could tell he was lonely.

People came and went. Everyone admired the Christmas tree and decorations. Christmas music was on, there was a fabulous food spread on the table, and small gifts for everyone who came. Bully was getting all the attention he could handle, along with scraps of food.

At 8 pm, Houston got a call. He went out to security and spoke to the men. There were only a few families still visiting.

By 9 pm, all the guests, except Fons and Carol, had headed to their other commitments. It had been a fun evening.

A knock came on the door. Sophie opened it; the look on her face was priceless.

"Ojisan," she blurted out and hugged him.

Houston saw the delight in Katsumi's face at her response. She started to lead him in when Izumi said.

"What, am I, invisible?" He laughed.

"I'm sorry, Nori, come in please." She hugged him too. Houston came and greeted them both. Bully ran to Mr. Katsumi, who immediately patted him on his head and spoke to him.

Sophie led Katsumi to the best chair in the room and took his coat. She introduced him to Carol as her uncle, Fons didn't need an introduction, he stood and greeted him. Sophie hurried over to fix him a plate and brought it to him. She started to sit then realized she had forgotten his tea, so she rushed to get it. Then she put a pillow behind his back and started to refill his drink when he stopped her.

"Musume, musume! I am fine. Please sit, you are wearing yourself out." It was evident that he enjoyed her doting on him.

"I'm so glad you're here, Ojisan. How did you do it."

"I am the Kumicho; I do what I want," he insisted.

Houston knew that wasn't the case. He could imagine what

kind of chaos it caused in the compound by his request to leave.

Katsumi noticed the piano; Suki had always played for him. He had the piano destroyed when she died.

"Will you play for me?"

"If you wish." She moved to the piano. The others noticed and moved closer to the piano.

She played Christmas songs, and they sang along. A sweet presence filled the room.

Fons hated to leave, but his family was expecting him, and he still needed to drop Carol off at her condo. He knew he would have to explain who the man was Sophie called uncle, without giving away confidential information.

Sophie hugged Carol, "I could never have made this evening half as nice without your help. Thank you, Carol."

"Sophie, it was my pleasure. My holidays are not nearly so entertaining." She laughed as she nodded to Mr. Katsumi.

"It's midnight! Time to open presents!" Sophie said as she took some from under the tree and handed one to Nori and one to Katsumi. She had wrapped all their gifts in the traditional furoshiki fashion.

Izumi put his down for a moment and went to the door. One of his men handed him the gifts they brought.

"Please, Ojisan, open it. It's a small gift." She watched as he opened his first gift.

He unwrapped it carefully and saw the box. It was the candy he loved from Japan.

"Musume, how would you know of these?" He looked pleased.

"A little bird told me." She smiled at Izumi.

Izumi opened his gift. It was an exquisite soft leather wallet from Houston.

Katsumi handed her a gift.

"Itadakimasu," she said as she opened the beautiful hair sticks. She thanked him. Houston opened his from Katsumi; it was an expensive silk tie from Japan.

"Thank you, Mr. Katsumi. It's exquisite."

Sophie handed him another gift. The watch.

"It is wonderful, musume," he examined it. He turned it over and saw the inscription, 'to Ojisan love Musume'.

Sophie thought she saw his eyes water. But he composed himself, immediately putting on the watch.

They took turns opening gifts, all beautiful and thoughtful. Finally, Sophie gave him the last gift. It was the Bible. She wasn't sure if he would accept it. He opened it carefully and took it out of its box. He ran his hand over the leather cover that had his name engraved on it. As he flipped the pages, she saw his delight when he noticed it was in Japanese. She went to him.

"Ojisan, do you like it?" She squatted down next to his chair.

He patted her hand that was on his arm and looked up at her. "It's wonderful." That was all he said.

They finished the night with more good food and beverages, and then Kato came to the door and said it was time to leave.

"Musume, I thank you for such a pleasant evening," He patted Bully on the head and thanked Houston for having him. Houston and Sophie walked them up to the roof, where a helicopter was surrounded by security the whole night.

Izumi said his goodbyes and followed Mr. Katsumi to the helicopter. Sophie handed Kato a gift before he left and a bag of goodies to take home with him. They waited until the helicopter was out of sight before they went back downstairs. Sophie was shivering from the cold.

Houston stoked the fire for her. They sat on the couch in front of it, warming themselves, watching the lights on the tree, twinkle.

"This was a wonderful Christmas Eve, sweetheart. I'll never forget it," Sophie said, looking up at him.

"Me either, princess. And we have many, many more to look forward to." Houston had his arm around her and pulled her closer, kissing her on her forehead.

Katsumi didn't speak all the way home. Izumi understood, they had just gotten a glimpse of a life neither of them had ever had the privilege of living. When they got to the compound, Katsumi ordered Kato to have a piano delivered immediately. He wanted it in the dining room that viewed the gardens. Then he went to his quarters without another word.

Christmas day was fun with Houston's family. Houston brought the gift Izumi had left for his father.

The week sped by. It was time for their Saturday dinner again at the compound with Katsumi. Sophie was surprised to see a piano. She stepped over to it.

Katsumi followed her. "Do you like it, musume? Suki played for me, every day, late in the evening. Maybe you would play for us tonight." He no longer asked for a story. At first, she played the classics, then she played some old hymns and sang with them. Katsumi was pleased and invited them back again the next Saturday. The door was still open.

Kato got a call from the Oyabun from territory 21. He wanted approval for disciplinary action on a servant. When death or mutilation is a consideration, it had to be approved. The Kumicho makes sure the claim of wrongdoing is proven. Only the Kumicho could kill or maim indiscriminately. He asked for an audience with him at 3 pm.

Katsumi and Izumi were in the small dining room having lunch, discussing the current quarterly financial report. Thirty-two Oyabuns ran territories under the Kumicho's control. Every one of them sent a percent of the territory's income quarterly to the headquarters. The funds maintained the compound and pays salaries to those who maintain it. The largest salary going to the Kumicho, making him a very rich man.

Kato came into the dining room and told the Kumicho of the requested audience. He explained that the Oyabun wanted to meet at 3 pm to get approval for disciplinary action on a servant.

"Do you know what the servant has done?" Izumi asked.

"I understand he has run away many times, but this time he stole jewelry from the Oyabun's wife. He wants his punishment to be death." Kato responded.

"Does he have witnesses?" Katsumi asked.

"Yes, sir. He will bring them."

Katsumi dismissed Kato and discussed it with Izumi.

"Kumicho, you cannot kill this servant for stealing. It's

280

barbaric. Other punishments fit this crime besides death."

"Izumi, you have gotten soft. The Oyabun has every right, under our law, to ask for death. Without discipline, our organization would be like the Tongs or the Triads. Would you wish that for the Akuza? However, it does seem a little extreme, and I will try to temper his request, but if he insists, I must approve it. I cannot go against Akuza laws," Katsumi replies.

"You are the Kumicho, you are the law and can change it if you wish."

"I am, and the men look to me to keep law and order. If I revise laws that have stood for hundreds of years, they will question my resolve to run the Akuza." He stood up indicating he was done speaking about it.

"You can bring an even-handed view of punishment. Only the old guard wants to keep the antiquated laws. Do not do this." Izumi couldn't allow an execution to happen in front of him. His new sense of right and wrong wouldn't allow it.

"Enough!" He looked at his son. "I must keep my commitment to the law of the Akuza, whether I agree with it or not. I won't go against laws handed down to me from my Kumicho and his before him." He walked out of the room.

"Kato, I can't in good conscience allow this. It is not right; is there any way to stop it?" Izumi had followed Kato to his station outside the assembly room.

"Izumi, nothing can be done; if there is proof, then the Kumicho has to approve it. What is the matter with you, Izumi? You have seen executions before. What has changed?"

"Me, I have changed, Kato. I accepted what I knew before; now, I know better." He could see Kato didn't understand, but he didn't have time to explain. He needed to find a way to stop this. Izumi knew that all mafia organizations had their own set of laws. The Italian mafia, the Russian mafia and the Chinese mafia, all operated the same way. They executed their own members or used mutilation as punishments. But the Akuza had a history hundreds of years old, of extreme cruelty that overshadowed the others.

Izumi went to Mr. Jo, thinking he might know of a time when mercy was shown. These punishments tended to make news in their communities.

He saw Mr. Jo outside and told him what was happening.

"Izumi, the only way to stop it would be for someone else to take the punishment. The Akuza law allows a family member or a servant to give his life in place of the one condemned to death. It is usually a family member, a girl child for her father, a wife for her husband, a servant for his master. It is seldom their own choice. But the master of the home or a male life is considered more valuable." Mr. Jo responded.

"Like Christ did for me." The correlation struck Izumi. "Mr. Jo, I can't stand by and let this happen. I'll trade my life."

"Izumi, no, please do not get involved. This is not your responsibility."

He left Mr. Jo and went to his room to pray about it.

Mr. Jo called Sophie; she could stop him. It was 1:30 pm; there wasn't time to waste.

At 2:30 pm, the Oyabun, the witnesses, two enforcers from his territory, and the servant arrived. Kato ushered them into the sitting area. No one saw the Kumicho before the appointed time.

Katsumi was in the hall, hoping the proof wouldn't be sufficient to carry out an execution.

Izumi came down to speak with him. "Kumicho, please, do not do this. It is too extreme; you can make changes. It would be good for the organization."

"Stop! I told you I will not betray my commitment to the Akuza. If you do not have the stomach for it, go to your room." Katsumi was struggling with his decision, he knew Izumi was right about it being too severe, but that was the Akuza way.

At 3 pm, Kato escorted the men into the assembly room. The Kumicho was standing with his legs apart and hands clasped behind his back. The men came closer.

"You seek resolution and judgment from your Kumicho?" It was traditional for them to speak Japanese during a trial.

"Yes, Kumicho," the Oyabun said as he and the other men bowed low. The servant kneeled, with his head to the ground, hands bound behind his back. Kato's enforcers lined the front of the dais. Kato stood behind the Oyabun and his men.

"What is your claim against this man?" Katsumi opened the trial.

"Kumicho, Ito has been my servant for ten years, his father indentured him to me in payment for a loan he could not repay. Ito was to be my servant for 20 years, but he continually runs away. I have whipped him and even took bamboo slivers to his fingernails, but Ito continues to defy me. Yesterday he ran again. When my men found him, he had my wife's jewelry on him. He is beyond rehabilitation. I request a judgment of immediate execution."

"For what crimes?"

"Disobedience and nonpayment of a debt." The Oyabun said.

"Do you have proof?" The Kumicho asked.

"I do, this is my advisor; he was with the men who found him and found the jewelry on him."

"Let him speak."

The Oyabun's witness explained the events.

Sophie was almost there. After contacting Houston to let him know what was happening she headed to the compound. The traffic was slow, and she was running out of time. She wasn't sure what she was going to do, but she needed to keep Izumi alive. She made it to the front gate, still praying for an answer. The men allowed her to drive in and called Kato to let him know she was coming. Her security had to wait at the gate. They were not happy about it, but she insisted she would be fine.

Kato met her at the door, "Ms. Star, what are you doing here?"

"I have to stop Izumi; he plans on exchanging his life for the servants." She was hurrying to the assembly room.

He stopped her at the door, "I cannot let you in; the trial has already begun."

"I'm going in, Kato; I won't let you stop me." She said it with conviction.

Kato thought for a moment, he could easily take her down, but she needed to stop Izumi if what she was saying is true. "I will let him know you are here, and it is an urgent matter. He may stop the trial for you."

Kato went into the assembly room from the dais door as the second witness finished speaking. Kato whispered to the Kumicho, "Kumicho, Ms. Star is here, she says it's urgent, can you see her now?" The Kumicho paused for a moment. Then spoke to the assembly.

"I have an urgent matter. My men will direct you to the sitting room."

Kato knew the Oyabun was insulted, but he would never say it.

Kato escorted Ms. Star in from the side door so she wouldn't be seen by those leaving. "What is the meaning of this interruption! It is not acceptable, Ms. Star."

She moved closer to him and slightly bowed. "I apologize, Kumicho, please forgive me. But I have information you need to hear before you continue this trial."

"What is it you know, Ms. Star."

"I believe your son intends to give his life in exchange for the servant, Kumicho."

He turned to Izumi, who was on the dais with him. "Is this true, Izumi?" He shouted.

"Kumicho, I told you how I feel about this, while you are worried about your image, I am worried about a man's life. I cannot stand by and see a man die for tradition rather than justice. There is no justification."

"I will not permit it! Do you understand?" He walked closer to Izumi.

"You cannot stop it; it is my right as Akuza. The same law you say you must uphold."

Katsumi slapped his son. "I will not allow it! Do you hear me?"

Sophie was startled. She could see the red mark on Izumi's face, but it did not move him.

"I will do what my conscience tells me." Katsumi had turned slightly from standing face to face with him.

"No, I forbid it!" Katsumi backhanded him, causing Izumi to stagger to the side, bringing his hand to his face. Izumi took a moment to compose himself.

"If you sentence him to death, I will do it."

Katsumi sat in his chair, putting his head in his hands. His life was coming apart around him. Deep inside, he no longer believed he was deity. Or that the Akuza was the divine society made up of all past and present Japanese warriors and Kumicho's, now entrusted to him. But he had given his allegiance, and he was too proud to say he was doing a fool's errand all these years.

I am destined to lose everyone I ever love. He wasn't sure when he had let down the wall of ice around his heart to allow himself to love again; all he knew was that he had.

"Kumicho, I may have a way out of this," Sophie said.

The Kumicho stood, "Call in the Oyabun."

Izumi and Sophie walked down the stairs to the assembly floor. Izumi went to the door to tell Kato to bring in the parties involved. He saw Houston but could not stop to talk to him.

The men went to where they were before the interruption. Sophie was on their left, and Izumi was on the right on the assembly floor.

The Oyabun asked Kato what Ms. Star was doing there. Kato just moved him along, refusing to respond.

"Oyabun, do you have any other witnesses?" The Kumicho asked.

"Yes, my enforcer can tell of the other times he ran and his prior punishments."

As the man was speaking, Kato allowed Houston to stand by the back wall. He kept his hand heavily on his shoulder to make sure he didn't interfere. Houston couldn't understand Japanese, but their actions spoke for themselves.

The Kumicho spoke to the accused. "What do you have to say for your defense?"

The accused was allowed to raise his head but not stand

up. "Kumicho, it is true that my father indentured me to the Oyabun for a debt he could not pay. But the Oyabun is a cruel and bitter master, he refuses to feed me until I collapse, and he works me 15 hours' a day. I know the Akuza in Japan do these things, but we are in America. It is not legal for him to do these things or even for him to enslave me like this."

The Oyabun took the cane he had in his hand and hit him on the back with it. "The Kumicho decides what is lawful for the Akuza."

"Is what he is saying true, Oyabun?"

"It is my right to treat my servants however I please, is it not Kumicho?" He answered bowing.

"It is. However, I do not treat my men or servants that way, and their loyalty is without question. I might suggest you try a different course."

The Oyabun took the rebuke and continued. "It is also my right to ask for permission to punish him by execution for the crimes he committed. That is, if you find the witnesses to be telling the truth."

"I do believe them," the Kumicho said, "but he has not finished his defense. Continue." He spoke to the servant, who was still on his knees.

"I ran away to save my life; his treatment was killing me. Why not die trying to save myself instead of waiting for him to kill me by starvation."

"Did you steal the jewelry?"

"Yes."

"That was not self-preservation. If you had just run, I would have put stock in what you say, but you stole. It was not necessary to do that to stay alive."

The Kumicho sat down in his chair. The Oyabun's enforcer pushed the servants head back to the ground and put his foot on his back to keep it there. They all waited for the verdict. Katsumi knew what he had to do, but the result would be a personal loss to him.

He stood, "Oyabun, you have proven your case. Do you have your wife's jewelry back in your possession?"

The Oyabun nodded. "Yes."

"What is it you wish to be done?"

"I want him executed for his crimes."

"If you execute him, you will have one less servant, and the money will still be owed to you." The Kumicho paced the dais for a moment. "Would it not be more prudent to take the hand that stole from you and keep him alive to serve out his debt?"

"No. I insist on Ito's execution. He is no good to me as a servant."

"If you insist, I will approve it. It is your right."

Izumi moved forward, speaking in English. "Kumicho, I have a point of order."

Katsumi tried to ignore him.

"Kumicho, a point of order!" He spoke louder.

"What is it?"

"Under our law, a member of the Akuza may trade his life for someone appointed to die. I wish to exchange my life for his."

Houston was starting to get concerned; he tensed up. Kato felt it and pushed harder on his shoulder as a warning. Houston wasn't sure what was going to happen. But if Sophie interfered her life would be in jeopardy, and he would do whatever he had to, to protect her.

"I object!" The Oyabun yelled. "He is not related, nor is my servant's life worth saving.

"Keep quiet." The Kumicho demanded.

"I apologize, Kumicho." The Oyabun calmed himself. "I mean to say, I do not believe the point of order Izumi refers to, pertains in this case."

"I will decide that. Not you."

Katsumi was silent for a moment. "I have studied our laws

for many years, and indeed an Akuza member may offer his life for a condemned man. It does not specify the condemned man to be worthy. It was intended for use by family members. However, it does not strictly say that. If Izumi insists on this course of action, I have no choice but to accept it."

The Oyabun turned to Izumi, "Why? Why would you do this, you do not know this man, he is a worm. You are the Saiko Komon; your life is worth a hundred of his."

"I feel this is an injustice, I cannot stand by and watch. Your servant is right. These customs are not acceptable in this country."

"Kumicho, this is outrageous, you cannot allow it!" The Oyabun yelled.

Kato nodded to one of his enforcers to take down the Oyabun for speaking to the Kumicho in that way.

"Keep him there; he must learn his lesson," the Kumicho said. To the servant, he said, "You are free, your life has been paid for. Where you go or how you survive is on you. Do not ever go back to the Oyabun's territory. If you disrespect the Akuza by telling our secrets, you will die. If you live in peace, we will let you live. Do you understand this?"

The servant stood to his feet and bowed, "yes, sir." His face showed he was as confused as everyone else. He expected to die today. One of Kato's men untied him. "Have one of your men give him a ride to town and drop him off," Kumicho instructed Kato. He wanted the servant gone before the others were dismissed. He nodded his head to allow the Oyabun to stand.

Sophie moved closer. "Kumicho, I have a matter to bring up."

"What is it, Ms. Star."

"I wish to claim the debt you owe me for the work I did for you. You said you would honor any favor I asked of you."

"That is so, what is your request."

"I wish Izumi's life for my payment," she said.

"Kumicho, this is unheard of. First, your advisor saves the life of my servant, giving me no satisfaction for his offenses. Now his life is to be spared by a debt that is owed by you. I end up with nothing, no servant, and no satisfaction. Kumicho, I can't accept this!" The Oyabun shouted.

"You will accept this if it is my decision. Unless that is, you want to lose your position for being disobedient and a dissident. Both crimes that can end in a death sentence if I so choose."

"No, Kumicho, your word is the law, and I will obey."

"See that you do, if I hear otherwise, Kato will come for you," he threatened.

"Ms. Star, I did indeed make a promise to you for your work. The Kumicho is unable to default on a promise made in payment. I will grant your request. But I must give the Oyabun some satisfaction. For your interference in our affairs, you are to leave here and never return."

He turned to Izumi, "And you are banished. You are no longer Akuza." He addressed the Oyabun, "I hope that gives you some satisfaction."

The Oyabun bowed, "yes, Kumicho, it does." The Oyabun understood the severity of the punishment. In their society, being stripped of one's title, and banished from the Kumicho's presence and that of the community's was a terrible fate.

Sophie's back was to the others; she moved closer to Katsumi. She mouthed to him, "I'm sorry, Ojisan, I will miss you."

The Kumicho turned his back on her and walked away.

The assembly room cleared out. Houston went to Sophie. "I'm sorry, sweetheart, but you had no choice." He turned to

Izumi.

"Izumi, come stay with us. Do you need help getting your things together?" Houston asked.

"No, I must leave immediately. Kato will pack my things and get them to me. I wanted to say goodbye to Mr. Jo, but I must leave now. Will you go tell him what happened Houston? Sophie must leave immediately too."

"Yes, drive home in the SUV and wait for me, I have my own ride. I will talk to Mr. Jo."

When they got back to the condo, Izumi was discouraged. He hadn't wanted to leave his father; he still hoped he would turn his life over to Christ and resign as Kumicho.

"Izumi, you need to get away from here. You need to immerse yourself in your new life, away from all that has happened. Find a life outside the compound. I have friends in Lake View, Washington. The Church I got saved in is there; you can take time to reset your life." Sophie suggested.

"I'm not sure I want to leave," he responded.

There was a light rain falling. Izumi and Sophie were sitting outside by the heater under the covered balcony.

When Houston got back from the compound, they discussed what happened. Houston relayed his conversation with Mr. Jo. He agreed that leaving for a while could be beneficial.

"I will have my friend Suzie, find you a place, and introduce you to my Church and the Pastor there. If you wish, you can volunteer at the Church and spend time with men of God who can train you in the Word." Suzie was her first friend in Washington. She was the one who invited her to Church.

"Getting away from here, is not a bad idea, Izumi, you need to heal. Being exiled from your old life might be necessary, but you won't find it easy," Houston said.

"And," Sophie added, "there is a beautiful young woman that we sent there for her protection. I would like you to check on her. Make sure she's doing alright."

Kim Lee worked at Ivanov Enterprises. A criminal empire that had started dealing in counterfeit money. Ivanov's son wanted to make a side deal for himself and forced Kim, with threat of physical harm, to embezzle money from his father's business account, for him. She was one of the company's accountants. The Task Force targeted the company. When Houston and Sophie found out the trouble Kim was in; they sent her to Lake View for her protection.

Izumi gave a halfhearted smiled, "my dear sister, are you trying to set me up?"

She smiled, then got up and called Suzie, "I have another guest for you." Sophie just brushed the surface of what happened.

"I'll see if the Monticello has any extended stay rooms available until I find him something more permanent."

Houston made airline reservations for him a couple of days out. He wanted to spend some time with him before he left.

They settled Izumi into the spare bedroom and went to bed. Sophie whispered to Houston, "now the door *is* closed. I pray what we were able to do is enough."

"The word says, 'so shall my word be that goeth forth out of my mouth; it shall not return unto me void, but it shall accomplish that which I please, and it shall prosper in the thing whereto I sent it.' (Isaiah 55:11)

It's out of our hands. All we can do now is pray." Houston wrapped his arms around his wife, kissed her, and went to sleep.

When Katsumi left the assembly hall, he went to his quarters and wept. The only other time he had ever cried was when Suki died. He never felt so alone. He remembered now why he had put up the walls around his heart. The pain of a heart ripped open and bleeding from loss was too much to be borne. Was his pride worth it? He stayed in his room and didn't go down for dinner. Kato had a tray sent up, but Katsumi refused it. His mind was at war with itself.

CHAPTER EIGHTEEN
THREE MONTHS LATER

I zumi had been gone now for three months, volunteering at the Church and making friends. He talked to Houston and Sophie almost every night. Pastor Don met with him twice a week. Izumi was growing and beginning to see another way of life he liked very much.

Sophie called Suzie to see how things were going on in a different front. Suzie told her she had introduced Izumi to Kim Lee at Church. She invited Izumi to go with the group for lunch every Sunday.

"Izumi spent most of his time looking at Kim Lee," she laughed.

Izumi had confided the same thing to Houston. Izumi would often go home from working at the Church, clean up, and go to the duplex where Kim lived. He would cut her grass or clean off the roof stalling until she got home from work. Kim would bring him out something to eat and visit with him. That routine went on for weeks. Finally, he got up the nerve to ask her out to dinner.

"Kim is the most beautiful, kindest woman in the world, except for my sister, of course," Izumi told Houston.

Houston got a call from Max, "Hi, Houston, the puppy

your requested is ready anytime now. He finished his basic training yesterday."

"Thanks, Max. I'll pick him up after work. How are you and Annie?"

"We're great. Annie's pregnant." he paused a moment. "I never considered myself a family man until I met Annie, now I can't imagine a life without her, and now that she's pregnant, I couldn't be more excited."

"I'm so happy for you. I'll let Sophie know, she will want to see Annie, I'm sure," Houston said.

"Oh, sweetheart, he is so cute. Can we keep him?" Sophie asked as she took him in her arms. Even as a puppy, the Belgian Malinois almost swallowed her up.

"If you want, princess. But what about Mr. Katsumi?"

"Houston, he looks just like his brother." She carried the puppy to the couch and put him on her lap. "It would be selfish of me to keep him." Bully came over to sniff him, his tail wagging. If he was worried about being replaced, he didn't show it.

"You know I can't take him to Katsumi myself; I'm persona non grata."

She wrote a note and tied it to his collar. Houston took the puppy and all the paraphernalia he bought for him and headed to the compound.

The guards stopped Houston at the gate, they called Kato to get permission for Houston to come onto the grounds, but Kato came to meet him instead. "Mr. Townsend, what are you doing here?"

"Kato, we made a request months ago for one of Bully's brothers for Katsumi. I picked him up today. Sophie doesn't want Katsumi to be alone."

Kato moved Houston away from the guards at the gate. "No one knows how bad it is, Houston. Katsumi went into a deep depression right after the trial; he quit eating for a while. This is not good for us. He has had no meetings for months; rumors are circulating. The Kumicho will not talk to anyone except Mr. Jo or me. I'm afraid for him that he will take his own life."

The news was a surprise to Houston. He had no idea things had gotten that bad; he and Sophie prayed for Mr. Katsumi every day. "I'm sorry, Kato, we had no idea. I hope this gift will help in some way.

"I do too." Kato helped Houston take the dog and his belongings from the SUV and put them in Kato's vehicle.

"Will you call us now and then and keep us informed?" Houston asked as he got back in the car.

"I will. Mr. Townsend, thank you on behalf of the Kumicho for the gift."

Kato went to the small dining area where Katsumi sat for hours on end, looking out on the garden. The last place he and Sophie had walked together, the last place he had a son and a daughter. The last place he was happy. Katsumi turned his head to see who entered. His face lit up; he thought it was Bully, and that Sophie had come to see him. Then he realized the dog was too small to be Bully.

"What is this, Kato? Why is that animal on my compound?"

"He is a gift to you, Kumicho." The dog pulled the leash out of Kato's hands and ran over to Katsumi. He was too small to lay his head on Katsumi's lap, but his nose reached the edge of his thigh, startling Katsumi. Katsumi saw the note attached to the dog's collar.

Dear Ojisan,
I miss you so much. I'm sorry to have forced your hand in such a way.
Bully's brother needs a home. I hoped you might do me the great favor of taking him in. I know I impose on you too much, but if you could do me this one last thing. I know the puppy would be well taken care of and loved.
Houston and I send our love. I know you don't think of me any longer as your musume. But you will always be Ojisan to me.
Love
Sophie.

He put his head in his hands and wept. Kato instructed the servants to leave the room, and he left him alone. The puppy wined, trying to get his attention. Katsumi instinctively started stroking his fur. It was the beginning, a way out of the sadness and despair that had settled over him.

EPILOGUE

Izumi asked Kim Lee to marry him five months after he first laid eyes on her. He loved her with his whole heart. Sophie knew from talking to Kim Lee that she was deeply in love with him too. They planned the wedding for October. Deciding together that their life was back on the east coast, they planned on moving to Trenton, NJ. They wanted to be close to friends and the Trenton Church. They would build their home and start a business there. Izumi planned to open a 'Men's Fine Clothing' store and manufacturing plant for his designs. He was hoping to hire and train women who came out of the brothels.

Houston and Sophie were overjoyed.

Izumi and Kim arrived weeks early to prepare for the wedding. Izumi had purchased 20 acres in Trenton online. He planned on building a beautiful home for Kim Lee, designing it himself.

Kim was staying with Yon Moon and Yon Dee (Dajao's new name) until the wedding. Izumi was staying with Houston's parents. The invitations were sent, and they were busy with preparations. It was only three weeks away. Izumi sent an invitation to his father; his only sorrow was their separation.

Kato had seen the slow climb from the pit of despair since the gift from Sophie arrived and the persistent support from Mr. Jo. Tora (Tiger), the puppy, was Katsumi's shadow. He was with him twenty-four hours a day. Kato even heard Katsumi laugh when the puppy would chase his tail, or do the same trick Bully did, to get his treat.

Katsumi began sitting in the garden and reading the Bible Sophie had bought for him. Mr. Jo would spend time with him each day. He even started taking meetings again, which was helping the rumors subside.

The butler brought Kato the mail; he was now the Saiko Komon. He saw an invitation from Izumi. He hesitated to give it to the Kumicho, afraid it would set him back. He finally decided it wasn't his place to make that decision and took the invitation to the Kumicho.

Katsumi went into the garden to read it.

YOU ARE INVITED TO THE WEDDING OF
IZUMI NORI TO KIM LEE
ON OCT 28TH AT 6 pm
AT THE TRENTON CHRISTIAN CHURCH
RECEPTION TO FOLLOW
A note was inserted.

Dear Chichi,
I hope this reaches you. I have found a woman
I love as much as you loved my mother.
My only sorrow is the loss of you in my life.
If you have a change of heart, I would gladly
give you half of my property to build your
own home so that you could live close to your
future grandchildren. I love you and hope you

will come.
Reisoku,
Nori.

He sat rereading the invitation over and over. He got up and went to Mr. Jo's cottage. He sat with him and showed him the invitation.

Finally, he spoke, "Jo, I am a prideful and stubborn man and have wasted my life on a lie. I cannot live with this any longer. I will not lose my unborn grandchildren to this life. I want to be free from my pride and all the evil things I have done and ask Jesus into my life."

Katsumi got down on his knees, head to the ground and wept for his sins and his wasted life. He asked deliverance from this pride and ignorance that had ruined his life. He asked Jesus to come into his heart.

Mr. Jo saw a blue cloud come down and overshadow them. The presence of the Lord was so great he too was forced to the ground. They both laid prostrate on the ground. It felt like a huge hand had laid itself on the two men. The weight of it should have been crushing. But it was not. It was indescribable. They laid on the floor and worshiped God with tears flowing from their eyes.

When the cloud lifted, they sat up, exhilarated, but exhausted, by the experience.

The next three weeks flew by. Katsumi had to find a way to resign. A Kumicho is one for life. Only on rare occasions has one retired, usually due to health. Katsumi sent a substantial monetary gift to the highest-ranking Council member in Japan. With that gift's acceptance came a letter permitting him to retire.

A letter went out to all the Oyabuns for a mandatory celebration. The celebration would honor the current Kumicho and induct a new one. He talked to Kato for many hours, telling him why he was leaving and about his experience with Jesus. Finally, he told Kato he chose him to be the next Kumicho.

"Kato, if you choose to continue in this life, my best advice is to move the Akuza into the twenty-first century. Change some of the old ways. Use true justice and not tradition to make your decisions."

Mr. Jo and Katsumi left the compound after the induction of Kato as the new Kumicho. All their belongings were in tow behind them in a trailer. They hurried to get on the road; there wasn't much time before the wedding.

The Church was buzzing with last minute details. Kim Lee was getting dressed in the room set aside for her and her bridesmaids. Sophie was a bridesmaid, and Suzie was Kim's maid of honor. Houston was Izumi's best man, and Fons was a groomsman. Sophie went to tell Houston it was almost time for the ceremony and to give Izumi a big hug.

The men were waiting outside by the side door. It was a beautiful fall day; the sky was blue. There was a slight chill in the air, but it wasn't cold. Most of the guests were already seated. Bully stood watching all the goings-on, unhappy he wasn't allowed inside for the ceremony. Something caught Bully's attention. He took off, Houston hollered at him to come back, but he kept running. In the distance, he could see two men walking with a dog on a leash. Izumi strained to see the late-arriving guests. When they got closer, he couldn't believe his eyes; it was his father and Mr. Jo. Izumi and Sophie ran to them. Houston headed that direction behind them.

Sophie wrapped her arms around Katsumi and cried,

302

"Ojisan." She kissed his cheek. Izumi wrapped Sophie and his father up in his arms.

"Chichi, you came." Izumi was so thankful. He knew that something extraordinary must have happened for his father to be here.

Sophie and Izumi released Katsumi and turned to Mr. Jo. Izumi thanked him; he knew Mr. Jo had a hand in this. Sophie hugged Mr. Jo.

Izumi and Sophie, each took one of Katsumi's arms and escorted him to the Church. Houston accompanied Mr. Jo.

Izumi led his father to the place of honor on the first bench, after introducing him to Houston's family. Houston did the same with Mr. Jo after introductions. After doting on Katsumi for a while, Sophie had to go back to the bride. It was time for the wedding.

The reception was winding down, and the bride and groom just left. Their first stop was South Korea to meet her family. Then they were going to travel to Europe for a few weeks. They wanted to be back for the Thanksgiving tailgate and 50-yard line seats. Everyone now expected it to be a tradition. Sophie would gladly order four more tickets for Katsumi, Mr. Jo, Izumi, and Kim.

Sophie was sitting by Katsumi, Bully had his head on Katsumi's lap, Tora was laying by his feet. They all were listening to him recount his salvation experience.

By all accounts, it was a great day.

FROM THE AUTHOR

I hope you enjoyed reading Flesh Peddlers. I enjoy writing complicated characters.

When I first became a Christian a woman came up to me and said she needed to ask for my forgiveness because she had quit praying for me. She said she thought I could never get saved.

I've never forgotten that. If God had not been merciful to me she would have been right.

Above all I want to thank God for sending his Son Jesus to make a way for our salvation and my Pastors who taught me the power in the undiluted Word of God.

LJ

www.ingramcontent.com/pod-product-compliance
Lightning Source LLC
Chambersburg PA
CBHW020410260626
47156CB00007B/2308